M000226981

I Keep My Exoskeletons to Myself

■

I Keep
My Exoskeletons
to Myself

A Novel

.

Marisa Crane

Catapult

New York

This is a work of fiction. All of the characters, organizations, and events portrayed in this novel are either products of the author's imagination or are used fictitiously.

Copyright © 2023 by Marisa Crane

All rights reserved

ISBN: 978-1-64622-129-5

Library of Congress Control Number: 2021951981

Jacket design and illustration by Dana Li
Book design by Wah-Ming Chang

Catapult
New York, NY
books.catapult.co

Printed in the United States of America
3 5 7 9 10 8 6 4 2

For Ash and Wilder

Part I

.

> . . . bright sunlight
> can also be very sad
> have you noticed?

MARY RUEFLE

> Define loneliness?
> Yes.
> It's what we can't do for each other.

CLAUDIA RANKINE

The kid is born with two shadows. You better believe I head straight down to the Department of Balance office to appeal their decision. It isn't right, giving an extra shadow to a baby. It's not like she killed you on purpose, Beau. She's a newborn baby, for fuck's sake. She's basically a more sophisticated potato. And that's exactly what I tell the receptionist resting his boots on top of his desk. He is long and slender, with a droopy face.

"Where's the father?" he says.

"I'm her other mother," I say, trying to steady my pulse. I always hate this moment of vulnerability, of simultaneously waiting for and anticipating a reaction.

"Oh, I see." He clears his throat then lowers his boots and leans his elbows on the desk. "Sorry, those deaths are automatic shadow assignments, ma'am."

"What do you mean?" I ask, knowing fully well what he means.

His lips part into an approximation of a smile, as if daring me to challenge him further.

"Is it because I have one? Because that's not her fault—" I say, my face gathering heat.

"No, ma'am. It's standard procedure," he says.

"That's not true, and you fucking know—" I say, stopping myself before I accuse the Department of living up to its reputation. Everybody knows they're homophobic, racist, transphobic, ableist, xenophobic, sexist, all the goddamn phobics and ists, but they'd sooner strip away my extra shadow than admit it.

And yet, punishing a newborn still seems excessive. But maybe I'm giving the Department too much credit.

"I'm afraid I don't make the rules, but I do make people hell-bent on breaking them wish they hadn't," says the receptionist.

I haven't been a widow—what a miserable, lonely word—for more than an hour. I don't want to lose our baby, too. But what I want matters very little to my temper, which I can feel building behind my eyes before it finally overflows, wet hot tears streaming down my face. It has always been this way, my anger and sadness twin forces inside of me.

I look down at the squish-faced kid, expecting to find a sleeping baby, peacefully unaware, but no, she is wide awake, her big, swollen eyes full of questions, her blue-gray alien hand pressed to her cheek.

"Come on," I say, in between sniffles. "Please don't do this to her."

He knits his eyebrows together in a painful display of empathy. It would have been kinder if he punched me in the face.

"You've got to be fucking kidding," I say.

"We don't exactly kid around here," he says. "At least not until happy hour." He laughs when he says this, and I imagine him and the boys at a high-top table, spilling pints all over each other and sharing the day's stories, the kid and I no more significant than a cockroach squashed under his foot.

"Fuck you," I say.

I watch him clench and unclench his jaw, perhaps deciding his next move. Although I can't see him, I can feel the security guard inch closer to me, his movements quiet and fluid like a good hunter. I readjust my grip on the kid. My breath grows stale in my chest.

"Get her out of here," says the receptionist. "This Shadester's not worth my time."

The security guard grips me by the bicep and escorts me out the door, releasing me back into the world with a small, pointed shove.

Upon confronting the car seat, I realize that it had been your job to learn how to use it. It takes me twenty minutes to get all the kid's parts where they need to go. Except for her second shadow. It has a smug freedom about it that sets my teeth on edge. I swear I catch it high-fiving mine.

You aren't waiting for us when we get home. You aren't lying in bed reading. You aren't cooing in Mischief's fluffy face. You aren't sifting through the mail, perusing the circulars for sales. You aren't, against your better judgment, making an afternoon coffee. Suddenly, all this unoccupied space. I want to get blackout drunk for months on end. Yes, that's what I want. I want to sit in my own filth and like it.

"And what did we learn today?" I ask the wailing kid, patting her baby body with a damp sponge. On the other side of the sink are the dirty dishes. Mischief leans down to lick the solidified butter off a plate, and I shoo her away.

"That's exactly right," I say. "We learned that I am the second most well-behaved person in this room."

I wait for a reaction, but the kid seems unmoved. I want to be someone who moves people, even tiny, helpless people. Now, where is that switch, the one that turns off such a humiliating desire?

A dozen or so drinks would no doubt do the trick, but I can't get properly wasted—I have a baby to keep alive. But how? A therapist might diagnose my panic disorder with a panic disorder of its own. When we first decided to start trying, I said things like, *I can't even wash a wine glass without breaking it— what if I break our baby?* You pulled me close and reassured me that babies' bones were made of rubber. I imagined an impossibly small baby with a skeleton comprised of pink erasers. I imagined rocking our baby to sleep, my fears smudged and unreadable. Get me there, get me there, I thought.

∎

I knew you were impractical, but I didn't realize you were this impractical, you once said, removing an entire lemon from our garbage disposal. I'd heard good things about the cleaning potential of citrus. That was back before the Department slapped another shadow on me. We argued so often we thought we'd made a mistake marrying for love when there were things like fear and loneliness to bind you.

———

For the record, you had no business coming into my life just to turn around and leave. On our first date, you took my hand across the table and smiled with every atom inside of you. Your boldness was almost revolutionary. I thought, what are the odds that this is happening everywhere, all the time?

On the second date, you said, *I could hang out in a dumpster with you.* The very idea excited me.

Once I've safely strapped the kid to my chest, I do what is expected in these situations: I pick up the phone and change people's lives forever.

"What are you talking about?" says your mom. "What are you saying?"

I was always the one who was irrationally afraid of dying. Never you. You were too stubborn to be afraid of anything. We used to joke I was afraid of my own shadow. We'd talk about early death over dinner or TV like it was a cold front moving in.

Make sure my dad doesn't put me in that ugly snakeskin dress for my funeral, I said, fighting off the breathless terror of panic. *I think I'll probably end up throwing a clot. Yeah, I see that for myself.*

If you were in a good mood, which meant only two parents had called the school that day, you'd smile a slight smile, shake your head, and stroke my hair. You'd say something like, *If you die, I'll kill you,* or, *That's not going to happen on my watch.* If you were in a blustery mood, which meant another asshole kid had provoked a fight or spread a rumor about a certain slut who wouldn't sleep with him, you'd roll your eyes, maybe get up and pour some wine.

It's just a joke, I'd say, scrambling to recover. A quiet sip at the counter, a glance out the window then back at me. *Did you defrost the chicken?*

You knew I wasn't joking, but you also didn't know just how far I'd let myself go. Every evening, despite my low blood pressure, I slipped into the bathroom and swallowed a baby aspirin to prevent a stroke or heart attack. Science didn't matter. I imagined the pill surging through my blood and dissolving anything that threatened to tear us apart.

What I mean is, it never once occurred to me that you, too, were mortal.

■

I watch a lot of reality TV in the days following your death, the kid alternating between guzzling down her bottle of hospital formula and sleeping in her rocking sleeper thing (I'll admit, I don't know its proper name). I wonder if this is what it feels like to work in the Department's surveillance unit, although our lives are not filtered and dispensed by editors with a dramatic agenda—the contextual horror of it all!

I lick the salt off pretzels then feed the naked pretzels to

Mischief while the people on TV bitch and moan and drink and hurt each other's feelings. They lie, they cheat, they lose their jobs. It feels nice to feel sorry for people who are far better off than me.

It seems Mischief, for the first time, has discovered our new litter of one. She tiptoes up to the kid's swinging contraption and wets the kid's hand with her nose. She shakes her head a few times, wipes her face clean.

I focus on my own recent discoveries: broken egg yolks now make me cry, the kid's crying makes me cry, the mail makes me cry—who gave businesses permission to print your name? It feels like time has slowed so dramatically that it has begun to move in reverse. My face, although pink and puffy, looks younger than it has in years, as if relieved that all that worrying had been justified all along.

Truth is, I'm terrified the Department will confiscate our baby if they suspect even the slightest hint of neglect, but that doesn't stop me from dissociating for hours on the floor while the kid learns about her new home, the bassinet. Any floor will do—the kitchen, the bedroom, the living room, even the bathroom. I'm not interested in small answers to small questions, like will formula ruin her standardized test scores? (You were right, the parenting forums do have an agenda, Beau.) And will those ruined test scores condemn her to a lifetime of harassing her friends with pyramid scheme pitches? Those answers will hash themselves out in due time. What I'm interested in are the unanswerable questions—how can I manage to keep on living in a world without you, a world that hates both me and my family?

Before you, whenever I heard the word *family*, I pictured generations of strangers crowded in a living room, jockeying for position.

"Move over, I can't see the tree."

"Which presents are mine?"

"When can I go home?"

"This brandy has eggnog in it."

"The holidays depress me."

In middle school, my only queer friend taught me to use the word *family* when identifying a queer stranger in public. As I got older and gayer, I heard a lot of talk about *chosen family*, but I didn't understand why something so beautiful had to be compared to family. Why couldn't it just be its own good thing?

■

At your funeral, in your hometown three thousand miles away, everyone wears soccer jerseys and shotguns beers and passes the kid around like a hot potato.

"Stay strong," people from your past say, gripping me

by the shoulder while trying to avoid eye contact with my shadow.

But I don't want to be strong, I want to be a time-traveler.

After your mom chokes her way through your eulogy, I pass out in the funeral home bathroom. She picks me up off the floor and holds a beer to my mouth.

"You know she would have insisted you finish your beer," she says.

Before the kid was born, your mom was all, "Here's your twentieth box of diapers," and "You better make sure she calls me Nonna," and "I can't wait to hear her birth story." She even mailed us a cheesy poem called "I'm the Mom of a Mom to Be." Today, she keeps her distance from our baby, from me. Every time I try to hand her the kid, your mom has to run off to greet so-and-so or change the song that accompanies the slideshow of your life.

The birth story thing is an old habit of hers—every time she meets someone new, she asks them to share their birth story. I trust that she genuinely wants to know about everyone's transition from womb to world, but I also suspect she's dying to regale everyone with yours. You can see the *ask me, ask me* in her eyes.

You were four weeks early. Your mom didn't make it to the hospital in time. She pulled over at a lookout spot on the side of the mountain, climbed into the passenger seat, and gave birth while a family took self-timed photos nearby, bunny-earing each other. She claims you arrived in three minutes flat, as if it were an Olympic qualifying race.

"Notice anything different?" I ask back at her cabin, your old house. I waltz with the kid around the kitchen so her shadows dance across your mother's face while she sips her 7 and 7.

"You know I don't judge," she says, glancing at the Department camera in her kitchen.

"Okay," I say, afraid of what will happen if the kid and I stop waltzing, afraid of what still moments will bring.

Your mom stares into her drink, running her finger around the circle of the glass. Her skin hangs loose around her jowls, like a bloodhound.

I want her to look up and smile at us. I want to know that, despite your death, we are still hers.

But she doesn't look up. She stands from her stool, still examining the glass as if it contains your last words, then takes her drink to bed.

"There's extra blankets in the hallway closet if you need them," she shouts over her shoulder.

We sleep in your childhood bedroom. It looks like a teen-aged you still lives here with her baseball mitt, cleats, shin guards, several soccer balls, and posters of athletes. Your dresser is crowded with framed photos of you and your mom, arms thrown carelessly around one another, as if you'd always have each other.

———

We haven't had that much time together, we said. *I want to be sixteen with you,* we said. *Do we really want to bring a child into this mess of a world?* President Colestein was becoming more and more of a tyrant, his new shadow implementation shattering everyone's hopes for recovery and rehabilitation. Maybe we wanted another person to join us while we watched the world burn.

■

We is the longest word I know.

■

I used to love talking on the phone. When we first met, I called you every time I was in between places—the car, the train, the bus, all became opportunities to hear your voice, to reaffirm that you were, in fact, real. Now, every time the phone rings, I sink further into the floor. At first, I try to ignore it, but the unknown caller persists.

"Hello?" I finally say, leaning on the kitchen counter for support.

Long, deep breaths on the other end of the line.

"Who is this?" I ask. No response.

I rack my brain for who might be on the other end. Everyone I called is now avoiding me. That, or they found religion and are consulting with a higher power.

"Fine," I say. "Be that way."

The same long, deep breaths, broken up by static. I am only slightly concerned; mostly, I am irritated, surprised by how much I want to hear another person's voice.

"If you're going to interrupt my nightly cry, at least make it interesting," I say.

They hang up.

I'm due back at work exactly a week after your funeral. I tell my manager, Jackson, I don't feel ready to return and he tells me I am never going to feel ready, but I have to do it anyway. He believes in me, I am strong, I can take control of my life.

"There's a mindcast for this," he says over the phone. "I'll get you a copy—on the house, of course."

Another phone call.

The same breathing. This time, I am a bit more spooked.

I triple-check the locks on the doors and windows. I feed the kid formula. I lie and tell her I made it myself: does she like it? I kiss her alien hands and alien feet. I tell her you'll be back soon, you are just at the store picking up a few things.

It's true: if given the chance, I would trade her for you.

■

The parenting blogs aren't particularly helpful—they are written for NoShads by NoShads. They tell me to live in the now. Okay. They tell me to make healthy choices. Organic vegetables, fruits, whole grains, as if I can get my hands on any of that. I'm lucky if I can find a fresh carton of eggs on our designated grocery day. The blogs tell me to focus on me and my family. *Every family's journey is different, avoid comparing notes.* They don't say anything about the absence of family.

I want to be domestic with you, you said the first time I invited you over. I had one fork, and I was so nervous I didn't dare eat. Instead, I organized my bookshelf and watched you make yourself at home. *Don't lose my fork*, I threatened.

∎

Whenever I feel out of control, I recite all the creatures I can think of that have exoskeletons. "Grasshoppers, cockroaches, crabs, lobsters, snails, clams, chitons, spiders, ants, scorpions, shrimp, dragonfly nymphs, cicadas, butterflies, moths," I say to the kid while putting her diaper on backward. I have one eye on the Department cameras, our third, fourth, and fifth family members. "It appears we're outnumbered," I whisper into the kid's ear.

Later, the kid poops so loudly she wakes herself up from a nap. She is inconsolable. But I want to wait—I sense more is on the way.

"I have filed your grievances with the customer service department. They will get back to you in two to three business minutes," I tell her.

But those two to three minutes are a mistake. The poop—it goes up to her neck.

■

We are at the liquor store, comparing wine labels. One of us is exercising our new lungs quite loudly. The cashier gives me a look, but I ignore him. The kid likes the label with the golden retriever on it; I like the one with the abstract face that seems to change every time I look at it. The wine labels remind me of you, how people were intimidated by you and your matter-of-factness until they took a step back and studied you from a new angle, understanding that you were both hard and soft, loveable and disagreeable. Some people took one or two hangouts, some never learned. *I've known them for five years*, you used to say. *At this point, it's no longer my problem.*

The kid abruptly stops screaming. Her eyes focus, or rather, try to focus but end up crossing on something behind me. I turn around and it's you. You're buying a six-pack of our favorite cream ale. Your blond hair is pulled up in a bun and you're wearing your gray workout leggings, the ones that inspired a spank every time you put them on. We follow you through the aisles to the checkout. We forget about our car, our bodies in space, and follow you down the street and through a crowd outside the school. We follow you past the basketball court, past the library, past the alley where you and I had once walked, hand-in-hand, pretending our then-partners didn't exist. Daring someone to spot us, to blow our lives up so we wouldn't have to. We follow you all the way to the train station where we watch you wait in line, tapping your hand against the side of your thigh, rising onto your toes to see what is taking so long. Eventually, you reach the window and buy a ticket. Then you get on the train, and you leave us, Beau. I look from the kid to the train back to the kid. We don't understand why you did that. It doesn't make any sense.

Pop Quiz:
Q: What do you know about distance?
A: I know that I feel it everywhere.

■

Are you going to be okay? they asked me at the hospital. I exchanged a *yes* for the kid.

■

You couldn't wait to be a mother. You had big plans. And by extension, so did I. But they were never truly mine to claim, were they? I'd always considered myself too selfish to have children, too jealous to share you. I loved children, was good with them, as long as they belonged to someone else. At work, before I'd been fired for my extra shadow, I held group therapy sessions for the troubled kids at school. We'd write songs and poems and the kids occasionally forgot they were supposed to hate group therapy. I disliked the word *troubled*, but that was the word the school assigned to any student with a lick of personality.

At social gatherings, you always gravitated toward the babies, laughing, and smooching, and tossing them into the air. Every time you and I reunited, even if we were just coming home from work, I secretly hoped you'd show a similar enthusiasm when you set eyes on me. What was I missing? I couldn't see what was so exciting about them. I did my best to blend in with the other adults, cracked a beer, nodded along.

The kid's screaming has burrowed its way into my brain and found a nice den in which to live. If you were here, you would laugh and say, *Sounds about right. According to my mom, I screamed for three years straight.*

I text your mother: "Seems lung capacity is genetic."

She replies a few hours later: "Ha. Good for telling people to fuck off."

Mischief joins in the screaming. She throws her bowl at me. She spider-monkeys the screen door. She learns the hard way that her claws work too well. She is stuck in a compromising position.

Oh no, a knock at the door. After peeling Mischief off the screen, I open up to a care package from Jackson. A basket full of fruit, a jar of strawberry jam, a mindcast. When I bend over to lift it, my boobs fall out of your robe—which has already lost its Beau scent—and I realize I can't remember the last time I wore actual clothes. Inside, I make toast just the way you liked, burnt black and smothered in extra jam. I have this idea that the toast will somehow summon you, but it doesn't.

The toast tastes so bad, Beau. Like a tire.

■

According to the woman on the mindcast, our bodies are made of purple, red, and blue light that we can harness and transform into anything we want, so why on earth would we choose sorrow? Fear? Resentment? I listen to this mindcast one too many times myself before trying to sell it to some other vulnerable person. Next, she will tell me that if I continue to ignore my light, my organs will shut down. I wish they'd consulted at least one physician during the making of this product.

Today, I spend some time online shopping. It takes me longer than it should to remember that tops and bottoms are names for articles of clothing, too. After some debate, I splurge and order ten bottles of your favorite cologne then spray your bathrobe, the bed, the towels, everything.

When you got your new teaching gig, I peeked over your shoulder at your life insurance policy and said, *Not bad*, smirking a little. *I'm never letting you make my morning coffee again*, you said. I remember feeling a little insulted that you thought I would use something as impersonal as poison.

■

After three weeks of waiting, I receive your ashes. I set them on my desk and stare at them for hours while I hold the kid, gripping the back of her skull like a softball. I am convinced that the kid's secret agenda is to snap her weak neck when I'm not looking. She will make a big production of it, going so far as to invite strangers via neighborhood flyers to come round and watch.

I wonder if the kid can smell the imposter on me. If she can, she doesn't seem to mind. She sleeps soundly in my arms at last, a smile letting me know that she's okay, for now, anyway. As for her second shadow, it obscures your urn. I give it a few good kicks. It doesn't whimper.

As long as people have had bodies, people have had shadows. I think this should mean something, but I'm not sure what. A quick internet search reveals the folklore surrounding shadows. Ancient peoples from one of those violence-obsessed empires once believed that shadows protected them and that evil forces feared the untouchable power of shadows.

Of course, shadows cannot exist without a light source. And the presence of two shadows implies two light sources. Who, then, is my main enemy: the sun or the state?

Pop Quiz:
Q: How is a Shadester made?
A: Two parts fearmongering, one part delusion, three parts manipulation. Season heavily with deceit

labeled as *promise*. Stir consistently on low heat, so low hardly anyone notices it's on.

When paranormal researchers began investigating shadows hundreds of years ago, some freaky things happened. All of them reported being visited in their dreams by their own shadows, which urged them to stop their experimentation. If they didn't stop, they'd risk disrupting the balance between the shadow world and ours.

"What is she like?" I imagine you asking. "I can't see, so tell me, Kris. Who is our child? Is she perfect?"

"I don't know her very well yet," I tell your urn. "But something tells me that if I asked nicely, she'd agree to sing karaoke with me."

My username: newperson1234
My questions for the forum:
How much tummy time is too much tummy time?
What if the baby hates being swaddled?
How do I dress her without pulling an arm or a leg out of its socket?
How warm is too warm for formula? How cold is too cold?
Wouldn't we rather the formula be too cold than too hot?
What is the baby doing with her tongue?
Should I be able to see all the blood inside her?

■

Half a block away, I hold the kid up and show her the ocean while a Shadester takes a piss off the cliff. I find that it's nice to sit and look at the water as long as I don't ask anything of it.

"This is how waves work: they build like a cry, then crash," I tell the kid, peeling my sweat-soaked shirt from my skin. The news has insisted that we aren't experiencing a perpetual heat wave, that we are imagining things. "Are you looking?" I say. Dolphins dance and weave under the waves. I envy their freedom, how all they have to do is dive deeper in order to make their shadows disappear.

The kid's eyes are closed, and I like that she isn't looking. I like that already I can't tell her what to do. The Shadester is peeing just above where you and I used to have our covert meetups back when we belonged to other people. Now, our spot is nearly underwater.

At night, while you were with your girlfriend, you would text me that you were sending work emails. This meant that I should be expecting one from you. *I* and *love* and *you*, said the emails. When we got married, you sat on the couch and sent actual work emails while I refreshed my inbox next to you, waiting for the past to meet up with the present. I didn't know what to do with all that misplaced magic.

Every boring slice of domesticity, the grocery shopping, the endless errands and chores, the accusations— *Did you move my . . . ?*—these moments made up our life,

and I'd wished them gone. I hadn't understood the tenderness of climbing into bed with you after a stretched-thin
day. Of pulling the comforter down and sliding in beside
you. Of falling into a dream before we could properly kiss
goodnight, but knowing the kiss was still there, hovering
between us.

Back inside the apartment, I forget what I am doing and accidentally remove a pan from the oven with my bare hands.
    "So, is there anything you want to know about me before
we get in too deep?" I ask the kid, squeezing an ice pack
between my hands. The pain feels better than good. "The
pressing issue right now is the fact that I've no longer got
any fingerprints."
    No response.
    "Do you have any crimes you want me to commit on
your behalf?" I ask, but she has no thoughts on the subject.

If I had to choose, I would say the moment between when
you decided to kiss me and when we actually kissed, that is
where I wish to live forever. Inside my anticipation, dying
to receive you.

I discover that a moderator has flagged one of my baby
posts as "cause for concern." I cover the computer screen
with Post-it notes, then type what I hope says, "Why do you
think I'm here?"

■

Another phone call. More breathing. This time, a small cough, followed by a few sniffles. The connection is bad, staticky.

"I would ask if there is something I can help you with," I begin, "but I'm not in any position to help anyone at the moment."

Although the kid is already strapped to me, I pull her closer to my breastbone, willing it to split and make room for her to enter. I turn all the lights in the apartment off, as if darkness can protect us.

"I—" says a man's voice. Then he hangs up. I recognize the voice, but I resist giving it a name. Naming it would mean having to confront it and the person attached to it.

"Shrimp, lobster, crab," I whisper, over and over again.

■

When I was young, I made a habit of draping my baby blankie over my head and pretending I was a lamp. I did this whenever my parents confronted me about sleeping in class or talking back to the teacher. When I got home from school, my parents told me to take a seat. *I don't want to be one of the humans*, I said in a sing-song voice from under my shade. I could see my parents' muted figures shaking their heads through the thin pink of my blankie. *I only want to be the light for the humans.*

■

While the kid gets her one hour of sleep, I take some time for myself. I toss a T-shirt over the bedroom camera then masturbate until I lose feeling in my clit, my legs. I use our vibrating dildo since all my fingers are bandaged up. I close my eyes and pretend it's you touching me. I miss your skin, your heart, your rhythm—when you fuck me, here, in this fantasy, you fuck me so hard that I temporarily forget the sad bird of my body. I can feel you in my pelvis, my spine, my belly. I feel you in my claw-dug desire, in my hunger for a release. But this pleasure, this building toward brief oblivion—it can't last.

Moments later, the Department employees let themselves in and find me fucking myself through my tears. I don't bother covering up. At first, I think they are going to give me another shadow.

"You know the rules," they say. "No obscuring the cameras, for any reason."

"I know."

The kid exercises her lungs in the other room. They print out a ticket for noncompliance. A five-hundred-dollar fine.

"Next time we won't be so forgiving," the scrawny man says, licking his lips and laying the ticket on my chest, his hand resting on my boob for a few seconds before pulling away.

The photograph of the abandoned house, which has a copper key stuck in the lock, is still hanging above our bed. Or is it my bed now? When you bought the photo for me, you said it was a reminder that you'd always be here, even if it seemed like you'd left. That was during our affair when I spent days worrying that I'd invented your face. I know you must have felt the same way about me, because you once sent me three emails in a row. Then you made a rule: no more emails today. Then you sent one more, with the subject line "Pelican excuse."

Dear K,

I'm at the beach watching the pelicans. I imagine us as pelican characters. I would be the one repeatedly dive-bombing, partially for fun, partially to get the best fish. You're the one just sitting there, floating, observing all the others, waiting for me to bring you some fish.

I broke my rule, but for good reason.

Key in lock,
B

According to you, the photographer had looked bewildered when you'd chosen that print. Apparently, he'd been trying to sell the print for ten years. He didn't understand why no one had wanted it; he said it was the best photo he'd ever taken.

After the men leave, I feed the kid, put her back down, and try to pick things up where I left them, but I can't get off. I feel like I'm in a sensory deprivation tank. When I finally give up, I hear the mechanical sound of the Department camera moving above me. Without looking up, I lift my fist above my head then slowly raise my middle finger. Whoever is sitting back there watching me, I want them to know that I am a person with thoughts and feelings, and as a person with thoughts and feelings, I am not going to let them fuck with me or my kid.

Now, I try to find the photographer's business card—I want to ask him if he's ever sold a second print—but I can't find it anywhere. For some reason, I find myself thinking that it must be trapped inside the abandoned house.

Every night, I climb into bed and lay my arm across my stomach, pretending it is yours. I close my eyes and when I finally open them, I have not turned into a pelican.

■

Once a month, you would put on your apron—only your apron—and bake Mischief a sheet of fish-shaped treats.

Now, the days blend together and sometimes I forget where I am and wind up eating homemade cat treats. Mischief watches me and my crumby lips with the eyes of an assassin.

During the day, she falls asleep curled up on your pillow. At night, she screams until I open the bedroom window for her to jump out. A new rebellion. I wait for a few minutes and allow her to feel intoxicated by her newfound independence before getting up to retrieve her from the neighbor's lawn. She digs her claws into the meat of my shoulder. Her "Help me, help me" cries can be heard round the world.

"Okay, so I gather you want to be an outdoor cat?" I say. Mischief licks her paw then cleans her face. "Who am I to get in the way of your happiness?" I open the front door and walk out into the courtyard. Mischief debates whether this is a trap or not, then slithers her way out the door and into the light. I set food and water bowls outside the door. I point to these with my human fingers, then with her front paw.

"You can always come home," I say. "Free meal service, use your meow as a doorbell." But Mischief has already leapt onto a nearby wall and followed it to the alley.

Mischief returns later that night for a meal. I stroke her back and nuzzle her face with mine. Then she leaves to explore the world and never comes home again.

I tape MISSING signs to streetlights and stop signs

throughout the neighborhood with Mischief's most flattering photo, her face slender and mysterious, her Marilyn Monroe mole in full view.

When my mom left us, the police said I shouldn't hang up signs because they might be misleading. *Why?* I asked. Turns out, she was at such-and-such an address, drinking martinis, and getting on with her life. That didn't stop my dad from calling her ten times a day. *You don't give up on family*, he told me. I wasn't bitter he was searching for her—I was bitter he was speaking like a low-budget greeting card. Were any of his beliefs actually his own? Were any of mine?

■

"There has got to be a better way to keep track of the passing time," I say to the mailwoman, who smiles politely and hands me my mail. I am wearing your bathrobe and slippers. It is probably around the time people justify drinking.

It's so bright out, I get an immediate headache between my eyes. What a terrible place for Shadesters to live. The sun's always shining, the people are always out, the palm trees provide little shade. I think of your mother on her morning walks, of the autumn leaves crunching beneath her feet. She can at least feel the passage of time over there.

"There are calendars," the mailwoman offers.

"What, are you in cahoots with my boss?" I say. She squints at me then cracks her neck.

"Honey, there's a brown smudge on your face," she says. "Maybe that has something to do with all of this."

I stuff my mail down the front of my robe in what I think will be a power move until it falls out the bottom and scatters all over the sidewalk. The wind steals what I am sure is an invitation to a lavish party. A bumblebee buzzes past the mailwoman's face. I, too, would be fearless if I had an exoskeleton.

Tomorrow, I decide, will be better. Tomorrow, I will recover from today.

■

I never feel like I know how to live in the world. Only on top of it, hanging on as it spins madly.

■

I never thought the Department would resort to openly spying on us. Foolishly, I thought there were limits to the cruelty. Or maybe my depression made me selfish; I was too focused on my own problems. But you were a well-read skeptic and questioned everything. You didn't trust technology. You exclusively paid with cash while the rest of us were sending and receiving money with the click of a button. *I don't want anyone to know what I'm doing*, you'd say. You had the same attitude about social media. Set to private on everything, you never posted more than once a month. On the rare occasions in which you posted a photo of us, the caption was always clinical and cryptic: "A pretty good time." Whenever I read one of those captions, I was convinced you were hiding divorce papers somewhere.

The tough part of learning to cope with my delusions was the unconvincing, the unlearning that never really occurred. I tried interventions on myself. Ones I'd learned in grad school. Reality testing is the ability to assess a situation for what it is, rather than the way we fear it to be. "Be objective," said our textbooks. "Note errors in thinking. Think *then* react."

My brain was never much help: *Divorce is expensive—she'd probably prefer to fake her own death.*

After your real death, my brain continued to attack me in new and exciting ways.

My brain: I will never be happy again.
Reality: You can fuck all the way off.

My brain: The kid and I are alone with ourselves.
Reality: There are always scared, lonely people inside the internet.

Reality testing never worked for the troubled kids either. *Is there any evidence that your fearful thoughts are true?* I'd ask. They had a lot of fearful thoughts: I'm never going to make any friends, pass my reading test, steal my pencil case back from so-and-so. I'm never going to not be angry. My parents hate me. I hate myself. No one loves me. I'm a fuck-up, a loser. *Yes, plenty*, the kids said. *We'll be here all day*, they said.

Ah, my people, I thought.

Of course, the correct response was, *No, no, there is no evidence, Miss K.* As staff members, we were expected to reject the urge to categorize these kids—everyone was a dynamic, ever-changing person whose behaviors would not fit snugly into a bell curve. One day, a kid might instigate eight fights; the next, she might spend all day at her desk, taking notes and raising her hand. There was no telling. But what I liked about going to work was that every kid started the morning with a clean slate. I wouldn't hold the previous day's behaviors over their heads, as much as I sometimes wanted to.

That stuff was old news, we'd laugh, planning for the day ahead. And sometimes, I really think the kids believed it, believed that if they kept their eyes up, they could keep moving forward like a board game with rigged dice. Four squares forward. Five squares forward. You've found a secret shortcut!

That all went to shit with President Colestein's announcement, though.

Tell me, he had begun, flashing a calculated smile. *Would you be so careless with one another if the shadows of those you've hurt followed you around for the rest of your life?* Pause for dramatic effect. *I think not*, he said, raising his eyebrows. *Accountability is necessary to promote change. And I love our country so much that I want to help us change, for the better.*

Mr. President, Mr. President, said reporters.

Who is Mr. President? he grinned. *Call me Cal.*

How do these shadows work? Do they really look like the victims?

Maybe they do, maybe they don't, he said, winking at a blond.

The next day, the collective fear was palpable. When we went outside, we could feel gravity pressing down, as if it had somehow doubled overnight. We looked at our neighbor, who was a smaller, more tragic version of ourselves, then we looked at another neighbor, then another; everyone was hang-headed and limb-dragged. They looked so heavy I thought they'd fall through the ground straight to the center of the earth.

■

I've avoided the grocery store for as long as possible, instead choosing to live off the canned soups and chili you'd squirreled away, just in case. But with food running low, I have no choice. Today, we brave the grocery store for the first time since your death, the kid strapped to my chest. It's a Monday, the only day Shadesters are allowed to go grocery shopping, since stores restock on Tuesdays. You'd think NoShads would let us have this one day to ourselves, but no, in their heads, they are the fittest animals, and the fittest animals don't show mercy. I squint at my grocery list, still adjusting to the subtraction of you and the addition of the kid. We are lucky: there are some eggs and just-expired bacon left. Even with the Shadester tax, we can stock up on some decent food. As we shop, I try to stand a certain way so that my shadows will successfully swallow the kid's, but it's no use—I can't navigate the store shuffling sideways like a deranged sand crab. It's bad enough that I—a mother, a caretaker, a raiser of baby—am a no-good Shadester, but together, the kid and I look like a couple of outlaws. It's kind of romantic if you can forget the danger of it.

While I examine the ham for fungus, a woman who could be my grandmother waddles up to us, a massive watermelon tucked under one arm. She must be royalty to get a watermelon that majestic. I know they keep the good stuff in the back.

"If I were you, I would keep her and that *thing* locked up," she says, eyeing the kid's shadow.

Without saying a word, I look her up and down. I think she can feel my rage, can see the tiny person lighting a fire behind my eyes, because she takes a few steps back, her hands surrendering.

"Listen, I'm only saying what everyone else is thinking," she says.

My phone rings—this time I am thankful for the interruption—and it's the breathing again, this time shallow. A scared, suffering breath.

"Is this about Mischief?" I say into the phone, glancing at the kid. Nothing.

"I've had better stalkers, you know." We go through the usual rigmarole of me begging and the caller not responding.

When I stuff the phone back in my pocket, the woman is still standing there, studying us, as if she can't quite place us or our role in her story.

"You can go now," I say, shooing her.

"Oh, now they've resorted to elder abuse," she announces to no one, walking away.

■

The next time I see the mailwoman, I am ready. "It's Friday," I say. "Commonly known as the do-nothing day."

"And has your life improved considerably with this new knowledge?" she asks, handing me a wad of mail. Buy this, buy that, get a loan, donate, donate, donate, meat on sale, adult diapers for cheap. A photo of Colestein, handsome, rugged in all the right places, yet delicate around his trust-me gray eyes. Above his head, it says, "Help us keep the balance for a safer and better nation."

"Only fools trust good looks," I say, holding up the photo.

"He looks like he keeps someone tied up in his basement," she whispers.

■

Years before I met you, a friend introduced me to kink. She showed me shibari models online, and I thought I would very much like to feel the sharp of my teeth against their flesh. I wanted someone both to tie up and to tie me up. Then I met a woman who was a live-in sub for a dom couple. Her name was Lily—she was a switch. Every fall, she went to a leather and kink festival. *I don't know what I'm doing*, I said. *It's okay, I'll show you*, she said.

We hung the set of rules in her bedroom and recited them into each other's mouths. It was a beautiful initiation. Every time we went out to the bar, her goal was to make me jealous with other women; my goal was to hide my jealousy, to avoid interfering with her flirtations. If I pulled her away from a conversation, to kiss her, to bite her, to mark my territory, I would be punished later, which I frequently was. I lived for the sting of the flogger, the rip from and return to my body. I felt good as long as I knew what was expected of me. Within the realm of kink, I felt unstoppable and invincible, like a teenager drag racing on an icy road. Outside of it, though, responsibility felt wrong, heavy—something I couldn't wait to dispose of.

Things didn't work out with her for the same reason things never do: she felt like a distraction from my life, instead of a part of it.

We never talked much about your exes, did we? You had too many to keep track of. There was the one you moved

across the country with ten years ago, the one who ran thir-
teen miles a day, the one with the pet hedgehog, the one
you worked with, the one who wanted more from you than
you were willing to give. The list went on and on. I didn't
know a single ex's name, just a basic description of each.
One of them nicknamed you *dark and stormy*. You took it
as a compliment, no matter how she'd meant it. Then, of
course, there was the one you were dating when we met.
The one you left when you realized you wanted us to keep
meeting, again and again.

■

Pop Quiz:
Q: Can you name an emotion other than lonely?
A:

■

Hippies masquerading as pseudo philosophers love to tell
anyone who will listen that reality doesn't exist, it's a con-
struct, like everything else. But if reality doesn't exist, then
explain my shadow, the kid's, the looks we receive. I remember coming home to you after receiving my extra shadow,
both of us sore with shame and guilt. You were able to shed
those feelings within a few days once the freshness wore
off. But me, I'm simple—things designed to manipulate me
tend to succeed. And my shadow is no exception. It follows
me everywhere, a constant reminder of the one thing I can't
find it in me to talk about.

I showed up to school and, seeing the shame in my eyes, one of my troubled kids pulled me aside and said, *Old news, right, Miss?* and I started crying on the spot.

But you never blamed me, did you, Beau? It actually made me feel worse, as if I had to double the blame to make up for your understanding. If I was the only one blaming me, the guilt had no outlet, nothing to do but grow its own vascular system and circulate through my body.

"What's today going to be like?" I ask the kid. "Like yesterday, except today?"

She is covered in snot, needing me.

Judging by the frequency with which the kid wails, I suspect she, too, understands loneliness, its curious depth and texture. At night, I open you a beer. I slide it across the table, then check for my pulse. Your history scattered everywhere: books piled against the wall in the bedroom, countless near-empty lotion bottles on the dresser, fertility paperwork, ultrasounds, essays and quizzes you were in the middle of grading, will forever be in the middle of grading. Not to mention, coffee mugs everywhere—on the bookshelf, next to the toilet. I even found the one your students made you—what was it doing in the closet, Beau? Your students had adored you. What did the school tell them? How do you tell a classroom full of students that their teacher died giving way to another person?

The phone rings, as it tends to do. Finally, your mom. I haven't heard her voice since your funeral.

"You know, I've been thinking. You could have been the one to have the baby and everything would have been alright. I'm not one for blame, but . . ." and she doesn't finish her sentence.

I sob and sob. "Stop," I ask of the water. "Please, stop."

What your mom doesn't know is that the first and only time you'd mentioned the possibility of me carrying the baby, I didn't respond. Instead, I went into the bedroom, lay down on the floor, and dissociated for an ungodly period of time. Responsibility made me feel fragile, but why did I behave as if only I could be fragile? Post-sex, when I used to lay my head on your chest and listen to your heart, I felt smug, as if I'd created you.

■

Some days, I cannot find the start to the toilet paper roll, the start to anything.

■

You didn't answer the door after the surveillance announcement. Do you remember? After ten minutes of knocking, the Department employees trampled our door down. You screamed at them like I'd never heard you scream before. I stood with the broom over my shoulder, waiting for bloodshed. The men smelled like silly putty, as if they'd come from somewhere they'd been molded instead of born.

The taller of the two pulled you aside and spoke to you in the voice I could tell he reserved for women. *Don't patronize me*, you yelled. He told you to watch your tone, and did you know he had the power to make a Shadester out of you? You didn't want that, now did you? Your eyes were sharpened knives when you said, *No, sir.* He leaned in real close and whispered something in your ear that made you stiffen. I could see your jaw muscle flexing from across the room. I didn't have to hear his words to know he was coming onto you, that he didn't view me as a threat, as a partner that counted. Then he stood up straight and announced that we needed to cooperate so they could work. He said, *This is for the good of everyone, you'll see. People behave better when they know they're being watched.*

My first thought was, how will we ever learn to live like this? I didn't want to take a shit in front of them, let alone shower or have sex. But it turns out, human beings can grow used to just about anything if given the opportunity, and lucky us, we were given the opportunity to grow used to the blinking cameras in every room, to let it all hang loose in the bathroom, to make sex tapes we'd never get to see.

■

I begin waking up every night at 2:22 a.m. from the same nightmare—the kid, who is maybe four or five, dressed in a black, hooded cloak, levitates a few feet above a pool and speaks a language I can't understand. Her chin is pressed to her chest so I can't see her face, although I know it's her. Then she leans over, grabs her extra shadow by the head, and tears it from her body the way one rips off a bandage. The shadow, upon separation, takes a step back and examines the kid, then turns toward me, rubbing its palms together like a fire-starter. As soon as the shadow begins strangling me, I wake to a dark figure sitting on my chest, the air tight and clipped in my lungs. The first time this happens, I yell and accidentally wake up the kid. We spend the rest of the night on the porch watching the stirred-and-shaken sky.

Not long after the dreams begin, I start waking with finger-shaped bruises between my ribs. The first stage of grief, I realize, isn't denial—it's clinging.

■

At first, the Department faced opposition. We spent countless evenings watching Shadester rights bounce around a courtroom like a beach ball, knowing in that dizzying, tingly way that they could be talking about you or me or both. *They don't deserve to be marked forever,* the opposition said. *We know from research that rehabilitation is better than punishment.* We held each other's hands tightly. The same hands we sometimes dropped in public when we felt unsafe—we had that privilege unlike so many others; whiteness meant we could remove our otherness like a sweater if we wanted. We could walk five feet apart and temporarily become *gal pals.*

Pop Quiz:
Circle the option that best answers the question.
Q: How do you define freedom without ever having felt fully free?
    A. N/A
    B. N/A
    C. N/A
    D. N/A

I'm grateful for this new policy. Now I know, without a doubt, who I can and cannot trust, said a man on the news, following President Colestein's announcement. The man had given a thumbs-up to the camera like a little kid on a cereal commercial. *Fucking bigot,* you said, shaking your head.

■

For decades, scientists have been tagging animals in the wild to track their locations. Once I peel the Post-it notes off my computer screen, I spend some time perusing Shadester forums. I learn that untagged sea lions have begun rejecting their tagged peers.

■

"Emotional regulation skills," a woman shouts out her car window, her voice trailing off. "You should acquire some," she says, driving past again. She reminds me of the people who used to say, *Have you tried a mindcast?* whenever my temper got the best of me. They were the same people who thought that everyone's horrific circumstances were a direct result of their behaviors, that you could manifest a better life, if only you'd try harder, you lazy piece of shit.

I don't know what makes her think I don't have any emotional regulation skills. Just a few more broken bottles and I am bound to feel like a person again. You'll have no choice but to come back and clean up the glass. You were always cleaning up after me. I'm sorry I wasn't better at chores.

I often avoided chores in favor of going to the neighbors' apartment for happy hour. Antonio made a mean charcuterie board. One by one, they became a family of shadows, first Maria, then Antonio, then their six-year-old son, Carlos, and then they were gone. I heard from the couple in apartment six that Carlos had received his extra shadow for accidentally throwing a baseball through another tenant's window, the broken glass scattered on the walkway like seashells along the beach.

Pop Quiz:

Q: What is worth more: a human life or physical property?

A: Say what you really mean.

Q: I'm the one who demands things around here.

A: *Which* human life?

∎

The troubled kids, they knew what was up well before I did. They knew that *evidence-based* was nothing more than a formal way of saying, *Despite not knowing you, we will fix you.*

But it wasn't until the shadow implementation that I realized that word could be weaponized. *We've done the research. The shadows are an evidence-based practice. People behave better when they are reminded of their mistakes*, said the president, as he was making a very big mistake.

Much like I do not want an extra shadow following me around, the troubled kids did not want reality testing; they wanted to drain my body of any and all serotonin. Usually, this meant firing the most specific insults at me, hoping the words would poke holes in my human suit.

One of my troubled kids, Randy, was in your eighth-grade class. He hated me because I didn't care what he did with his day or whether he came to group or not. When I entered your classroom, he'd look me up and down, say something like, *Did your mom get you those pants or something?* And you'd stifle a laugh, having also commented on my fashion choices. I wasn't sure what the implied insult was—I'd have loved to hear from my mother, even if it were just a pair of pants sent in the mail. Later, I learned Randy's mother had left, too.

Other kids, the tiny ones, hugged me around the waist and asked if they could come over for chips and soda and video games. My reason for saying no never sounded much like a reason at all.

People always asked how we went from strangers working in the same school to engaged several months later. The first thing you said to me: *So, you're my new escape.* You were referring to my role as the person who periodically removed the troubled kids from your class, but that didn't stop my body temperature from jumping to two hundred degrees.

∎

Ever since I was young, I've had a plan for myself—I was going to be someone that people liked but never asked anything of. Before you, I was devoted to my devotion to nothing. Then, the first ultrasound: *It's real*, you said. *It's finally real.*

There is a reason devotion sounds like motion. *Where are we going?* I wanted to ask.

Pop Quiz:
Choose the word that doesn't belong:
    A. Safety
    B. Attachment
    C. Comfort
    D. Mother

■

You're going to be a great mother because you're you, you once said. We kissed and I silently thanked you for your most magnificent lie to date. I remember giving your ass a little spank to show you that I would always be fun and kinky, despite my pathologies. You didn't react. Instead, you said, *I hope our kid wants to be our friend.* It would have been the saddest thing in the world if it were coming out of someone else's mouth. Out of yours, it sounded like an incantation.

■

The Shadester we've seen pissing off the cliffs joins me for a joint. We sit on a bench at the end of the street. Turns out he lives in a tent on the cliffs. According to him, his name is Siegfried. He's pale with freckles under his eyes and long brown hair that reaches the middle of his back. The bench is situated so you can watch seagulls poop on the rocks.

"What are you supposed to be doing right now?" Siegfried asks, braiding his hair.

"Making cold calls," I say, sucking on the joint.

"Where'd that baby go?"

"Asleep."

"Who do you call?"

"Anyone who has ever ordered a mindcast from us or signed up for our mailing list."

"A what?" he asks, scrunching up his face.

"It's like a self-help recording. Some fancy NoShad shit."

"Okay, so that's what, ten, twelve people?" he asks very seriously.

"Yesterday a man told me I sounded like I needed a good fucking," I say.

"What does that even sound like?"

"You're listening to it, baby," I laugh.

"I'll go with avoiding my avoidance for a thousand dollars please," he says. He plucks the joint from between my fingers.

"Those were simpler days, huh."

"Everyone always thinks the past was simpler days."

"I wish you'd let me have this one thing," I say. I actually stomp my foot.

By week eighteen of waking at 2:22 a.m., I've formed a routine. Catch my breath. Take a baby aspirin. Check the closets for intruders. Count the kid's shadows. Pour a whiskey. Smoke a cigarette on the porch. Scan Shadester forums.

YOU'RE NOT ALONE, the forum banner says.

"Being a Shadester is ruining my life," writes a seventeen-year-old boy. "My whole life feels like a race. I'm watching everyone else run away, but I just can't catch up, no matter how hard I try."

Another Shadester teen: "Most days I sit there wishing I was normal and it's really affecting my grades. I barely do any work in class and have no direction in life. I don't know what the fuck to do."

"I love you," I reply. "I love you," I say, lamp-shading my head with a blanket.

I would have already ordered dozens of Shadester children's books, but I don't know where to find them—the Department is a big fan of censorship, only they don't call it that. They call it strategic stabilization.

My post on the Shadester forum:

"My kid was born with an extra shadow (don't fucking ask). Any advice on how to teach her about it? I think I'd rather lick C*lestein's nipple." No matter what, the forums are deleted by morning, then a new one sprouts up, and so on.

The forums remind me of the lesbian chat rooms I frequented as an adolescent. I'd found them when I searched "girls kissing," something I'd justified early on as nothing more than a funny joke—*ha ha, wouldn't it be funny if I looked up girls kissing? Ha ha what a funny thing. Anyway, boys are cute.* The chat rooms had absurd names like W4OlderW and LesRoom. I could be anyone I wanted in those chat rooms. A sexy, experienced goddess. *Yeah, do you like that?* I'd type. I was a twelve-year-old acned virgin. I met older women in those chat rooms, although it occurred to me later on that they, too, might have been twelve-year-old acned virgins.

■

I try talking to our baby while I apply ointment to her tush. I tell her what I know about shadows: "When I was a kid, my friends and I played this game we called the Shadow Game. It was a terrible game with no real rules, but we loved it. All you had to do was chase someone down and catch their shadow by diving on it. The best part was when the person whose shadow had been caught would do something silly like pick their nose or do an embarrassing dance, because *they* weren't the one doing the embarrassing thing—their shadow was. One day, my buddy Rob hid scissors in his hoodie pocket, and once his shadow was caught, he stabbed our friend in the bicep. *It wasn't me, it was my shadow!* he cried when they took him away."

■

The anonymous calls keep coming. None of them reveal why Mischief has changed her name and run off with an older man. I finally shut off my phone so the kid and I can misinterpret each other without interruption.

At this point, I'm almost certain about who is calling. There isn't anyone else it could be. Over and over again, I ask myself: What if I can't find it in me to forgive him? What if I can?

Pop Quiz:
Q: Can there be healing without forgiveness?
A: This is an out-of-office reply. Check back later.

■

The first time you and I fucked, it was 5:00 a.m. We were wasted, and I came while straddling you on the beach for all the town to see. Topless, still wearing my shorts. *How did we get here?* you kept saying between sloppy kisses. *Do you and [redacted] have a lot of sex?* I asked, knowing the answer. *No, we don't, not at all,* you said. Your body was vibrating under me. *Say it again,* I said, a wetness between my thighs. Beside us, our single shadows attached at the waist. I watched your shadow grab my shadow's hand and stick a shadow-finger in its mouth.

That first time, I couldn't stop talking about wanting you while I was in the middle of having you, as if the act itself wasn't enough—I had to make the universe know, too.

Sex during our affair had been a rushed, neurotic thing. I'm not sure either of us could get out of our own heads. I'd never seen someone get dressed so quickly after—that is, if you undressed at all. Sometimes we parked behind a pizza place and fucked in the backseat of my car, but our preferred place was the secret spot on the cliffs. *Is anyone looking? Who's there?* we'd say, as if our partners had sicced private investigators on us. It took pushing through the affair and coming out on the other side to realize just how unimportant we were. We weren't curing a rare blood disease, we were listening to our hormones. No one had ever followed us. And our partners were better off without us. They found new people to love and be loved by. The sex improved once we extricated ourselves from our relationships. We had room to breathe. Time to explore. It wasn't long before I told you I was interested in kink. You didn't know what I meant, not specifically anyway. And maybe I didn't either. But my clit throbbed when I told you what I wanted you to do to me: *Slap me in the face and tell me to shut the fuck up.* You narrowed your eyes. *Really? Are you sure?* you asked, but you were already making your way toward me.

I tried to teach you about kink, using someone else's words. I googled BDSM and the first article I came across was called "Could Owning a Cat Be a Gateway to BDSM?"

What are you trying to tell me? you asked. You were petting Mischief, who was asleep in the laundry basket.

■

First, we tried IUI, which was, as I understood it, the equivalent of shooting some sperm up there and seeing what happens. After a few failed conceptions and uncomfortable inquiries from clinic staff about where your husband was, we switched to a new fertility center and tried

IVF. Whenever anyone asked the difference between the two, I just laughed and said, *Imagine driving a new car instead.* When IVF didn't work the first time, you were convinced your eggs were defective. I'd never seen a person break that way before. *There's nothing I hate more than hearing about other people's babies*, you snapped, slamming your laptop shut. Looking at all those happy faces hurt you, and you couldn't pretend that it didn't. *Give me one of my own*, you said. I never dared tell you this, but you saying the words *my own* hurt me in all the hard-to-reach places.

In social work school, one professor said it was our job to learn to treat humans like humans. *Not that any of you are particularly good at it*, he said.

The usual questions plagued me: Help whom, do what? Can there be help without hurt? Can I trust the impulse I have to help others? The troubled kids at school used to say, *If it's not money, I don't want it.*

We spent a long time scrolling through sperm bank lists. *What if we choose the wrong donor?* we wondered. What if our kid grows up to be a serial killer? Or a Department of Balance employee? We wanted a donor who resembled me, bonus points if he worked in human services. A trait we could do without: my tendency to grow attached, or rather, fixated. When we created our account, you warned me not to get too excited about any particular donor because his sperm might not be available when we needed it. *Just browse, okay?* Five minutes later I said, *Look, look, look, I think he's the one.*

You'd wanted to know why I was so interested in kink. What I didn't say: *I want to be bonded to you forever.* What I did say: *There are classes we can take.* You perked up at this. If there was one thing you loved, it was taking notes in an organized environment.

One time, after group, I overheard one of my troubled kids ask their friend, *What's that white stuff that comes out of a boy's penis?* They were eleven, maybe twelve. The friend giggled. *No idea.* They left for lunch before I could make the decision to intervene. I wanted to shake them. *Half a milliliter of the white stuff goes for a thousand a pop.*

We couldn't have done any of it without your mom's help. She sent us check after check. *I'm not doing anything with it anyway,* she said. Most days, she went fishing or for a walk or a hike. I don't know what she does now if grief is robbing her of her usual joys. She used to collect various rocks that she lined up on her windowsills and identified in a big, fat book. Visiting the cabin was like entering a vortex—it was covered in homemade wind chimes made from old teapots and cutlery, rusty keys, and jewelry. Upon entering, I felt as if, for the first time since birth, I could think about my life and keep my heart from nosing in.

For one grad school assignment, I had to film myself performing mock therapy with an agreeing party. My father sat in an armchair across from me, eyeing the camera I'd instructed him to ignore. *So, what brings you in today?* I asked, forming a concerned face. *I forget my lines*, he said. *But I know that I'm unhappy.*

When you finally got pregnant, it was brilliant, it was magic, it was like finding a secret tunnel between dimensions. But you—we—had a miscarriage at sixteen weeks. I'd never seen you cry so hard. You took a week off work and curled up in bed. You spent most of the time staring at the wall or ceiling. I tiptoed from room to room trying to find somewhere to put my body. It took me a few days, but I finally broke down one morning making eggs and sausage. I don't know what it was about breakfast that pushed me over the edge, but it did. I think it's because I realized breakfast is for families.

I crawled into bed, wrapped my arms around you, and sobbed into your back. I felt your jaw pull into a smile. I think you were happy that I was mourning. You'd wanted confirmation that we were in this together. It was a fucked-up thing.

■

The phone rings and rings. I answer, "Tell me," and a woman's voice I don't recognize tells me Mischief has found a new home. One with a mother and a father and a window three feet off the ground for her to jump in and out of as she pleases. They've even provided her with a cat tree.

"Is it *your* home?" I ask.

"Listen, you didn't hear this from me, but the cat usually walks women home from the bar."

The kid wakes up every hour, on the hour.

"Beau, you got this?" I mumble through my daze. "Beau, your turn," I say, kicking the empty space beside me.

If someone broke in and tried to rob us, I'd empty my savings if it meant they'd take the kid with them. The kid's only saving grace is her widow's peak. It's a masterpiece, just like yours.

■

Tonight, we live in the car. It's the only thing that helps the kid sleep. I drive her around the neighborhood and search for Mischief. I shout her name out the window. I do that little noise cats like. An old woman on her stoop drinks a glass of white wine and scowls at me.

"What do you think?" I ask the kid. "Main street?"

She enters the last cycle of this crying phrase then settles into a smush-faced sleep.

I don't get three blocks before I see two drunk blonds, arm in arm, weaving on the sidewalk. Behind them, a trotting cat with her head on a swivel.

"So, the rumors are true," I say, tailing the group. Once the women are safely in their apartment, Mischief loiters outside as if waiting for a bartender to call her with another job to do. I park the car and tiptoe toward Mischief, whispering her name. She approaches me and circles my legs, rubbing up against me.

"Someone's polyamorous," I say, scooping her into my arms to take her home.

But Mischief doesn't want it. She's gotten a taste of the streets and there's no going back. She scratches up furniture, she knocks glasses off the counter, she paws me in the face. When I open the door to set her free, I only cry a little bit. I call your mom to ask her how she did it, how she dealt with her baby moving out. But I don't find out because her phone is off and I am sent straight to voice mail, where I listen to several seconds of your mother trying to convince one of her rescue dogs that he must put his toys back in the appropriate bin like all the others. And here I was thinking my tears might move her enough to forgive me for not turning my body into a home.

That's something you used to say. When you were thirty-six weeks pregnant, you spent most nights in bed pressing on the kid's belly or butt. *You wouldn't want someone pressing on the walls of your tiny home*, I'd say. *Home? I AM the home*, you'd laugh.

∎

After the miscarriage, you were desperate to conceive. To conquer your body's betrayal. You turned on a mindcast—this was before I began selling them—and lay down in bed, your hands folded across your stomach. *Remember: the world would not be the world without you*, said a voice intended to soothe. Shortly after, Mischief joined you and hacked up a fur ball breakfast medley. You turned off the mindcast and said, *If I were the type to believe in messages from the universe, I would be upset. But I'm not, so.* You looked inconsolable.

Then we tried again. This time, everything was different—I was a new Shadester. During your IVF transfer, I waited outside, chain-smoking in the shadow of the building. It was a success, you got pregnant again, and we dared not celebrate. We didn't tell anyone, not even when it looked like someone had stuffed a basketball under your sweatshirt. But in the privacy of our home, I rubbed your round belly like a magic lamp. I wished for a healthy baby, a perfect life together, a world that didn't implode before we—you, me, and the kid—could explore every inch of it.

———

One evening you came home from work, red-cheeked and snorting like a bull. The gym teacher had called a student a fag. You wanted to beat his skull in. You were six months pregnant. *You aren't allowed to beat anyone up for at least three more months*, I said. *I don't see it on the list of forbidden activities*, you said.

The kid inside your belly grew and grew without any complications. When I was hungry, I rubbed your magic lamp stomach and wished for steak tacos. They never arrived. Neither did the pinot noir. When I told you that you were sexy, you rubbed your round stomach and said, *I don't feel sexy*. I felt so helpless. I kissed your neck and your swollen boobs, I tongued your new, pointed nipples, lightly playing with your cunt. When you sat on my face, I couldn't see anything past your belly, and I liked it that way, the relative anonymity; I was object and as an object, I licked and sucked your clit while you grinded against my mouth and nose, my breaths coming at sporadic intervals, each time my air getting cut off for a little bit longer, but I worked and worked—I wanted to please you more than anything, to show you that you were the sexiest person I'd ever encountered. Your pussy throbbed in my mouth, and as you came, you squeezed your thighs against each side of my head, the thunder of orgasm leaving a dulled ringing in my ears.

Whoa, you just gave her some serious waves, you laughed, falling onto your back. Breathless, hair stuck to your cheek. *Is she ever going to have a name?* I asked. Our list of baby names was three stories long, mostly consisting of ones that weren't really names. We couldn't agree on how many names one person could reasonably have. *What about Bear Fox Lightning Rosen-Allen?* you said, laughing. *Or Burgundy Bear River Rosen-Allen*, I countered. How would we settle on one?

I had high hopes you would know what to do once our kid was born, but when you looked down at the bloody, beautiful mess that came out of you, you were too in awe to speak. Then your eyes went blank and you left us. Just like that.

A Department agent, having already taken the kid straight from the birth canal and given her the extra shadow, handed the kid to me and slipped out of the room. The kid was crying and then the kid was crying louder and then louder still, so loud I almost passed out. The medical staff were rushing around pretending to do something other than nothing. One of the nurses, frantic, said *Oh my god, oh my god, holy fuck, she has two shadows, how did that happen so quickly?* and another tisked at me and said, *That's not how you hold a newborn.* She grabbed the kid out of my arms and demonstrated proper technique, resisting when I said, *Give her back,* the vertigo of inadequacy overtaking me. I nearly forgot you were dead until I looked over and saw them covering your body with a hospital sheet. I was crying but I couldn't remember starting.

———

This isn't fair, I just found her, I yelled, because it was true, I had. We'd spent twenty-six years without each other, and we spent our short four years together trying to make up for lost time. Once they wheeled you out, I looked down at the baby.

This is not happening, I said.

■

While I have the kid awake, I take photos of her the way people do with babies. "Pssstttt, look here, smile, pretend you just took the best poop of your life." She responds by blowing bubbles, by tonguing the air. I even get her to smile.

I don't understand what it is I'm supposed to feel.

"I am Beau's wife," is something I can no longer say. My head feels the way watercolor looks when it bleeds. I wish someone would come dip their brush in me.

Pop Quiz:
Q: What + what = a life?
A: *Till death do us part*, we said.

I have the photos printed then I mail them to your mom. When you finally left your ex to be with me, you called your mom and said, *I'm getting married*. She said, *You did it, you did it, you did it*. I spent all night tracing your MOM tattoo.

I wanted what you had with her. And if not, I didn't want anyone else in the world to have it.

The first time I met your mom, she hugged me so tight my organs begged for mercy. When she released me, she said, *So, I hear you don't scare easily.*

I liked visiting your mom. I liked being one of the select few. Two seconds in the door, and she was handing me a giant bag of my favorite pretzels. *Thanks, Mom,* I once said, when I thought I was alone. *Don't worry, I'll share her,* you said, coming up behind me and sticking your hands up my shirt.

At night, I flip through old scrapbooks, attempting to sear the images of you into my mind. And it works. I see baby you everywhere, in everyone. Obviously in the kid, but also in the kid's extra shadow. Your long face and ski-slope nose. Perhaps I am imagining things, but side by side, our shadows look like you at the beginning and you at the end.

■

Wildebeest babies are born ready to run. I wish the kid were more like a wildebeest. I observe her sleeping in her crib, sucking away at her thumb, and I squint my eyes until her blanket transforms into dark brown fur covering her entire body. I try to communicate with her telepathically, hoping she'll get the hint and stand up, climb out of her crib, and join me on a walk to a place where there aren't any people.

———

"What *can* you do?" I ask the sleeping kid. I feel like the boogie monster standing over her crib. I personally think I'd make a good boogie monster. When I was young, the other kids used to call me creepy. They couldn't provide me with details. *It's just you*, they said, avoiding my eyes. This secretly delighted me, until I learned that *creepy* really meant *sensitive*, which, of course, is far worse.

■

I wake up at 1:00 a.m. to a skull-shuddering crash outside. At first, I try to ignore it. Not my business, probably just a raccoon. But I can't fall back asleep. And despite not having woken from my usual dream, I feel as if someone is sitting on my chest, a leg draped on either side. Is it a heart attack? A pulmonary embolism? I wouldn't be so lucky. I slip into my robe and creep out into the living room. I have no baseball bat. Why don't I have a baseball bat? (This is where I imagine you rolling your eyes and saying, *I must have told you a hundred times, it's in the hallway closet!*) I turn on the patio light then crack open the front door. No sound, just the wheeze of the wind, the distant growl of the ocean. The moon, swollen and bright, hanging low in the sky. To the left of the door, I find the window screen on the ground. It has a huge slash in it.

I don't know why, but my first thought is that it looks very, very sad.

Back inside:

1:10 a.m.: The kid spits up then giggles about it.

1:11 a.m.: The kid shrieks so loudly I lose my legs.

1:12 a.m.: The kid's shadow trembles. It is so small I could swallow it whole.

1:13 a.m.: The kid backhands me in the face.

1:14 a.m.: I bounce her up and down like I've seen real parents do.

1:15 a.m.: The kid spits up again, and so do I.

1:16 a.m.: "Your mom was an acrobat. She fell from a tightrope. That's why I'm so mad at her. You understand, don't you? The last thing I need is you attempting any tricky balancing acts on my watch. Blink once if you hear me."

1:17 a.m.: The kid's eyelids grow heavy.

1:18 a.m.: Heavier.

1:19 a.m.: Heavier yet.

1:22 a.m.: Victory!

1:25 a.m.: Mistaking stupidity for bravery, I turn my phone back on.

I have eleven new messages from the unknown number. Finally, the voice I've been waiting to hear.

"I know we haven't spoken in a while, Kris. You know I'm bad with words. And, well, non-words, too. I just wanted to check in on you is all. Call me back, please? Here's my number."

"How's the baby? You holding up okay? Need any help?"

"When you were born you were so, so, so tiny. We didn't know what the heck we were doing. They send you home with this baby and don't tell you what to do with it. I suppose rule number one is don't call a human baby an *it*."

"Listen, I don't know how you got your shadow and frankly, I don't care anymore. You could have stabbed a man, whatever. Well, okay, maybe I care a little. Just don't stab *me*, and we'll be okay. Deal? I'd really like to see you. Don't make this more than what it is."

"Sometimes it takes us old people a while to catch up. You know? I'm here for you now. Give me a call, would you?"

"Saying sorry about Beau doesn't seem like much. Or anything at all. You know I know how you feel. Shit, maybe that's bad of me to say. Motherfuck, how do I delete this one?"

"At least let me know you're alive, okay? That's the least you can do. Send a burning arrow through my window, I don't care."

"The human brain is nature's biggest mistake. An honest mistake, but a mistake, nonetheless. Nothing that has happened should have happened."

"Sometimes when I mail a letter, I get this overwhelming fear that it never goes anywhere. Simply falls straight into the earth. Poof! That's how I feel about these messages. Poof!"

"Best way to get a kid to fall asleep? Start telling them about yourself. Worked for me back in the day."

"Like I said, I'd take it back if I could, but I can't. Here's my number again, just in case."

I text him a link to the definition of *conditional* then chuck my phone at the wall.

I can't remember my father ever talking about himself. Sure, I know some typical facts like where he grew up (everywhere), his major (chemical engineering), his GPA (3.34), his last job before he retired (director of supply chain management for an artificial flavor company), but I can get all that from scanning his resume. *Who is he?* I wonder. What does he care about? What makes him cry? How does he process his pain, if at all? Who does he want to be?

All I know is, as a kid, the only thing that helped me sleep was the sound of the vacuum cleaner, and it was my dad who stayed up until all hours vacuuming my room and the hallway outside.

Another night, another voice mail from my father. He must be having trouble sleeping, too.

"Remember when you were little—maybe four or five?—and I'd take you to birthday parties? You were so scared of people that you'd cling to me in the corner for the whole damn thing. The best part was when you went home and told Mom how much fun you'd had. We called you Velcro. Sometimes I wonder where you stick now."

∎

My birth story according to my father:

When my mother went into labor, I was positioned with my head down and my hand by my head so that all the doctor could see when he examined her at eight centimeters were my grasping fingers. I reached out and grabbed the doctor's hand and wouldn't let go.

■

Shopping list:
- a new home in the darkness of the Arctic Tundra
- canned tuna for Mischief (to lure her home)
- a variety pack of pacifiers
- baby food, baby food, baby food
- a single person who hasn't at one point or another asked, "Is this the life I imagined for myself?"

■

I spend several hours looking up grief counselors online. Despite my previous career, I'd never liked therapy much. All the therapists did was ask me about my parents, as if that were the same as asking about me. I'm sure there are good ones out there, but I don't know where to find them. I don't like the way the grief counselors look in their photos. Any of them. Their sad, ugly faces stare back at me through the computer screen. The looks in their eyes urge me not to feel so sad and ugly, but given the circumstance, I don't think that's fair.

———

Against my better judgment, I've chosen to meet with a woman named Frances. She purses her lips and says, "Why don't you tell me what you think?" I tell her I think I am paying her, and she chuckles as if this is all part of my journey. An emotional support dog sits next to her chair. The black lab sniffs my legs aggressively.

"I hate it when you sniff me that way. It makes me feel violated," I say to the dog.

"Good," says Frances. "*Good.*"

In another session, I sit on a blue carpet with my back against the wall talking to the youngest woman I could find listed. Alice.

"Do you ever find yourself sitting in the middle of a coffee shop, surrounded by plugged-in patrons, and suddenly you are overcome with the desire to make everyone stop what they're doing because—" she interrupts me, which you learn not to do in what, Therapy 101?—and says, "I think I know where this is going, Kris."

"No, you don't. I want to ask people if they ever feel sad. Like, I know they do, but I want to hear them say it."

Alice points her pen at me and smiles. A breakthrough.

"That's because you want to know you're not alone in your grief. Perfectly normal," she says, jotting things down, perhaps writing "Perfectly Normal" under my name. I don't see her again because she made a good point, and I wasn't there for the good points.

■

The kid has begun to form some type of personality. She smiles at me when she isn't screaming. She looks more and more like you as the days go on, which surprises me, and then I am surprised by my own surprise, and I have to go back to the beginning.

I do my best to ignore her extra shadow, which grows as she grows. Most people's second shadows are on one side of their body and attached at the hand, like paper cut-out art. When the sun hits the kid just right, her shadows look like wings billowing out from her body.

"Why is this water falling from my eyes?" I say.

The kid reaches out her fat hand and grabs my nose, her tiny, razor-sharp fingernails scratching my skin off until I have no armor left.

Grasshoppers, cockroaches, etc.

"Cooooo boooo booo bee bbuh cuhh," says the kid, her chest puffed up. Then she sticks her entire fist in her mouth, something wildebeests cannot do. If pressed, I would not admit to feeling comfortable with the kid. I'm not sure what it is babies want from their superiors.

While you were pregnant, you'd done everything you could to reassure yourself that I would be good with our kid. We babysat our friends' kids. You watched me bounce and play. It felt like an audition for a role I already had. It's not like you would have left me. Or maybe you would have? *I love how Winston loves you and your belly button*, you said as I held our friend's baby, who repeatedly pointed to my stomach, instructing me to lift my shirt and show off my belly button. *It's because I have outie belly button representation*, I said. *Write that down somewhere*, you said.

It is not lost on me that the kid might someday become someone else's troubled kid. When the school counselor calls home to report the kid's poor behavior, I will not respond like the other parents. I will not say, *What exactly is your purpose then?*

The kid sprouts some teeth, and I fish around in her mouth to investigate. She doesn't seem to like it. Crying is involved. Running her lines for the world's most tragic play.

"I can't help it, I'm a tactile learner," I say, kissing the top of her head. "You're going to have to learn to adapt, you melancholy goose."

I start crying just as the kid stops, as if we are two hoses that share the same faucet. You used to call everyone a goose. A love goose. A wife goose. A cute goose. A sleepy goose. A hungry goose. Even Mischief goose. You ruined long-necked birds for me, Beau. The oval of your mouth when you said *goose*. Your calloused hand cupping my face. The cushion of your lips against mine.

You got the goose thing from your mom. When I asked her about it, she said, "That's what they are. I can't explain it."

Later, I get drunk and impulse buy a gorgeous wooden chest. I've always wanted one. Antiques give me the sense I can turn back time. *Chest goose*, you would have said.

After much debate, I decide on responsibility. I store the kid's birth certificate in the chest, along with all our fertility documents: preparation information, procedural guidelines, glimmering price tags, the sperm donor's identification number. And your name. Your signature. Your sloppy threes and nines. And mine, right under yours.

■

During the winter, tracked geese will sometimes die because of large ice blocks that form around their collars. The scientists continue to track them anyway, citing the importance of research.

■

At night, after turning on the kid's noise machine and explaining the brain benefits of sleep, I spend my time smoking on the porch. I watch the sky drip into the horizon. I miss you; I miss our plans.

I often wonder what would have happened if I never met you, if I'd ended up with someone else. How our lives would have played out. I probably wouldn't have an extra shadow, at least not yet, and I probably wouldn't be staring at the sky, wondering if you were the one responsible for its dark and stormy canvas.

Well, the extra shadow is doing its job. There isn't a day that I don't wake up and wonder whether I deserve even the simplest of joys.

That reminds me—when I was young, I had a dead-eyed friend who used to grab my hand and make me slap myself in the face. *Stop hurting yourself, stop hurting yourself*, she'd say.

■

Pop Quiz:
Q: What will you fill yourself with today?
A: Imagine this is a five-paragraph essay response, with an oddly touching conclusion.

■

Today, on the news, a reporter interviews NoShad parents of a Shadester child.

"Is it true what they say about the little ones? They're possessed by demons?" the reporter asks, stuffing a microphone in the flustered faces of two men. Neither of them responds. One of them closes his eyes and stands like that, swaying a little. The other pulls his son closer, but the boy slips out of his grasp, approaches the reporter, and kicks her in the shins. I'm sure that doesn't help his demon case, but it sure is satisfying to watch.

■

Once a female octopus has laid her eggs, she will stop feeding. She guards her eggs until they hatch, slowly starving to death. *Show-offs*, I think.

In the past few months, I've only left the house for essentials. It seems I've lost all my friends. Not in a violent way, but in a burning-out way. They have their own lives to attend to. No one besides my father has reached out, and I'm trying not to think about how he rejected me when I needed him most. I haven't heard from your mom since she called to not blame me. I suspect she will not rest until she gets your old motorcycle working—even when you were alive, she refused to get rid of it. It was her way of hanging on to you, her Beau, from across the country. What was it like for her to lose you, her only child, her miracle baby? It's one of those things I can imagine but can't find a place for. She'd gotten pregnant with you at age forty, a one-night stand. *I'll take it from here*, she'd said to no one, smiling as she held the pregnancy test up to the light.

"You know where we live," I finally text my father. I assume it will send him running for the sunshine.

In captivity, toward the end of their lives, some female octopuses will tear off their own skin and eat the tips of their tentacles.

On TV, President Colestein talks about nothing.

"We are leaving behind the gray area on this quest for perfect societal balance," he says, his delivery so smooth that the words don't matter. "Think of our country as a scale. Everyone contributes to the balance in their own way."

The kid chugs down her bottle then pushes it away and feels around for my nip, opening and closing her mouth like a fish.

"Shh, not for you," I said. "Well, they're not for anyone at the moment. Or ever again."

Pop Quiz:
True or False
1. If you want to know what someone wants, all

you have to do is look at their actions. Whatever they do means they most likely want the opposite. _____

2. It matters very little whether you mark true or false. _____

When my cousin was released from prison, he was never able to find a job again. Every time a potential employer saw his criminal record, they stopped calling. *I've been forever marked*, he told me a few days before he overdosed. And to think, we thought the prison system was corrupt, but the reality is, it was just preparation for what came next.

Octopuses cannot be tracked the traditional way—they are famously intelligent and difficult to catch. They will rip off their tags if a scientist manages to attach one. Don't worry, the scientists always find a way.

■

I once confided in a friend about my interest in BDSM.

"I don't know, I like loving sex?" she said.

"Oh," I said.

The BDSM Basix class was held in a room above the sex store. The class was exclusively for queer and trans people, which I liked. The teacher was a chubby, beautiful woman with gray hair and cat-eye glasses. *Let's go around the room and introduce ourselves. Say why we are here*, she said. *I was a teacher for twenty-five years, and now I teach this.* I nudged you like, *Hey, look, a fellow teacher!* Her contact information was written on the board, presumably various usernames on various kink websites. This was what—four or five months before the shadow implementation? Otherwise, the room likely would have been one big shadow. My phone vibrated in my pocket. A text from my father. *What are you up to?* This was back when we used to talk every day, before I was a Shadester. *Getting dinner with Beau*, I said. *Oh, where? Can your old dad join?*

There were easily twenty-five or thirty people smushed into that room. The excited ones giggled uncontrollably every time the teacher made a dirty joke. A few people looked nervous, perhaps first-timers like us. You had your notebook open on your crossed legs, pen poised on your lips. For the most part, everyone seemed so kind, so welcoming. There was one man, spit-shined bald with a brown mustache who gave me the creeps, although I couldn't say why. He sat with his arms folded across his chest, frowning for the duration of the class. When it was his turn to share why he was there, he said, *I didn't know there was a class. I just happened to be downstairs poking around when I heard the commotion upstairs.* The commotion, I guess, had been everyone sitting quietly in their seats before class began.

Welcome. In case you didn't know, this class is for queer and trans people only, the instructor said. The man shifted in his seat, arms still crossed, looked over his right then left shoulder, then told the floor, *Yes, I'm, uh, gay.*

He looks like a fucking cop, you whispered.

I was torn between wanting to give the man a hug and wanting to steer clear of him forever. I guess the two desires stemmed from the same feeling—pity. You could practically see the soundproof closet around him.

When I was nine years old, a few months before my mother left, I had a sex dream about a girl in my English class. I began going to bed earlier and earlier, in hot pursuit of that same dream. Her name was Cash and every day she drew a new picture of a dolphin jumping out of the water, a slew of *v*'s flying in the poorly blended sunset. She stored the pictures in a binder labeled DOLPHIN. Every single picture was the exact same. I thought her commitment to this single task meant she would make a great girlfriend.

Something no one has ever said about me: *She wants her partner to have many interests that are not her.*

If you are going to do it to someone else, you need to know what it feels like first, said the teacher. *That's my number one rule.*

■

When the doorbell rings, I accidentally spill my coffee, and the kid crawls over to investigate the carpet. She slaps it with her meaty hand. The second I scoop her into my arms, she begins to cry. The end of the world is nigh. I answer the door in your robe, hood up.

A short, stocky man rocks from heel to toe in my doorway, partaking in his infamous self-soothing activity—twirling his mustache.

"Oh, you took me literally," I say, petting the kid on the nose like Mischief used to like (still does like?).

"Can I come in?" he asks. For a moment, I consider shutting the door in his face but then I remember his voice mail about my nickname, Velcro—he's right, I've always been desperate to stick somewhere.

I move aside and let my father in. I move shit around to make space for him to sit. The couch is covered in photos and books and wrappers from various snacks that make me so bloated I look a few months pregnant.

"I usually sit on top of the wrappers," I explain.

"Give me the baby," my father barks, reaching his veiny hands out. That's when he notices her extra shadow and nearly chokes on his spit. Once he recovers, he pulls her close, as if to protect her from herself.

"Kris," he whispers.

"Stop, I know," I say, waving him off, and in turn, waving off my vivid mental movie of a NoShad hitting her over the head with a beer bottle.

The kid stops crying the second she's safe in his arms.

"Rude," I say to the kid.

My father gives me a stern look then switches his tune and bops the kid up and down and begins dancing around the living room. Great, I think, now there is a stranger holding my baby.

"When was the last time you left the house?" he asks.

I know that this is his way of easing me toward more difficult questions. I try to invent a plausible lie explaining how I got my extra shadow. He can't possibly know the truth; if he did, I'd have to move to a remote island and change my name, become one of those people who drives a golf cart around, waving at locals as I pee myself over each speed bump.

I don't respond. I fuss around in the fridge, which houses moldy cheese and spoiled milk.

"I see," he says, scratching his cheek with his free hand. "Has she told you how much she hates you yet?" he asks with a twitch of a smile.

"No, she hasn't reached that developmental milestone yet," I say, trying to sound like a baby expert.

My father laughs a full body laugh, his shoulders shaking like he's riding a rickety roller coaster. And just like that, he becomes my dad again. He says that was his least favorite milestone, that I was a temperamental teen, and he wishes he could have skipped that one altogether.

"At least you were there for every milestone," I say, thinking of my mother. My mother whom I love even when it is least convenient.

My dad takes a deep breath and turns away, twirling his mustache. I can't discern whether I've hurt him or touched him. It isn't something we ever talk about—my mother leaving.

I pretend to play with a pen on the kitchen counter. Maybe I'll write Siegfried a nice note. He would like that. I will remind him of what it was like before, ten, twenty years ago, when the sun wasn't our enemy, and the world was fat with promise. *Remember when our shadows told happy stories about where we lived and loved and played?* I'd write. *I once took a photo of my shadow waving. I gave it to my mother. What is this?* she said, flipping it over as if the answer was written on the back.

It occurs to me that I am ill-equipped to write a nice note.

After a few moments, his back still to me, my dad says, "Did you get my message?"

"Yeah, all ninety-seven of them."

"When your mom was pregnant with you, she liked to hollow out a pickle then pour Coca-Cola inside and scatter shredded cheese on top," he says. I can't see him, but I know a smile is hesitating across his face. "Did you know that? She could be so funny sometimes."

"I wish you wouldn't," I say.

My dad turns to face me, his eyes frothy. He stands there looking at me, lips slightly parted, as if daring me to ask, *What? What is it?* When I don't speak, he doesn't so much go in for a hug as fall into my arms.

"This doesn't mean we've made up," I say, squeezing him tightly.

■

Pop Quiz:

True or False

1. You need more than any one person can reason-
    ably give. _____

■

The Department spends so much time and money trying to convince us that Shadesters can have fulfilling lives that I almost begin to believe them. That is, until I leave the house. "Gloomshow!" shouts a man in a raincoat and top hat on my walk to the drugstore. That's a new one. Siegfried said he's gotten it recently, too; it's a hip insult going around. The news anchors tell all kinds of tall tales about Shadester success stories: a president of a real estate company, a top defense attorney in the state, and a doctor that discovered a cure for a rare hereditary disease.

Siegfried and I sit on our bench, smoking cigarettes in the heavy-blanket heat. My dad is inside putting the kid to bed. I point out the secret spot on the cliffs where you and I used to meet up to drink beer and kiss each other's faces.

The great thing about Siegfried is that he doesn't ask me about my shadow, and I don't ask him about his. I assume he was fucked by the system like most everyone else. I am sick of all the *so-how-did-you-get-your-shadows* and the *I'll-show-you-mine-if-you-show-me-yours*, because I am never going to show anyone mine. What I tell myself is that I am too ashamed, but a smaller, quieter part of me knows I am too afraid to give up that shame, to share it with someone who could possibly take a sledgehammer to its surface and release all that broken light.

"You haven't happened to see a beautiful white and gray cat slithering around, have you?"

"I see a lot of cats," he says. I nod, wondering if they all use the beach as a collective litter box.

"I get it," I say, for something to say.

"I found a place to crash by the way," he says. "I met some Shadesters at a support group. A couple. They've got an extra room for me."

"A support group."

"Yeah, it's okay if you're into, like, shedding the rest of your identity."

"What identity?" I laugh. "What did I even do before Beau?"

"This will still be our bench, don't you worry."

"I *was* worrying, how did you know?"

When I head back inside, I find my dad in the fridge, shuffling things around. He brought us some of the good food, the NoShad food. Fresh spinach, raspberries, blueberries, even a pineapple. What I said about my father back when you and I first met: *He could be anyone—I hardly know him at all. But whoever he is, he is good.*

"You owe me a new window screen," I say.

"How did you know it was me?"

"What was your plan exactly?"

"Make you love me again," he shrugs, twirling his mustache.

Surprisingly, my dad had no problem with the whole gay thing. My coming out had been as thrilling as folding laundry. *I like girls*, I said to him over lunch. *Great, cool, girls are great*, he said, sipping his beer. *No, you don't get it. Like, I date girls*. I was fourteen and had dated exactly zero girls. Over a decade later, I called him during a brief period of stability. I think you were outside watering your plants and whispering affirmations. *I didn't know how to tell you*, I began. *But I have an extra shadow now*. I thought saying it that way was softer, easier to absorb than *I'm a Shadester*. The blow of the dial tone ripped the fabric of my world right off.

Pop Quiz:
Q: Is it smart to categorize people as either good or bad?
A: Of course it isn't.

◾

"Look at her go," cheers Siegfried. The kid has just taken her first step, toward a bag of BBQ potato chips.

"Beau, hurry! You're missing it!" I shout, as if you are simply grading papers in the other room.

I smile, waiting for your approaching footsteps. Siegfried stands up from the couch and gives me a wordless hug. When he lets go, my vision tunnels then goes dark. I wake up on my back on the floor, the kid lying across my stomach and smacking me in the boob. I imagine she is mentally chanting something like, *If I can't have chips, I'll take the nip!*

"What happened?" I ask everyone.

"You remembered your relationship status," says Siegfried, making silly faces at the kid.

The kid, as if understanding my question, slides off my stomach and onto her feet. Then she takes a few more steps before taking another tumble. This time, I don't call for you.

The kid and I eat toast and strawberry jam for breakfast every morning. The ritual keeps me clinging to this life for a while longer. The kid's shadow quietly munches beside her. Shrimp, butterflies, scorpions. Shrimp, butterflies, scorpions.

The kid loves walking, even though she arguably spends more time falling. Every time she falls, my chest tightens for a few moments, thinking she's finally broken, or more accurately, that I've been neglectful enough to allow her to break. To give the Department an excuse to take her away from me.

According to research, penguins wearing tracking bands produced fewer chicks and were more likely to die than penguins with no bands.

■

On the kid's first birthday, I sing the words all wrong, but thankfully she doesn't notice. One day, I will have to explain things to her but today is not that day. Happiness, in the kid's eyes, is shoving icing in her face. As for me, I fall in love with the kid. I finally understand what all the fuss is about: a tiny someone is predisposed to trust you and you have the chance to prove them right.

Once I put the kid to bed, I slip on your soccer jersey and watch a video of you on my phone. Would it be like this every year? The kid's celebration dampened by the anniversary of your death. In the video, your head is tilted back, studying the planes overhead. You have your business face on. Just as I am about to stop recording, you turn to me and say, *If someone were to look at us, would they know we were in love?*

This remembering. It's like sneaking up to a million different houses and knocking, then running away before anyone can answer.

■

The kid's first word is *wow*, which is really quite something when you think about how little there is to be astounded by.

"Wow!" she says to my father when he arrives with some of my old clothes for the kid.

"Don't get a big head about it. She's impressed by dirt," I say.

He bends down to the kid and holds up a yellow and black dress with pineapples printed on it. She grabs it and throws it to the ground.

"Guess we know how she feels about it," I say. He isn't listening, though. He is smiling as he gently folds the clothes into neat little stacks on the couch.

"Wow, oh wowwwww," she says to the people walking their babies and dogs.

"Wow! Wowieeeeeeeeeeeeeeeee!" says the kid at dinner, first fisting her bowl of mashed potatoes then twisting her hands in the air like she is starting a baby-sized motorcycle. Off into the sunset, she rides. If only.

She grabs a pea from another bowl and holds it out for me as if it were a gem. I hate to break her heart.

"Yeah, I see it. That's a pea," I say. Me, always the sage in this relationship.

Her second and third words: *No* and *wrong*, used together.

"I am, in fact, very right," I argue.

She shakes her head as if she has lost patience with

me then places it in her mouth. I'm such a good mother, I think, moving closer to admire this miniature god. She removes the pea from her mouth and rams her hand into my bottom lip. Ouch.

"No, thank you, I am not required by law to let you mama-bird me," I explain.

She shoves and shoves and, finally, I open my mouth and let her feed me the mush. She sits back as if to observe the product of her own greatness then repeats the action several times, wearing a small, satisfied smirk on her face. I chew up the peas and save them in my cheek. Once she's run out, I stand up and spit them in the sink. I decide to return the favor and feed her some peas, one by one. I clap for us each time.

We are putting on an incredible performance of survival. Where is our prize?

■

New NoShad neighbors move in. Married or dating or both. They are very hip, very tattooed; they look like the types to actually notice a butterfly and also to call you out for referring to your prejudices as *opinions*. A deer-like dog trots beside them, howling every so often for attention. The couple even smiles, which infuriates me. What is wrong with them? Why did they choose to live here when they could have lived anywhere? Everyone else in this apartment complex is a Shadester—there are the

Mexican sisters upstairs, the young white woman in number four, the elderly Black man in number eight. I never see much of anyone except for when I'm coming or going, which is when I perform the human greeting ritual of waving.

I press my ear to the wall while I wave a bag of chips like a flag, encouraging the kid to charge. When I was given my second shadow, you and I were forced out of our old apartment and into this shitty one, which is two blocks from the spoiled ocean that people used to want to live near. In fact, buyers would put themselves into unfathomable debt so they could live in this neighborhood.

We want to keep the complex up to a certain standard, the landlord had said. *You understand.*

So, we moved into this place, technically available to everyone but where no NoShad in their right mind would ever want to live. Someone had committed suicide in the bathroom after becoming a Shadester. I don't know why, but I imagine telling the kid this information when she gets older. I harbor awful, disturbing thoughts, and this is one of them. I imagine that the kid winds up forming an unhealthy obsession with suicide. She spends a lot of time asking why someone would do such a thing, and I spend a lot of time shocked but grateful that she doesn't understand wanting to die. In this scenario, I say, *Your other mother would never do that to us*, over and over, even though the kid hasn't asked, not once.

———————

Despite my commitment to eavesdropping, the new neighbors don't provide any context for why they moved here. All they do, besides play the guitar and drums at all hours, is plan their next meals and drinks and then consume those next meals and drinks while talking about their next meals and drinks. Their predictability soothes me.

■

I'm sitting on the couch with the kid on my lap. She's laughing at all the wrong parts on TV. A true nightmare.

"The neighbors are arguing over what to eat again," I say, loudly, so they can hear me. Maybe if they know that I know they are having communication problems they will come over and seek counsel and we will fall madly in friend love, and it will be beautiful but not so beautiful that it makes other people barf just to look at us.

"Wow," says the kid.

"No, I'm not certain the argument is actually about food. I think it's a cover for the big things they'd rather not talk about."

Perhaps I'm slow to catch up, but I've just realized the only people I want to befriend in my complex are NoShads. It's very boring, being a cliché.

"No, no, no!" says the kid.

"Good point, but honestly, the older you get, the harder it is to talk about what hurts. Look at Grandpa."

She looks around the room then holds up her hands, palms facing the ceiling.

"Maybe Grandpa's in the lost and found bin," I say. The kid thinks about this for a beat or two while I bounce her on my lap. She looks like she's sitting on a dryer.

"Momma?" she says, wiggling her way from a seated position to a standing position, her feet digging into my thighs. Her first time calling me anything.

"What did you say?" I ask, trying my best not to assign any value to the word.

"Momma," she says again, attempting to turn around and face me. Then, all of a sudden, she is on the floor, her legs twisted in impossible directions. She looks absolutely dumbfounded that it is even possible for her to fall off anything. She seems fine until I start crying. That really gets her going. I bend down and tell her my first lie: "Everything's going to be okay. Shhhhh, shhhhhh, shhhhh." I cover her face in kisses, but it is no use.

I begin to panic. The Department must have seen what happened. I hadn't meant it when I'd said I would pay someone to take the kid away. I need you to know that, Beau.

I can hear you now: *Come on, Kris, everyone drops their kid at some point. It's no big deal. It's basically a rite of passage.*

I'm not in the mood for one of your lectures.

About ten minutes later, there's a knock at the door. Then another. Then another.

"Open up, Miss. I'm here on behalf of the Department's Child Services Unit," announces a man.

"Fuck," I say.

If I were a social worker assigned to myself, I would say, *Kris, it is in your best interest to cooperate.*

Honestly, I can hardly believe the Child Services Unit actually exists. One day, Randy came into school with hand-shaped bruises on his neck. *It's nothing*, he said, waving me away when I asked him what happened. *You don't know what you're talking about*, he said. He started seven fights throughout the rest of the day. As with all the other reports I made, it felt like his never went anywhere. Poof! That's how I felt about all those child endangerment reports. Poof!

"Don't make me break the door down," says the Department agent, still banging.

I text my father, "Code red, code red."

I scoop up the kid, who thankfully has calmed down a bit, force a smile across my face, then open the door. They only sent one man this time.

The white man before me is a human dial tone, the type

I run from at parties, but there have been so many that fit that description over the years that I can't quite place him. Still, something about him seems vaguely familiar. Maybe it's in his rigid posture.

"Is there something I can help you with?" I say, with a snarky tone even though I don't feel snarky—I feel afraid.

"I'm Agent Brown. I received a report that you dropped your baby. I'm here to assess the situation," he says, pushing past me into my apartment, where he crinkles his nose and covers it.

"Everything's fine here, sir," I say, dropping the attitude. I look at the kid, who is sucking her thumb and doing her best *aren't-I-adorable?* face. "It was an accident, but she's okay. Not even a scrape."

"May I investigate the subject?" he asks, already plucking her from my arms.

Agent Brown examines her arms and legs. You can tell she doesn't like it. But she doesn't squirm or make a peep. He checks out her head. Runs his hand through her blond curls. He presses lightly on her skin. All over. As if he's selecting an avocado at the grocery store. He traces her extra shadow with his finger, slowly, with precision. If I didn't know any better, I would say he's savoring it.

"Hmmmmm," he says. "Hm."

He holds her with one arm while he checks his tablet with the other. He holds it in front of my face, waiting for it to scan and pull up my information.

"I see you're a widow," he says.

"A window, yes," I say, staring out the living room window. It's overcast today. A good day for Shadesters.

———

The day I received my shadow, I stood in line at the outdoor stage in center city, where new Shadesters over two years old are brought after their arrest—according to research, children could feel shame as young as two, which is why they'd chosen that age as the cutoff. Armed guards surrounded us, poking us in the back with their assault rifles. NoShads gathered around the stage and passed beers and joints around as if it were a concert or festival. Some brought signs with cruel messages that they punched toward the sky and screamed things I tried not to hear. Nearby, protestors, still invigorated by the newness of the policy, were arrested then shoved into the line. One by one, new Shadesters were required to march on stage, where an armed Department officer announced our names and what we did to get another shadow, inviting everyone to boo and hiss and shout insults. I don't know how long I stood up there, but it felt like an eternity. I closed my eyes and pictured our favorite campground in the desert, the fox we'd seen last time we were there, gentle and curious, darting from tent to tent, a cute orange blur, but it was no use, my brain couldn't be tricked—a voyeuristic crowd had invaded my campsite and told me all the various objects they wanted to stick inside my holes. Once I stepped down from the stage, a Shadester woman approached me. *One piece of advice*, she said. *Life is better without the sun. Learn to become smarter than the weatherman.*

———

Over the course of a few months, the protestors slowly dwindled. Many, it seemed, grew weary after the fourth or fifth shadow. After the thousandth or so "mysterious disappearance," as the Department had begun calling them.

"Not a window, a *widow*," he says, rolling his eyes. "Has that shadow jumbled your brain around in there?"

Even his laugh is stiff and unpleasant.

"Yes, sir." I stuff my hands in my pockets to keep them from shaking. I feel the familiar pull from my body, but I fight it. I need to stay.

"Oh," he says, frowning at his tablet.

"Oh, what?"

"Your late spouse was a woman."

"Yes, sir," I say, bracing myself. I've been through this hundreds of times. On the phone with plumbers and customer service reps and bankers and airlines and and and. *Your husband will know what to do.* Or, *Is your husband around? Can we speak to him?* Or, *Is this a joint account with your husband?* Or, *You and your husband have been reimbursed the cost of your flight, thank you ma'am.*

He adjusts the kid in his arm, cupping her butt with his hand. I watch him open up a new file on his tablet—a child endangerment report. He doesn't even try to hide it. I am never going to see the kid again. Our kid.

"I didn't realize you were," he pauses and swallows hard, "a lesbian."

That's when I remember where I know him from.

∎

For the last thirty minutes of the BDSM class, the instructor gave us free range to try out various toys—from floggers, paddles, and crops to sandpaper, nail files, and steel wool. She told us to introduce ourselves and make new friends, perhaps try out some sandpaper on a new friend. *Who wants me to flog them?* she asked. My hand shot into the air, and you gave me a little shove like, *Go on.* A few of us lined up against the wall and lifted our shirts and the instructor went up and down the line. She finished with back rubs and hugs.

Well, that was fun, you said on our walk to the car. *Thanks for being open to it*, I said, bringing your hand to my lips. Then you told me how uncomfortable the bald creep had made you feel, how he had picked up a piece of sandpaper and used it on your arm without asking. *I almost punched him.* You pointed to the red spot on your forearm where some hair had been removed. *Oh my god, why didn't you?* I said. *I'll do it right now, let's turn back and see if we can find him.* You laughed. *No, it's fine. I think he's gone, anyway. I saw him slip out the back.*

∎

"Yeah, I'm gay, what's that got to do with anything?" I say, a newfound confidence in my voice.

"How do we know you didn't intentionally drop the baby? Wouldn't be the first time you've hurt someone," he says, raising his eyebrows.

I wish the kid would leap out of his arms and into mine, or perhaps onto the ground where she has better access to his shins. Instead, she tugs on his earlobe then peers inside his ear, giggling: "Wow!" It appears her self-preservation wires had also been cut at birth.

"There's nothing to see in there, babe," I say.

"Excuse me, what gave you the right to talk to me like that?" demands Agent Brown.

"I was talking to my baby."

"You've given me no choice but to confiscate her," he says.

"She's not contraband. Please, give me my baby back," I say. "Or else."

I am having fun on this side of things. I feel guilty that I am having fun.

BDSM is about the exchange of power, the class instructor had said. *The one who gives it up is the one with all the power.*

Agent Brown practically grows right in front of my face. Like a video game boss in the final level.

"How dare you fucking threaten me," he says. I inhale sharply and grind my teeth down to a very fine powder I would gladly snort if it would get me high enough to forget what I am about to do to this man.

"I haven't even gotten to the threat yet."

"What is that supposed to mean?"

"Don't you remember me? The class wasn't that long ago," I tease. "Or did someone take sandpaper to your memory, too?"

He tilts his head back and squints his eyes. He studies me for what feels like hours. The kid pokes his cheek, but he doesn't react.

"I take it the Department doesn't know you're gay," I say.

"Quiet the fuck down, would you?" He hands the kid back to me and glances at the camera in the corner of the living room then straightens his tie and closes the file on his tablet. The kid grabs a fistful of my sweatshirt and looks up at me as if to say, *What's his problem?*

"I'm assuming they don't know about your deviant interests, either?" I whisper, pretending to spank the air.

His pink face fades to an icy white.

"You won't get away with this," he says.

I really just did that, I think, closing the door and locking it.

You would have done it, too, Beau. Don't pretend you wouldn't have.

If I'm being honest, it felt good. I felt unconquerable, if only for a few slick moments.

Pop Quiz:

Q: How do you know if you're a good person?

A: The less you worry about it, the more likely you are one.

A: I am worrying about it.

And then, I feel an intense wave of nausea, followed by stomach-wrenching heaves, and finally, release. All over the living room floor.

■

"Tubby time," I announce, trying to shake off our run-in, but it's no use. I can't stop wondering who he sleeps beside and who he loves, if they are one and the same. To combat these thoughts, I fantasize about him running over large groups of people with his car, about him stabbing people in the streets and licking the knife clean. But it is no use, I still feel monstrous.

The kid runs into the bathroom on her tippy toes before I can even finish my tubby announcement. I fill the bath with the kid's favorite tubby time toys—a rubber seahorse, a couple of neon-colored boats, and suction cup jellies—then strip her baseball tee and joggers off. I lift the kid into the warm soapy water then climb in behind her, my legs spread and pressed against each side of the tub so she can plop down between them. With my assistance, she sticks several of the jellies to the wall, squealing each time, "Momma, look!"

Loving the kid means loving the flickering light in the bathroom that dances across her chubby cheeks and widow's peak, the light-hungry bubbles clinging to her chest. Loving her means that, in this moment, even her shadow looks cute. How did you manage to grow a living thing inside of you? Not just any living thing, *this* living thing. At our second ultrasound, you said, *People make other people inside their bodies.* The doctor smiled and said, *That's you. You're the one doing it*, but all you did was shake your head like there must be a better explanation.

The kid rips the jellies off the wall, one by one, then stands up and climbs out of the bath, slipping one leg over the edge of the tub, then the other. Naked and still soapy, she runs into the kitchen and tries to grab a box of cereal off the counter, but she can't quite reach. I pour her some and watch her eat, the spoon steady in her hand. For now, the kid depends on me, but she sure as hell doesn't need me. Once she can reach the counter, it will be over for us.

■

KRIS'S TREATMENT PLAN
Daily Progress Note:
List goals as notes on treatment plan.

Progress toward goal: Regression = 1, Consistency = 2, Improvement = 3.

1. Kris will learn to recognize life's joyful moments as they are happening.
   Rating: 2
2. Kris will manage her frustration in positive, socially acceptable ways.
   Rating: 2
3. Kris will remain so busy that she cannot possibly think about Beau's death, the state of the country, the kid's future.
   Rating: 1

About that last one: these thoughts never leave my mind. They have season tickets in the nosebleed section. They eat popcorn and cotton candy and get trashed on beer. They chat loudly amongst themselves, taking photos instead of watching the game, and I am able to keep them drunk and glued to their seats as long as I stay busy, busy with errands, busy with work calls, busy with cooking, busy with playing. Once I stop moving, that's when the fans sneak past the distracted security guards, down to the field, where they blow the whole place up.

Today is full of calls with straight, white men. They have problems, too, they tell me. They use the call as a time to unload on me. I let them, because they agree to order a mindcast at the end, granted I listen and provide the appropriate amount of sympathy when necessary.

"My daughter is dating a Shadester," one man confides. "My wife and I are so embarrassed that we hardly meet up with our friends anymore. We're practically convicts," he says.

I imagine him motioning to the walls of his mansion.

■

A few days later, I tell my dad about what happened.

"It's not hard to keep one alive," he says. "Feed them every day and don't confuse your bottle with theirs."

"Aren't you the least bit worried?" I ask.

"Of course, I am. But what do you expect me to do?"

"I don't know, Dad. I don't know."

"Are you ever going to tell me how you got your shadow? It's driving me crazy."

"I didn't kill anyone, if that's what you're asking."

He shows me his new phone, the sleek shine of it. The screen is nearly the size of the kid, but with the click of a button, it can fold into a device no larger than a quarter. My phone, on the other hand, resembles a brick and is about as useful as one. Then he holds up a finger and goes outside, returning with a huge TV box.

"NoShad privileges," he grumbles. "You can send any file directly to the TV."

"Finally, a place for all my files," I say a little too harshly. He sets it down and pulls out the directions, flipping through all the different languages. The kid wanders over to him, interested.

"I've been listening to those mindcasts of yours," he says. "They're so bad, they're almost good." He pulls the kid in for a big hug, and she squeals, slithering out of it.

"I think that's the point, Dad."

"I suppose it is, isn't it," he says, twirling his mustache, staring at something undetectable to me. I have a feeling there's something he isn't telling me.

I wish I could turn off his despair with the ease of a light switch. It has always made me uncomfortable seeing his sadness on display. As a teenager, I wanted to ask him if he liked being alive, but I couldn't bring myself to do it. I could talk about suicide with strangers online but with my own family? Impossible.

Do you want to die? I used to ask the MILFs in lesbian chat rooms while pretending to do English homework. *This isn't exactly what I meant by dirty talk, but yes.* Many of them were married to men. They were jealous I was twenty-five and out. *What are you doing talking to me all night? Go out with your friends. Find someone your own age*, they said, followed by a picture of their cleavage.

More about octopuses: they can taste a person's body chemistry through their skin. I cannot imagine having to taste everyone's depression and anxiety.

Once we—well—once my dad, sets up the TV, we sit down with some beers. He messes around on his phone then sends a picture of me to the TV. I'm four years old, wearing a pink party dress. I look absolutely miserable. He doesn't seem to see it that way, though. He smiles at the TV warmly then looks at me.

"I'd love to try again."

"Try what again?" I ask. He examines the back of the remote.

"If I just had another chance to start over," he says, but he doesn't finish his thought. He's staring at the picture of me.

"You raised me just fine," I say.

"That's not enough," he says, and I think he's going to cut himself off again, but he continues. "I want to try again with someone who wants to try with me."

Pop Quiz:
Q: What would you tell your younger self if you could?
A: The future is a place you can never catch up to.

∎

The kid acquires more and more words, as I am told children tend to do.

"Rape," she repeats while we watch the news. Two No-Shad men brutally raped and murdered a Shadester woman.

That is how the news anchor words it—*brutally*. As if there were any other way to rape and murder someone. Because of who these men are, the case will actually go to trial—most people don't get such a luxury. It's typically as swift as a pickup, an arrest, and a drop-off at the stage—then off a murderer walks, three extra shadows later, which means even higher taxes, extremely limited health care access, and the right for businesses to turn them away. Neither, of course, offers rehabilitation, or anything close to healing.

"Never say that again," I beg of the kid.

On one of our walks, we pass by a light post with one of Mischief's missing posters torn half off, flapping in the wind. Someone has drawn a huge penis on Mischief's back.

"People are dicks," I say.

"Wow, dicks!" says the kid, smiling.

"You'll get a lot of use out of that one," I say. "People are awful. That's why your Nonna prefers the trees and the animals and the moon."

■

My father barges into the house, bearing a gift. The kid is crawling through one of those indoor play tunnels. Back and forth. Each time she emerges, she claps for herself, then it's back to work she goes.

"It's a photograph. One of mine," he explains before I've gotten a chance to unwrap it. He's recently taken up photography. I am expecting a nice landscape, perhaps a pretty bird or two. He twirls his mustache, watching me, while I tear the wrapping paper off to reveal a picture of the Department stage. Some blurry people on it, wishing they were anywhere else.

"Out of all the things," I say, my face growing hot. He does his rocking thing, a little frazzled.

"I thought this would be a way to, well, reclaim it, is all."

"Reclaim?"

"You're not the only one with access to the internet, Kris."

Later, when I shove the photo under my bed, I find the photographer's business card I'd been searching for.

■

By the time the kid's appointment for her one-year checkup comes around, she is nearly two. Shadesters have to wait longer for health care. Remember when we could make an appointment online and be seen by a doctor the next day? I didn't even tell you every time I went to see our boy, Dr. Billings, who, despite being kind and understanding, never agreed to give me that full body CT scan I requested and instead handed me a referral to a therapist.

At the kid's appointment, the pediatrician says, "I'm sorry, I just haven't seen one this young before." He is excited, stimulated by his discovery. It seems we have a collector in our midst.

He listens to the kid's heart, her lungs.

"One what?" I demand.

"It's not exactly something you can throw a coat over, huh?"

"In exchange for that comment, you owe me a prescription for those pills that turn people into gelatin," I tell the pediatrician.

"No, I'm afraid I can't do that," he says.

"What do you mean?

"You're what one might call drug-seeking."

"Perhaps you could change that title to drug-receiving?"

When we arrive home, we find Siegfried painting on an easel in the courtyard. I grab the kid's hand, but she slips out of my grasp and runs toward him. Up close, I see he is painting a bird of paradise.

"I hate whoever broke the news to them that they can't fly," he says, switching to a tiny brush for detail. Then he begins working on an elderly woman next to the flowers. His grandmother.

"You would like her, Kris," he says. "Good at upsetting partygoers."

"She's still alive?"

"Do you ever wonder why some people are allowed to grow old when Beau wasn't? How is that fair? Who decides who gets longevity and who doesn't?" he asks.

If anyone else had said something like that, I'd already have had them pinned to the ground, but it's Siegfried. He might be the only true friend I've ever had.

"Beau says for you to knock it off and paint me a still life of a dating profile," I say. He stops painting and looks at me.

"Do you really think she'd want you to move on already?"

"Fuck, no," I say. "That's why she said it. She knows I'm no good at online dating, that I write long, rambling messages about a single, black hair that regularly grows out of the mole on my chin."

Back inside, the kid and I play with blocks.

"Grandma?" the kid asks, knocking over a tower I'd just built.

"A grandma is someone who doesn't answer my calls," I say.

"Hmph," she says, detecting a falsehood somewhere.

■

All charges are dropped against the men who raped and murdered the Shadester woman. For fear of stating the obvious, I will not describe the men for you, Beau.

I'm on the bench with Siegfried again. Only this time, the kid has decided to join us. She's drawing what I suspect is a tree with a blue piece of sidewalk chalk. Siegfried drinks from a flask, one of his eyes black and swollen shut.

"Glad you could make it," he says, raising his flask to the kid, who clinks her sippy cup accordingly.

"Maybe you could hide that, so I don't have to threaten another Department employee so soon," I hiss.

"You drink around her all the time."

"Yeah, well, it's called coping."

He points to his black eye, and I concede. I consider asking him about the eye but then decide against it; I'd rather not know the specifics.

"I've seen the future, and this isn't how you die, I promise." I have no business promising him such a thing. "You hear that? Goes for you, too," I say, tapping the kid with my toe.

She draws a few more branches on her tree, then looks at me over her shoulder.

"I hear, I hear, I hear," she begins. "I hear everything," she says, flashing a charming, mischievous smile before returning to her work. Already she knows no boundaries, no authority figures. I wish time would slow down. I have no idea how I am going to talk to the kid about her extra shadow. About mine. How did parents do it? My parents must have sensed my queerness, possibly as young as three, but instead of sitting me down and saying, *We love you, we love you. Here's what you need to know about the people who won't*, my father ignored me, and my mother redirected me toward princess crowns and pink frilly dresses. If I ever run into her again, I might drop the word *femme* into the conversation.

My daily reports as a school social worker used to say, *According to staff, Randy required redirection fifty or more times during math class. When redirected, Randy grew angry and violent.*

Siegfried fingers his eye, flinching, then continues to press on it, as if he were desperate to relive the pain. "I made the mistake of begging for money downtown," he says, shrugging.

"But this type of thing doesn't happen anymore, Siegfried. You must be mistaken," I say in my mock-President voice. He grants me a sympathy chuckle.

"Today is the three-year anniversary," I say, toeing my shadow.

"Happy birthday," he says, pouring a splash on my undesirable partner.

I tell him that Darlene, the name I've given my extra shadow, thanks him. He laughs a Siegfried laugh then decides to name his shadow Bartholomew.

"Bartholomew can have some whiskey, too," he says.

"If he's good."

"Right, right, if he's good."

Sitting and talking with Siegfried feels good, the closest to human I've felt in a while.

"I once read that some trees are connected by a complex fungi network. Trees keep the chopped-down stumps of their loved ones alive by feeding them sugar solutions through their roots," I say.

"I'm here for you, you know, if you want to talk," says Siegfried.

"Trees keep alive?" the kid asks.

"Yep. Unfortunately, we can't do that for people," I whisper, quieter than I'd intended.

The kid shakes her head and returns to her masterpiece. Why do I feel like the child?

Siegfried takes another sip from his flask and holds the liquor in his mouth for a disgusting length of time before finally swallowing. We sit in silence for a while.

I'd say that Siegfried might be the last real human being on the planet if he weren't so kind.

Pop Quiz:
Q: What is the difference between nice and kind?
A: Only one is a result of fear.

A white guy walking his dog approaches us. I nudge Siegfried in the ribs, and he sits up straight, his one eye wide. "For what it's worth, I think Shadesters should have rights like everyone else," says the man, staring at the space above our heads. Then he scampers off.

"Are you still staying with that couple you met at the support group?" I ask. I have an idea. I can redeem myself.

"They moved to the mountains."

"Do you want to live with us? We don't have a spare bedroom, but we have a pullout couch."

"I couldn't ask you to do that," he says, looking at the kid.

"Good thing you can't, because you didn't," I say, already feeling better.

"We would make a cute ass family, huh?" he says, trying to tame his smile.

———

After you, whenever I hear the word *family*, I picture a library of people, holding hands to keep from falling off the shelves.

"Siegfried is coming to live with us," I tell the kid. "Isn't that exciting?"

"My bed no," she says, wagging her finger.

"You run a tight ship," I laugh. "I like it."

■

The kid begins babbling in her sleep, often so loud it wakes me up, but Siegfried sleeps soundly, snoring on the couch.

"Buckety! Buckety!" she yells, her language centers lighting up. The first time it happens, I rush into her room, convinced it's some emergency code word, but when I arrive at her crib, her eyes are closed, her lips forming a dreamy half smile. A small part of me wishes you and I had gotten pregnant at the same time so that the kids could babble to each other in the night, in a language all their own. I imagine them chatting about the most important things: sugary snacks they haven't yet devoured, doggies they haven't yet bossed around, bubbles they haven't yet blown.

My dad arrives unannounced with a pizza and a serious look. Siegfried is out somewhere, doing whatever it is he does when we aren't together.

"What's this all about?" I ask, suspicious.

"I thought we'd have a pizza party," he says.

"Pizza, pizza, pizza, pizza, pizza," the kid chants, while my dad digs through the cabinets for clean plates.

"You really know how to divert and distract," I say, stuffing pizza in my face.

"That's not fair." He looks at the ground, twirling his mustache. When I don't respond, he says, "Fine. I wanted to talk to you about something."

"You don't say."

"Don't yell at me, but, well, it's about your friendships."

"Excuse me?"

"Don't you think the braided one is an interesting choice?"

"Have you been spying on me?"

"No, only tidying up," he says. He means he's been scrubbing my car again.

"Dad, I'm a Shadester, too, you know."

"Okay well," says my dad, "it's different because you're my daughter."

I storm outside and light a cigarette and before I can take my second drag, he is beside me, coughing in my face.

"Awful habit, can I have one?"

I hand him the pack. The kid bangs on the front door and I let her outside, where she wanders around examining the potted plants that tenants have placed in the courtyard.

"All I'm saying is, I don't think he's necessarily increasing your popularity," he says.

I don't respond, instead choosing to aggressively smoke

my cigarette. I still can't tell if he knows Siegfried has moved in with us.

"I just hate how much harder your life is going to be. Do you really have to add to it?"

"There is someone tinier and squishier that we should be worrying about," I say, eyeing the kid, who is attempting to unearth someone's succulent.

"Have you decided what you're going to do about that?" my father asks, as if he is asking which type of pie I plan on making for the holidays—pumpkin or cherry? *Of course not*, I want to say. Everyday decisions immobilize me—what to eat for dinner, which order to run the errands in, what to watch on TV. How could anyone expect me to make the big ones, the life-altering ones?

■

Siegfried slips in the door around midnight while I'm drinking a beer on the couch. I don't say hi because I want to scare him and that's exactly what happens when he notices me. He jumps in place like a spooked cat then collapses on the couch next to me, taking in gulps of air.

"Where do you go?" I ask.

"Nowhere," he says, unbraiding his braid.

"I promised myself I wouldn't be overbearing."

"Well, intention is something," he says.

"Is it, though?"

He shrugs. I get up and hand him a beer, which he drinks down like it's water. I watch his Adam's apple slither up and down his throat.

"I wish I could turn my brain off," I say.

"Why?" he asks. I can tell he's trying to swallow a burp.

"I'd like a break from myself. How do you do it, day in and day out, forever?"

"Do what?"

I pause. Take a sip.

"Live with yourself," I say.

"Oh," he says, ominously. "We're going there, huh?"

"I think so."

"I don't know, Kris. I spent a long time beating myself up for shit I did, but then I realized it wasn't productive. Maybe that sounds callous, the productive bit, but it's true. I went around asking for forgiveness everywhere I went. It took years before I realized someone could say the words *I forgive you, Sieg* but they couldn't grant me forgiveness."

He gets up and grabs two more beers, setting them down on the coffee table in front of us.

"I had to do that," he continues.

"So, what, you're telling me you've actually forgiven yourself?" I know I must sound incredulous.

"Yeah. I mean, I just stopped looking back. I try to focus on what I can do in the present. Don't think about the future either." He seems over the conversation, but I can tell he's trying.

"Why not?"

"I don't know, I guess I don't want to waste time thinking about something that doesn't even exist yet," he says.

"How am I supposed to believe we are members of the same species?"

———

I begin testing Siegfried's self-forgiveness threshold.

"I can't wait to eat the last cupcake," I say. "Looks so delicious!" I say this as if the secret to happiness is inside that very treat. Then I disappear into my bedroom to make some cold calls.

When I come back out, Siegfried is eating my cupcake, vanilla icing on his cheek.

"Don't you feel the least bit bad?" I ask.

"You were talking about it so much, I thought you wanted me to eat it," he laughs.

"Would it be worse if I couldn't get over it?"

"Yes," he smiles, "but you're already over it."

The next morning, I wax philosophical.

"How can we trust our own impulse to be forgiven? There's this epidemic. I don't know if you've heard of it, but Person A will apologize to Person B so that Person B will continue to perceive Person A as a good person."

"What you're saying is, it's all about reputation?" says Siegfried, pouring us some coffee. The kid is crying in the other room because I told her we are out of bacon.

"I'm sorry!" I yell, but it's no use. Her day is ruined.

"Oh noooooooo, what will she tell her friends?" he says, wiggling his fingers next to his face.

■

Before bed, I read the thumb-sucking kid a children's book about a woman with two shadows who beats all the odds and becomes an astronaut. Her name is Skys. Like more than one sky, spelled incorrectly. I had to scour the dark web for something this progressive, a book the Department considers too dangerous, a form of propaganda. Someone had been selling it secondhand; I wasn't sure how they'd acquired it, and they spoke in code when they messaged me from their anonymous profile.

"Yes, the learn-to-speak Spanish book is very good, you'll love it," they said, before instructing me where they would drop it off.

When I found the book at the pick-up spot, I felt vaguely proud of myself, as if I'd ventured out into the world and hunted and gathered for the kid.

I hold her hand and use it to point to both shadows.

"One, two," I say.

Then I point to her own and repeat, "One, two—see, there's nothing wrong with two."

The kid tilts her head then looks up at me with her big blue Beau eyes, expecting something, although I don't know what. I thought I was off to a great start.

My dad sends me a text: "I notice you haven't hung up my photo. Did I do something wrong?"

Sigh. Up the photo goes. Above my dresser, directly across the room from the abandoned house photograph, so the blurry people on stage know there's always somewhere they can escape to.

———

"I don't even like pad thai," says the neighbor.

"So, you've just been pretending to love pad thai?" says her boyfriend or husband or both. We can hear everything because their front door is open, the temperature having broken triple digits this week.

"This is merely a symptom," I say to the kid, nodding wisely.

The kid stares blankly at me, clutching her blankie. Before I can finish reading, she is asleep.

Later, I overhear a new argument, the suspected source of the symptom.

"I don't know why we had to move here. The other place was just fine."

No response.

"See? You know I'm right."

"I just wanted to get ahead of them, is all."

"I don't know. It feels like giving up."

One study found that having a second shadow is akin to experiencing severe trauma. I wonder if they could tell me more about how leaves grow on trees.

Pop Quiz:
Q: Who controls your body?
Q: How much do you trust them?

■

I begin creating stories for the blurry people in the stage photo. I pretend they are my ancestors.

"That's Vanessa," I tell the kid. "She thinks exoskeletons are just okay, but she more than makes up for it with her ability to wink with both eyes."

The kid looks at me, then blinks slowly, perhaps wondering what's so difficult about that.

"And that's Burgundy. They are almost always having moon problems."

"What's that?" asks the kid, holding up her hands.

"I'm afraid the moon is always messing with the tides inside Burgundy. Finally, we have Echo, the star violinist who is hoping to overcome his name and create something everlasting."

"Boring," says the kid.

■

The kid grows a mean streak overnight. After lunch, I take her tray, and then for the next hour, she stomps around the house chanting, "You don't take my tray, Mommy," and I wave the tray as evidence that I *do* take the tray.

Then after a hug she tries out a new chant: "You don't hug me, Mommy." She repeats this for an hour. Siegfried, for some reason, is exempt from the no-hug rule. "You *do* hug me, Siegfried."

Sometimes she hits me. A smack on the thigh or arm, and then she's off. She isn't stupid; she knows I won't retaliate.

"What was that?" a customer asks over the phone.

"The sound of nature running its course," I say.

The only moments of peace come at night when I watch Siegfried paint outside. I hold my phone light up for him and tell him about my childhood crush. Afterward, he tries his hand at a dolphin painting, but he gets the sunset all wrong. Too realistic, too sad.

Siegfried mentions it's perhaps better that the kid and I are on the same team. That's how he says it, like we and our shadows are lacing up for a basketball game.

"Then what's our game plan, Coach?" I ask. He doesn't respond, which means he doesn't like the sarcasm in my voice. I watch him paint the fins on the dolphin. Small, delicate strokes.

"You know, white Shadesters are really in for a rude awakening with this shit."

"What shit?" I ask.

"Like, we've never had to have this kind of talk with our kids until now."

"The this-is-how-people-may-treat-you talk?"

"Yeah, we've always been the oppressor. I mean, well, we still are, but you know what I mean," he says.

"I need to alert the authorities. I've just spotted a white man acknowledging his privilege in the wild!"

"Excuse me," he says, feigning offense. I watch him paint a small smile on the dolphin's face.

"So, where are you going with this?" I ask.

"Nowhere, I'm just thinking out loud."

"What did your parents tell you?" I ask.

"I don't know, nothing really, just that life sucked and we'd better get used to it. I didn't realize how poor we were until I went to school and met kids with hoverboards and charcuterie lunches," he says. "All those tiny mustards," he mumbles, shaking his head.

"Who is we?"

"Me and my baby sister."

The way he says *baby* makes me want to kiss him in that way good news makes you want to kiss the deliverer of that good news. I know what you're thinking, Beau, and it's not like that. The desire to kiss him has little to do with attraction—and everything to do with recognition—in him, I see the soft ache of shared suffering, an incurable longing to go back in time and shield his baby sister from any and all threats. A kiss would mean *I see you.*

The next morning, I ask him to tell me and the kid about his baby sister. For a second, I catch a glimpse of torment in his eyes but then he arranges his mouth into a smile.

"One time, when we were kids, she was sad because we couldn't afford to have her birthday party at Princess Mansion like everyone else—that place where the princesses used to wander around and invite you on adventures. So, my mom and I spent a month making a princess dress and wig for me. And on the morning of her birthday, I put on my dress and wig and swayed into her bedroom. I held out my hand and said, 'Where would you like to go?'"

"Yeah, where?" asks the kid.

"To the sky," he says, his smile drooping a little. "I took her on this rollercoaster by the pier. I lost my wig on the second loop."

"Where is your sister now?" I ask. He glances at the kid, his eyes sad and spooky.

"Dead," he says. "Class is dismissed for today."

■

Then there are the nightmares. Agent Brown visits me every night. In the dreams, I am naked, strapped by the wrists and ankles to a hospital bed while he burns various parts of my body with an iron. *What kind of gay are you, anyway?* he yells. *How could you fucking threaten to out me?* Other times, he attacks my parenting: *I'm scared to see how bad you'll mess that kid up.* The worst, though, are the ones where he says, *No one could love a selfish bitch like you—not Beau—*burn*—not your parents—*another burn*—not the kid—*a burn felt in my ribs, my spine, my everywhere.

I wake up and think, what else can I do for Siegfried?

"What do you need?" I ask him in the mornings. I pour him some coffee and make all three of us breakfast.

"Nothing, I need nothing, you're doing too much."

If by *too much*, he means folding his laundry and leaving notes in his socks, then so be it.

Reality Testing:
My brain: I am not a mother.
Reality: I am Momma.

A sample note: "Take a page from Mischief's book—hiss at everyone who looks at you wrong."

∎

It's strange now to think you'd been so close to throwing it all in with someone who wasn't me. I thought it seemed easy for you to accept comfort as a replacement for love, while you thought it seemed easy for me to lie, over and over again, with my body. I saved your name in my phone as Brad. When we finally broke off our respective relationships, you bought a six-pack of cream ale and met me at the cliffs. I changed your name in my phone to Beau [peach emoji] [peach emoji] [heart] [splash]. *Goose*, you said. *My goose.*

In the margins of a notebook, I write *Darlene* with a heart around it until my hand cramps. The mindcasts say to love the parts of ourselves we find unlovable, even extra shadows. Darlene sticks to me like a suction cup. She loves me too much. I haven't sold a mindcast in weeks, but Jackson suffers from pathological generosity. He tells me he has a Shadester brother; he knows how it is.

Our loved ones were generous, too. They pretended not to know about our affair. We got married on a boat. There were coolers of beer and hard cider. What you said after we kissed: *Look at everyone holding their crotches. It's so beautiful I can hardly stand it.* No one else knew our wedding song. In it, the singer laments his lover's fading time on Earth and all the things they never got to do together, while she reassures him that if she had one more life, she'd spend it by his side. I suppose it sounds a bit morbid to do the first dance to a song about death, but it wasn't really a song about death, was it? It was a song about choice. About loving someone so much you'd spend another lifetime with them, knowing you could easily choose someone else, go down a different path, chase the euphoria of the unknown.

Who is going to love me now, Beau?

In the courtyard, I share a cigarette with Siegfried. He looks beautiful draped in the liquid moonlight. Almost too beautiful to be alive. The kid smiles at him with all the dopamine inside of her and hugs his legs. It thrills me to know that she loves him, although I know it's dangerous to let her love anyone that could disappear without warning.

Siegfried shares his theory about shadows. He believes they are sentient. That they want to break free from their humans, but they just don't know how.

Are you going to learn from the pain you've caused? they asked me at the Department. I exchanged a *yes* for a shadow.

■

Remember how you and I used to trade off having mental breakdowns? *It's my turn today*, I once said, sobbing into the washing machine after a stressful day at work. The kids fought, the kids lied, the kids kicked me and called me a dumb bitch. *You just pull and twist*, you said, bringing my hand up to the knob.

Now it's my turn, you said, days later when you dropped the mail in a puddle.

"It's my turn, time and time again," I say, cradling your urn and thinking of Agent Brown. "Absolve me of my sins."

Siegfried comes home one morning with a broken nose and two black eyes, cuts decorating his face. My vision blurs until I see the kid's face in place of his. Will things be different by the time she's older? How far-reaching is my denial? It twists around the future like English ivy.

"Siegfried has boo boo," cries the kid.

"Don't worry, this is just a coincidence," he says, tickling her belly. She giggles but her face still tells a sad story.

"I'm sorry," I say, which feels worse than saying nothing.

"The palm trees look extra fake today," he laughs. "Did you see them? It's like we live on a Hollywood set."

"Then where's your makeup artist?" I lead him into the bathroom, where I have concealer that's a few shades too tan for him.

"It's fine, I'm fine," he says. "Happy Shadow History Month. It's me, I'm the history."

"If only," I say, dabbing under his eyes.

"You know, there's a story about a man who managed to wriggle loose from his shadow. No one knows how he did it. Legend has it, he owns a casino now. Calls himself Dr. Slots."

"And is Dr. Slots taking consultations?"

"I don't know. I wish Bartholomew would get a life already," he says. "Some days I swear I can feel him stirring."

"Do you think it's true?"

"What?"

"That they don't have to stay stuck to us?"

"Yes," he says, shaking his head, no.

"Stay still."

When I'm done, he lets me give him a hug. It feels like they've already won.

————

It isn't until later that I think to ask Siegfried who punched his face in.

"Some Department agent down by the pier," he says.

"You didn't happen to catch his name, did you?"

"You know, you're right. It was rather rude of me not to ask."

Later, I receive a text from an unknown number: "Regret is an awful feeling, isn't it?"

When I tell Siegfried he isn't safe here, he asks me where, exactly, is he safe?

∎

I film the kid dancing around the house in her diaper, a bowl of spaghetti upside down on her head. Sauce drips down her cheek.

"One, two, three, you, shade, me," sings the kid.

"Where'd you hear that song?" I ask.

"La la la la la," she sings, laughing and pitter-pattering her feet.

I text the video to your mom.

Some messages in a bottle travel over twenty thousand miles before they are found. I only need this one to travel about three thousand.

∎

Potty training goes like this:

"No, I won't do it!"

"Yes, you will. If not for me, then for Grandpa."

"Nope, nope, nope."

"I'll buy you a present." Her ears perk up, she cocks an eyebrow.

"What present?"

"Whatever you want, just use the damn potty," I say. I am the kind of tired that tells on itself.

The kid wants a Skys doll, but a Skys doll doesn't exist.

"You got it. Now, let's see what you can do."

She folds her arms across her chest and looks around as if to say, *Well, where is it?*

Then she pulls down her pants and poops under the kitchen table.

"Do you know how to sew?" I ask my father the second he walks in the door. The kid's in her room, plotting my demise.

"Have you been on any dates lately?" he asks.

"Didn't think so," I say.

"This is ridiculous, Kris. Don't you think it's time you were nice to yourself?"

"You somehow make lack of self-awareness look even worse than it already does," I say.

"Okay, so this doll," he says, rolling up his sleeves.

It's not that women haven't hit on me. It's that I tend to run the other way before they can smile at me a second time. A smile leads to all kinds of malignant things, like having to hear the words *I* and *love* and *you* all over again.

When I present the kid with the homemade fabric doll sporting a miniature fishbowl on its head, she squeals, taking it into her arms.

"Why black?" she asks, running her fingers over the back.

"That's her extra shadow. It's always with her, but it doesn't stop her from doing whatever she wants to do."

"Why would it?" she says, pulling down her pants. She sits down and pees on the potty. "Happy, Mommy?"

We is the most tender word I know.

Then she systematically disposes of all the diapers in the house.

"What now?" she asks, opening a board game. I make her a vanilla caramel milkshake before joining her.

∎

Shadows & Me!: The Classic Game of Impossible Conversations

Warning: Choking hazard. Not suitable for anyone who crumbles easily under pressure.

Objective: Be the first player to teach her about cruelty, how it rides on the back of cowardice and calls itself bravery. No one tells you this, but the game is rigged from the start.

Number of players: There are always more than we think.

Audience: Anyone who wants to truly comprehend why a stranger could hate them without ever having met them.

Contents:

1 bottomless beer bottle

1 lock on her door, to keep the monsters out

1,000 wish-you-were-heres

Countless long-term plans, abandoned (by me)

3 books about Shadesters in my viewing history

56 questions, all essentially the same: how do I protect her?

Cards:

The higher the number on the card, the more times I must tell the kid I love her unconditionally.

If I choose a wild card, I must teach her how to walk with her eyes on the horizon.

The get-out-of-jail-free cards may as well be a pair of handcuffs.

Setup:

Take the kid for grilled cheese and milkshakes.

Sit on my hands to stop them from shaking.

Ask the kid: "What do you know about your shadow?" Rearrange my ribs to make room for what comes next.

"Two is better than one," says the kid, shrugging. She slurps the last of her milkshake then continues slurping long after it's gone.

■

At night, when our shadows disappear into the darkness, the kid and I often have the park to ourselves. We play ourselves dizzy. I traverse the monkey bars with unprecedented strength, speed, and grace. The kid slides backward down a slide and, although she doesn't need my help, I am waiting at the bottom anyway with worried, open arms, and a mind that keeps flashing the words *child endangerment*.

"Again!" the kid shouts, brushing the mulch off her.

"Go ahead. The world is ours, stinker," I say, pausing. I've never called her a stinker before. It had been my mother's nickname for me. Something about a TV show she'd loved.

"Stinker?" inquires the kid, scrunching up her nose. "That's silly."

"It's a sweet thing," I say. "I promise you don't smell."

"You do, though," she says, running off. For a while, she looks like nothing can touch her.

———

In this world, you learn to hold the good days and bad days together in your lungs, and you don't dare breathe out, for fear that in releasing the bad days, you'll also lose the good ones. On the walk home, I think, this has been a good day.

"You've at least heard of time out, right?" my dad asks me, watching the kid throw a tantrum on her bedroom floor. It's time for bed, and she doesn't like that one bit. I try to hold on to the buoyancy from earlier.

"We could always do a different night," I say, stalling.

"I'll be in the fridge," he says. It takes seven books to settle her down.

Once I've finally turned on the noise machine and wished the kid sweet dreams, I head to the living room where Siegfried sits on the couch sketching and my father works on his third beer at the kitchen table. He's been drinking even more since he learned of Siegfried's current mailing address. I quickly catch up to him, barely stopping to breathe while I drink.

"You sure you want to do this?" he asks, eyeing Siegfried like he's a tied-up dog.

"I don't fucking know."

"Alright, don't think. Just give it to me," he says, holding his hands out like a trick-or-treating child.

I finger my ring and think about our wedding day. How stunning you looked. It'd felt like my entire life had come to a head. *You've stamped me forever, like a library card*, you said in your vows. Despite her fear of travel, your mom officiated. It was her first and only time visiting. She tried to take a plastic bag full of sand on the plane home with her.

We got married in the sun out on the water and your mom sobbed inconsolably. At the reception, my dad steered me around the dance floor like a professional, and your mom sobbed some more. Just like you, your mom spends her days steady and impenetrable, hoarding her tears for the moments that matter.

"This certainly doesn't seem necessary," I say. "It's not like there are any laws about this."

"If there's one person who knows what's best for you, it's, well, anyone but you," he says, twirling his mustache. Under the table, I spin my ring on my finger, trying to memorize its feel.

"Hand it over," he says, reaching across the table. I reluctantly move my hand toward his, and we both stare at it for a while, its lifeless flop. "Need help?" my dad asks, gently pulling the ring from my finger.

The sudden nakedness of my finger is what makes me notice his is still dressed in gold.

"She's really gone, isn't she?" I say.

"Yeah, kid, she is," says my dad, placing his hand on top of mine.

The next day I expect I will run into you at the drugstore, and you will say, "Kris, I'm not dead, see? I'm right here, buying deodorant without antiperspirant again."

"You monster," I'll say, shoving my ringless hand in my pocket.

■

A few days later, I wake to a text from your mother. A childhood photo of you, strikingly blond, a few new teeth. You're wearing a baggy football sweatshirt and grinning into the camera, chocolate ice cream smeared all over your face.

"She always made me warm her sweatshirts in the dryer before leaving the house," says your mother. "I'm sorry about what I said to you. I'm sorry for disappearing. You were Beau's favorite thing."

"It's okay," I text your mom. "I would have said the same thing."

She sends me a photo of a T-shirt she had made. On the back is your name with angel wings.

"What size are you?" she asks. Then she sends a photo of rocks she's painted with messages to you on them.

"Come back," they say. "I have so much to tell you."

Weeks later, she calls again. "I'm trying my best to move on," she says. I can hear her banging rocks together in the background.

"How's the motorcycle running?" I ask.

"I think I'm starting to scare people on my trips into town."

One of the stories about your mom that sticks with me: She was working at a hip little boutique, selling lotions, perfumes, crystals, candles, those kinds of things. You'd hang out there after school and open all the candles and smell them. Then you'd close them, wait for what you called the candle's re-scenting time, and open them again. You could do that for hours and hours. You were fascinated by how the smell never ran out, jealous, I think, of its endlessness. Did you know then that something would end you prematurely? Were you, on those days in your mom's shop, grasping at infinity?

One day, a boy from school came in with his mom and started acting like hot shit—your words. He followed you around the store trying to get your attention, and when that didn't work, he shoved you in the back and called you a stupid dyke, said he didn't want to date you anyway. Dyke? Date? You couldn't have been older than seven. That was when your mom, coming out from behind the counter, threw a perfume bottle at him—which missed him and broke on the floor, splattering his chicken legs with scents of jasmine—then chased him and his mother not only out of the store but two blocks away. She returned panting, fixing her hair into a ponytail.

In the middle of the night, I spray a pillow with your cologne and hold it tight.

I text your mom: "I'm afraid."

She responds right away: "Me too."

It comforts me that she has no solution either.

■

The thing about Velcro is, it collects all kinds of detritus along the way and then it no longer attaches where it's supposed to. If a stranger happened upon a stray piece of Velcro, they'd have no way of determining where it belonged. You can usually make Velcro stick again by cleaning it, but if your Velcro is old and worn-out, you'll have to replace it.

How, then, do I rid myself of all I've gathered along the way?

Pop Quiz:
Q: What makes Velcro stick?
A: One surface is made of tiny hooks and the other is comprised of thin loops. When pressed together, the hooks lock around the loops, securing the two pieces together.
Q: What does this mean for humanity?
A: We cannot help but cling.

When I look at the kid, I can't decide if she is a tiny hook or a thin loop. If she is the actor or the acted-upon.

"Mommy, your shadow is pretty," says the kid, looking up from her sidewalk chalk creation: a castle with a moat.

"That's one interpretation I haven't heard before."

I turn my head to try to catch the profile of both shadows. My extra shadow looks different than my first—it's subtle, but I swear its nose is just a little more pointed. Or maybe it's all in my head. Shame, as I understand it, puts a question mark at the end of every observation.

The word *mommy* still feels weird on me. Like I woke up one day and decided to wear a shark onesie to a job interview. There I sit, fins crossed, humming a happy little tune, while the boss asks me questions I don't know the answer to, the faint scent of blood making my mouth water.

■

I'm outside watching Siegfried paint again. Cash's dolphin, round two.

"I've been thinking about what you said. And I'm wondering, like, what kinds of things you used to beat yourself up over?"

I don't know why I'm being so nosy. I really don't care what he did to receive his shadow. The simplest explanation is that I can't imagine him doing anything worthy of self-flagellation.

"I don't know, Kris. Anything and everything?" He pauses, tapping the handle of his brush on the painting in a way I haven't seen him do before. He swallows hard before answering. "Like, I would beat myself up for having cheated on a girlfriend when I was eighteen. Shit like that."

He returns to painting. A *v* of birds so close to the sun I worry for their internal temperatures.

"Been there," I say, raising my beer bottle.

"And you got the love of your life out of it," he says.

"Does that make it okay?"

My voice sounds challenging, but I'm really asking.

"No, but I suppose it makes the guilt worth it."

"I guess what I'm wondering is, how do you manage to ignore Bartholomew?" I ask, digging my heel into Darlene's chest.

"I don't. I create a new narrative for him," he says.

I turn my attention to Siegfried's shadow.

"So, what's your story, Bart. Can I call you Bart?"

Siegfried stops painting and grins at his shadow.

"You have to imagine he's in a dark alley, smoking a cigarette, okay?"

I laugh. "Okay."

"Imagine he's strikingly handsome. So handsome you can't look away."

"Get on with it," I say.

He lowers his voice and tries to speak like an old-timey movie star.

"My story? Oh, you want to know my story? Darling, you can't handle my story. The things I've seen, the places I've been. They'd blow your pretty little head off," he says, fighting a smile.

"A story typically has a beginning, middle, and end," I explain.

He raises the imaginary cigarette to his mouth and inhales deeply.

"Oh, darling! Not when you're still living it."

Later that night, we split a bottle of wine on the couch. Siegfried isn't done lecturing me.

"Tell me this. What is your guilt doing for your daughter? How does it help her in any way?" he asks.

"It doesn't," I say.

"Exactly."

He nods like I should know what to do with this revelation.

■

Tonight, the kid climbs in bed with me, and I show her how to make shadow puppets on the wall. We do the classics: bunny rabbit, dove, horse, elephant, and wolf. With our extra shadows, we have all the more characters to play with. I look up how to do a cat. Her cat, which is really two cats, hops on the back of my two elephants, and we're off.

"What's a puppet?" she asks, after she's tired herself out. She lies with her head on my shoulder, tugging on my earlobe.

"It's something, in this case an animal, that's controlled by someone else."

"No fun for puppet."

"No, I suppose it isn't."

■

Your mom calls me, sobbing. Her dogs destroyed the camera in the bedroom and when the agents burst into the house, her husky, Al, bit one in the leg. Al's getting put down tomorrow.

"I just can't do this anymore," she says. "All this loss is going to kill me. And for what? So a couple of creeps can spy on me?"

Some questions:

How long do I have to do this whole living thing? Where has my last serotonin molecule gone? Is your mom going to be okay? Is it time for me to learn to mother your mother? Will the phone ring indefinitely? Do ghosts have armchair opinions? How do they feel about the cameras? About the Department watching our every move? Do the neighbors talk to each other in their sleep? Could I have a beer with them sometime? Would they like me? Would I like me? Will the kid like me when she grows up? Should I be this afraid? Should I amend that statement to specify the fear? Is the fear a large afghan I wrap my body in? Are you bored in your urn? Should I take you outside, let you get some fresh air? Should I toss some ashes in the ocean and pretend I'm just as boring as everyone else?

∎

I commission Siegfried to paint a portrait of Al for your mother. I think she'll like that. He won't let me see it until it's finished. He says paintings of the dead are sacred, they deserve their privacy. When he's finally done, he unveils

Al's smiling face, and it is perfect. I make him sign the bottom corner then I package it up to send in the morning.

"I don't just paint. I graffiti, too, you know," says Siegfried. "Want to see my work?"

And so, into the city we go. The kid is sugar drunk from a drink with zero percent real fruit juice. She's clapping for no one as she bounces up and down in her car seat, Siegfried fiddling with the radio in the front. He directs me where to go, and I turn down a narrow alley with walls covered in graffiti. I can see the artwork stretch for blocks.

"I took a date here once," he says. "I graffitied one of her poems and she absolutely swooned."

"I didn't even know this was here," I say. He rolls down the window and points out his most recent piece: a painting of a scale, one side piled with dozens of shadows. On the other side, it says "See? Now You're Free."

"Graffiti is a beautiful way to say fuck you," he says.

"Fuck you!" says the kid, smiling.

■

The kid has developed a keen sense of observation, even for a three-and-a-half-year-old, and she uses this gift at the most inopportune moments. Everywhere I take her, she studies people and then imitates their mannerisms back to me, or worse, directly to them. The kid, it appears, is making sure no one will ever say hello to me again. How will I ever repay her?

Today, I take the kid to the bank with me, and we run into that squirrely teacher you used to work with—the one who always says she hates small talk and then assaults us with small talk for hours.

"I'm really sorry for your loss," she says, eyes taking in our shadows. "The students were torn up about it. You should have seen them." I thank her and, having witnessed the kid's gears grinding in her head, I search for a non-existent escape route. We are stuck in this line together. The teacher has this way of talking out of the side of her mouth that I never took much note of before. But now I am accompanied by the kid, who is undoubtedly taking note.

The teacher stands in front of us in line, and I am mentally begging the kid to wait, at least until we're alone, to perform. After all, I'm not a monster; I support her talents and future career in comedy or acting. I want her to learn when to use her skills, is all. The woman talks and talks, and I nod and nod, hoping I can nod her away from me, out of the bank, and thus, out of the kid's sociological study.

Once it's her turn with a teller, I think we've gotten rid of her, but then she's standing outside when we emerge into the midday heat.

"You two are so brave," says the teacher. I nod wisely. The kid looks at me out of the corner of her eye, smirking, then addresses the teacher.

"Nice to meet you," says the kid, out of the side of her mouth in a goddamn perfect-ten imitation of this woman. You'd be proud, Beau. I know I am. You should see the look on this woman's face before she scurries away, pretending to take an urgent and earnest interest in the trunk of her car.

———

Siegfried, the kid, and I are watching TV one night, and the kid keeps sneaking peeks at me. I try to behave normally, no sudden movements, no strange tics, and I think I've succeeded until she jumps up from the couch and clears her throat to gain our attention. She points to her face to signify where we should look. She chews on the inside of her right cheek. Then her left. Then her right. Back and forth, back and forth.

"It was easy to learn. You do it a lot," she explains.

"Good to know. Now do him," I say, nodding at Siegfried.

"Zig Zag," she begins. "You're easy, too." She pulls her hair from her ponytail then begins braiding it over her shoulder while she rubs her lips together like someone who has just put on lip balm. He blushes, rubbing his lips together.

Zig Zag, I love that nickname. Every night it's, *Tell me something, Zig Zag.* He never runs out of things. Tonight, he tells her about his support group, only he calls it his superhero meeting.

"The superheroes all have capes, they drink coffee and talk about superhero things," he says.

"Then what?" she asks, tying her blankie around her neck like a cape. He looks at me then lowers his voice.

"They say there are some superheroes in the Department. They don't have capes," he says, "but they're there, biding their time."

■

The kid requests a trip to the beach even though the beach is a garbage dump. Who am I to deny the kid her garbage needs? I wrestle her one-piece bathing suit over her underwear. She always requires underwear. Sometimes she wears underwear under her underwear, just to be sure. When this happens, I say, "That's okay, I'll buy you more underwear," and I do. I order them online, with a five-dollar surcharge, thanks to Darlene.

The kid runs circles around the trash and seaweed and carcasses. She runs on her tiptoes, strong calf muscles already blooming. I watch her shadows run, too. I snap a few photos. She looks sublime against the toxic landscape. Like a menacing angel. I want to swallow the moment and keep it in my burning belly, but I have my wrong mouth on—I am wearing the mouth that speaks without thinking.

"I wish Beau could see you now," I say.

The kid stops running and turns to look at me, a question mark on her face.

"Who is Beau?"

She furrows her brow and folds her arms across her chest, imitating me. I uncross my arms, then she does, still frowning.

"Well, she's your mommy that gave birth to you."

"But you're my mommy," she says, drawing a heart with her toe in the sand.

I clear my throat and look around as if to recruit help. Anyone? But the beach is empty.

"I know I am, but you once had two mommies."

"What happened to the other?" she asks.

"She, well," I begin. I feel the sad bubbling in my throat. "She died. Right after she had you."

The kid peers at me as if I am telling a fairy tale. One far less plausible than ten-headed dragons and winged humans soaring amongst the clouds.

"Was she a dream?" the kid asks in a small voice. I start crying the ugly sobs of my childhood. I squat down in front of the kid and brush her stray hairs from her face. Up close, it seems possible for me to climb into her left cheek dimple and hide.

"No, not a dream. Far from it, babe."

I can't think of what else to say, how best to describe you. I wouldn't blame you if you hated me for keeping a secret this long.

"Then what was she?"

I choke up and the kid falls into my arms.

"You cry a lot. Does that mean I'll cry a lot, too?" she asks.

"No, hopefully you won't."

Once I gain control of myself, she releases the hug and smiles up at me.

"Beau's a cool name for a mommy. Does that mean you have another name?"

"Yeah, my name is Kris," I laugh.

"Nice to meet you, Kris," she says, holding out her hand.

■

The kid wants to understand who this Beau character is, so I offer up a few videos I have of you. It pains me, even now that you're gone, to share you with someone else.

"Do you want to see Beau-mommy or no?" I ask.

She tugs on my earlobe. "Do you?"

"This isn't about me."

She shoots me a look as if to say, *Yeah, right.*

"If you say so," she says. "Let's watch Beau-mom."

She says Beau-mom like it's one word. I say it a few times, faster each time.

"Beau-mom, Beau-mom, Beaumom, Beaumum, Beaum," I say, and she tugs harder and harder until I say, "Ouch, watch it," and she pulls her hand away, wearing an apology on her face.

"Just not so hard, okay? Next thing I know, my earlobes will be hanging by my knees and I'll have to wrap them around my neck like a scarf." She giggles, tugging lightly this time.

On-screen, you are very pregnant, wearing an old soccer T-shirt and sweatpants and practicing guitar. *Are you filming me? Stop*, you say, removing your left hand from the neck and holding it over my camera. *Let me do this, okay? It's my only joy*, says a younger, lighter version of me. *Oh, wow*, you say, smirking. You return to the B and E chords you're learning. You tap your right foot, keeping rhythm as you strum. In the background, scattered circulars you'd been perusing for deals. *Your only joy, huh?* you repeat in mock jealousy.

"I don't know the song she's playing," says the kid.

"No one does, sweetie."

"Can I learn to play?" she asks.

"You sure can."

She smiles proudly as if she's already mastered a complicated guitar solo.

"Her belly was so big," the kid whispers.

"That's because it was full of you," I say.

"Ha!" the kid fake laughs and then real laughs at her own terrible fake laugh and then we are both laughing, but I'm not sure at what.

"I could hang out in a dumpster with you," I say, thinking of you.

"More," she demands, slamming her cup down on her thigh.

"The kid loves watching home videos of Beau," I text your mom. The next thing I know, she has airdropped me hundreds of files straight to our TV.

"Took me a while to convert them, but here they are," she texts. Every night, I wear the Beau angel T-shirt to bed.

"You should think about moving here," I say. "Your only grandchild is growing up without you."

"What the hell would I do over there?" she asks.

"Whatever it is Nonnas do," I offer.

She doesn't reply for several minutes, and I think I've lost her, pushed her too far—then my phone buzzes.

"I've got plenty of spare bedrooms, you know."

Whenever you used to criticize my fear of change, I'd redirect attention to your mother. Same routine, same clothes, same dishes, same everything for forty-plus years.

■

The neighbors are smoking weed on their patio while their dog prances around the courtyard. Round and round she goes, circling drooping trees. This is my first time sharing the courtyard with them. The kid leaps off my lap and chases the dog, yelling "You better listen!" Very domineering that one.

The woman—I learn her name is Dune—passes me a joint and says, "Careful, it's strong stuff," in that sucked-in stoner voice. I take a quick hit then pass it back to her. I feel stoned almost immediately, regrettably philosophical. I study Dune; she's white, with blue hair and collarbones that poke out of her black tank top. I find myself inspired to reach out and pet her dark, thick eyebrows, but I refrain.

The dog doesn't bother to stop and squat when he poops—he poops while running like a horse. I cackle.

"He's always done it that way," laughs Dune's partner, Julian. Julian is Black with short hair and a nice beard. A small hoop in his septum. They both have tattoo sleeves, but I couldn't tell you of what. When I say something about the tattoos, Julian and Dune agree that their shitty ink makes them all the more sexy. They look at each other with these mushy eyes and it makes me want to curl up between them forever.

"You two are nothing like I thought you'd be," I say, although I'm not sure why.

"What did you think we were like?" asks Dune, amused.

"Avoidant," I say. "Like me."

They sit with this for a while, which I appreciate. I don't want them asking for more details even though I'm the one who brought it up. Misty-brained, I feel the need to explain myself.

"I just always hear you two arguing," I say. "About meals and whatnot."

"You call that an argument?" laughs Julian.

They seem so comfortable in the face of a dispute. How? How does one develop such security? I call for the kid to come sit with me, but she's too absorbed in her study of the poop. She looks at it like a lost treasure.

"Where'd you get the firecracker?" asks Julian, nodding at the kid.

"From my late wife," I say, the words fuzzy on my tongue.

"Ah," he says, nodding.

"I've never said that before."

"It's awful."

"*Late wife.* What does it even mean? Late for what?"

"This archaeological expedition," says Dune, nodding toward the kid, who is now poking the poop with two sticks, breaking it apart.

"This is chocolate, right?" the kid asks the poop.

"No, it's not!" I yell. "Don't you dare eat that."

"But Mom, you never let her do anything fun," whines Julian in a mock child voice. He puts his arm around Dune and smiles from person to person. *You* get a smile, *you* get a smile.

"I heard that," says the kid. She giggles and skips over to

me. "You didn't get the joke, that's okay," she says, climbing onto my lap.

"I wouldn't mess with her if I were you," I tell my two new friends, which induces a smugness in the kid.

We get to talking about what it is we do with our time. Julian and Dune are musicians when they aren't working from home—Dune as a web developer, Julian as a graphic designer. They play music together under the name Tasty Cakes. I find this very impressive, mostly because birds fall dead from the sky when I attempt to mimic their songs. The kid tells them that one day she will join their band and they nod very seriously. I head inside and grab beers and a fruit juice. When I come back out, the kid is playing musical chairs with Julian and Dune's laps.

"This one is softer but that one has more room," she says. No one told me that, as a parent, you have to carry double the amount of humiliation with you at all times.

I tell them a little more about you and they tell me how they met, how Julian's package had accidentally been delivered to Dune's house and how Dune had watched Julian open the package.

"Ten pairs of old man socks," says Dune. "Ten!"

Later on, I learn that Julian is trans and Dune is nonbinary, but Dune isn't out.

"Use they/them when we're alone, she/her in public," they say.

"What's nombinary?" asks the kid, examining our faces.

Julian and Dune laugh, and Julian pretends to take a bite out of Dune's arm.

"A very delicious person," says Julian, smirking at Dune.

"Okay!" says the kid, a little annoyed. "But really."

"It means I'm not a man or a woman," says Dune. "I'm just me."

The kid seems satisfied by this answer. She slides off Julian's lap and begins to chase the dog around the courtyard again.

Dune rolls another blunt and we smoke in silence for a while. Everyone seems to be in their own world. Then Julian stands up, closes his eyes, and does this slow side-to-side sway, stretching his arm out to Dune.

"Dance with me," he says.

"You know I'm a terrible dancer," they say.

"But not with me you aren't."

Dune smirks then stands up and takes his hand. They slow dance like high schoolers for either three hours or three minutes, I can't tell. I think about how nice it might feel to do that again with someone sometime. The thought alone dizzies me with remorse.

We say our goodnights and I read the kid a bedtime story. I think she's fallen asleep but then she rubs her eyes, points at a period at the end of a sentence, and says, "Serious dot."

———

She continues to sing songs that frighten me. She dances in her car seat and sings, "I have this, you have that! Together, we have nothing!"

"Did you make that up?"

"No," she sighs. "We all did."

"More and more people have extra shadows nowadays," my father says, catching a bug between his cupped hands. "I wish you'd stop acting so persecuted," he says, releasing it.

"You don't get it," I say. "You could kill me, and they'd take you for a steak dinner."

"You're right, maybe I don't get it." He twirls his mustache. There is an adorable bald spot from decades of self-soothing. When I think of moving across the country, I think of his adorable bald spot, how I cannot bear to leave it.

The kid takes to drawing on our windows with permanent marker. She traces her hand on the window then calls me over and traces mine, twice.

"Why do I get two hands?" I ask.

She pauses and furrows her brow, pressing her hand against her cheek. "Hmm, so that it has a friend."

"But your hand is my hand's friend," I say.

"Yeah, but soon I'll be gone," she says so matter-of-factly I swear she is you, reincarnated. The kid isn't even five and she is already planning her departure.

———

We spend more and more time with Julian and Dune. They invite us over for beer and apple juice. We ask them questions and they ask us questions, and no one falls apart, if only for a little while.

■

Today on the news, a gang rape and murder.

"Don't worry, this is just an outlier—crime rates have never been lower," says the president. "Studies continue to prove that the threat of an extra shadow decreases deviant behavior. All you have to do is trust the balance," says the president. A grin, a wave, a round of applause.

Pop Quiz:
Q: What does it mean to harm someone?
A: Define *someone*.

"Tell me something, Zig Zag," says the kid. We are eating spaghetti and meatballs for dinner.

He tells her how he's been reading a book about human evolution. He says our brains love labels; we've basically survived because labels allow us to categorize things that exist in our world. Anyone else would have told the kid some stupid story for children but not Siegfried. And the kid delights in it.

"Like a couch, for example," he says. "The first person to ever sit on a piece of furniture large enough for several people labeled it a couch so that they'd recognize other similar-looking objects in the future and know it was okay to sit on them."

"Sounds like a hoax," says the kid.

"Which part?" I ask.

"I sit on chairs, rocks, counters, floors, ground, cars, sand, slides, you name it, I sit on it," she says, raising her eyes.

"What cars are you sitting on?" I ask.

"Oh my god," she says, rolling her eyes.

■

The kid has filed Julian and Dune's band name, Tasty Cakes, in a brain file labeled VERY IMPORTANT. Dune shows the kid their guitar after the kid confesses to what she is now calling her "lifelong dream of rocking and rolling." The kid runs her hand up and down the guitar's body as if she, its creator, is admiring her creation. My small god. Prideful, she doesn't tell Dune who was responsible for giving her that dream.

Dune helps place the guitar in the kid's lap and shows her how to strum.

"I'm already rolling," says the kid, beaming from person to person. The dog groans.

"She gets that from me," I say, thinking about that time my friend and I snorted a stranger's Molly at a music festival then had anxious, searching sex on her living room couch. And then on Saint Patrick's Day, we dumped Molly into our beers inside a terrible bro bar then lost each other.

"Did you know," begins Siegfried slowly, smiling that gentle smile of his, "that we named the first person to ever create beautiful sounds a musician so that we'd know to love them?" He packs up his backpack to head out for the night. I don't know where he's going; he never tells me.

Siegfried doesn't come home that night, but that isn't overly concerning—he probably found somewhere to crash with friends. In the morning, the kid and I go for a walk on the beach. She finds a baggy of assorted pills and waggles it in the air like a miniature flag. Years ago, I might have pocketed it for later, but today, I say, "Drop it."

"I can hear the serious dot in your voice," says the kid, stomping into the water, wading in thigh-high. She releases the bag into the white wash.

When we get home, Siegfried is passed out on our doorstep, propped up against the door, slumped over like a scarecrow.

"Zig Zag," says the kid. "You're so silly."

He doesn't stir. Then I notice the dried blood on the side of his neck.

"Zig Zag!" she shouts, louder.

"Honey," I say, slowly, numbing out.

"Why won't he wake up?" the kid asks, nudging him with her foot. He falls to the ground, exposing the back of his head.

"Get inside," I say, opening the front door and shoving her in. I can hear her wailing through the door.

As I stare at Siegfried's lifeless body, raw anger climbs my throat. What the fuck happened? Is this a message? Did Agent Brown have anything to do with this? Is it partially my fault? Had Siegfried known the price of our friendship, I'm afraid he would have grabbed his paint brush and climbed inside our lives all the same. What do you do with a love like that?

■

According to research, hunters and poachers have begun using radio signals to find and kill tagged animals. They do this for fun, profit, or sport. Sometimes all three.

■

The evening is a whirlwind of EMTs and cops and questions and answers and the same questions again and the same answers again and the kid screaming inside the house while Julian and Dune try and fail to distract her with the guitar. No, I wasn't sleeping with him, no, I don't know what happened, no, I didn't kill him. The whole time they're questioning me, they ignore him, so I sit down on the pavement and cradle his bloody head in my lap.

Finally, a cop bends down and pushes my arm out of the way so he can scan Siegfried's face with a tablet. He's quiet as he scrolls through Siegfried's profile.

"I miss him already," I say.

"I'm sorry, you *miss* him? Do you know what he did?" I

can tell he's trying to be nasty but that he doesn't actually have the energy for it.

"No, should I have?"

"Well," he says, scrolling on the tablet. "It's certainly not something he would have dropped casually into conversation."

"We were trying," I say, beginning to cry, "trying to live in a world beyond our shadows," I whisper.

The man laughs. He turns his screen toward me. On it, a bunch of information about Siegfried, tiny words with big meanings.

"Tell that to the sister he killed," he says.

I swallow hard, my eyes start to blur. I focus on the mole on the cop's chin.

Siegfried's only sister. Siegfried's *baby* sister.

"What," I whisper.

"Looks like he was a dealer down by the piers," he says, consulting the tablet. "Oh, shit, I remember this case. He dealt this kid some bad dope, cut with some real serious shit. He didn't know the kid was getting it for his sister. And boom."

"Boom," I repeat.

"Boom," he says.

"You didn't have to tell me that," I say. "You didn't have to change everything."

But even as I say it, I realize I'm acting more disturbed than I am over what Siegfried did. I'm supposed to hate him, supposed to find his life irredeemable, but I don't have the capacity to feel that way right now. Right now, I don't hate him. I just want him back.

Black widows, snails, chitons.

Like a dream funneling out of my head, I am already losing the details of Siegfried.

After the cops leave, I go inside to find the kid curled in my bed. We hold each other a little tighter tonight. What if I had never let him leave? I could have demanded he stay indoors. I could have said, *It's not safe out there.* I know my thoughts are both irrational and self-pitying, but I can't stop the dam-burst flow of them.

"Why did he die?" she sobs into my chest.

"I don't know," I say.

"Say something else," she says. "You know nothing."

I stroke her hair until she falls asleep, her eyes puffy and pink with sorrow. Here we are, mourning a murderer.

■

Pop Quiz:

Q: Is a person no more than the sum of their actions?

A: He didn't mean to kill her, he didn't mean to kill her, he didn't mean to kill her. He didn't mean to.

■

When extra shadows were first being assigned, a psychologist wrote a lengthy proposal to eliminate them, claiming they were inhumane.

The official report said he took his own life.

It is awful, I know, and yet I find myself thinking that Siegfried didn't exactly put the needle in her arm, now did he? But what about all the other people he sold drugs to? He knew what would happen. It's not like he thought there was a chance they might go pour them in the bath like bath salts. If ever there were a time in which Darlene might chastise me, it would be now. I can just hear her saying, in a voice not unlike my own, *And after all this time, your default setting is still blame.*

Bonus Question:
Q: Where do you draw the line for someone you love?
A: I want to remember him as I always have.
Q: The line, where do you draw it?
A: I am not the Department.

The more I think on it, the more fucked I feel. And even though Siegfried and I had agreed to not discuss our extra shadows, I feel betrayed by him. But this feels disingenuous. Siegfried was the one who read the kid bedtime stories and painted your mom a portrait of Al and listened with his whole being. I find myself feeling sad for Siegfried. Had he been dealing drugs to help support his sister? How did he endure killing the one person he tried to keep safe? How did he manage to live with that?

■

"Please don't say what I think you're going to say," I tell my father over beers. Julian and Dune are babysitting the kid. I hear them rocking and rolling next door.

He wilts a little, as if saddened by my expectations of him. He doesn't speak. Instead, he studies me, looking for I don't know what.

"As a chemical engineer, do you know how to make deadly drugs?" I ask. He twirls his mustache, eyes on the ceiling.

"Of course," he says. "What do you think soda is?"

■

Siegfried could somehow find a way to forgive himself for accidentally killing his baby sister. I'm not sure what that means for me and my future—if I'm beyond hope or not.

Reality Testing:
Brain: I didn't love Siegfried, I loved who I thought he was.

Reality: There comes a point where the before and after must merge.

■

When I call the Department, they refuse to tell me any information since I'm not related to Siegfried. The only thing I learn is that his real name had been Zackariah. What had I even known about this man? My best friend?

"Of course, we'll be investigating his murder," says the agent, almost taunting. I picture a group of men drinking beers and throwing darts at Siegfried's face.

The kid and I hold our own funeral for him by the water. The hot air thickens and then settles into our chests, our breaths deep and forceful.

"What do we say?" she asks, grabbing my hand.

"Nice things about Zig Zag," I sob. "A eulogy."

"I'm afraid he'll disappear," she says, squeezing my hand.

"We won't let him," I say. What I don't say: *I'm scared this may happen to you one day.*

"Do a ewlogy," says the kid.

"Here's one: Zig Zag could make you feel like you were the most important, beautiful, dazzling thing he'd ever seen. Even if you were just weeding the garden or opening an umbrella," I say. "No matter what, he made you feel like you were the only one in the world capable of doing that particular thing in that particular moment."

"I've never seen you in a garden," says the kid.

"You're a real smart-ass," I say.

"I'd cry if I wasn't so sad," she whispers.

"He wasn't impressed by anyone more than he was by you, though," I say, thinking about how I let this man live inside my house with my toddler.

"I don't want to forget," the kid says.

"Remembering is a courageous act."

She glances at me and exhales sharply.

"What?" I ask.

She removes her hair tie one last time, draping her hair over her right shoulder. She separates her hair into three even strands, then slowly, methodically, she braids her long hair while rubbing her lips together.

Part II

■

I told you I wanted to live in a world in which
the antidote to shame is not honor, but honesty.

MAGGIE NELSON

As for the pain
of others, of course it tries to be
abstract . . .

MARY OLIVER

The night before the kid's big day. She is pacing around the house in a nervous, excited frenzy. I want to do something for her, I want to remind her that the world is bigger than whichever classroom she winds up in.

When I was young, there was a place you could go to listen to the sounds of the universe. It was an exhibit at the museum called the Infinity Room. A couple had traveled into space and recorded all these sounds together. It sounded like a perfect way to spend one's time—alone with love and sound. I wondered if they ever found any black holes, if they found a way to access an alternate universe. My dad used to take me there whenever I was feeling bad in the head, which was more and more often as my mother drifted, then fell out of orbit. After she left, I felt rag-dolled, as if life were trying to buck me off its back. My dad and I would sit in the dark and listen, losing time. After, he'd ask me what I'd found, not what I'd heard. I liked that. *So much*, I'd say, afraid to give any more away. After all, it was mine, I'd found it, I could keep it for myself.

But like so much from my childhood, the exhibit is gone now. I decide to take the kid to a small cove nearby, where the acoustics are good. I know this because it had once been my screaming place. Every night for months after I received my extra shadow, I drove to this cove and opened up my throat, wolfish and hungry. One night, I saw my ex-coworker, this white woman Joanna who wore expensive leggings and dangly bracelets. *Just so you know, I'm really pissed about what they did to you,* she said. *Yeah, thanks,* I said. *It feels like it happened overnight,* she said, her eyes asking something of me—forgiveness maybe—no, that wasn't right. Praise I think it was. She wanted a gold star. I knew for a fact that she'd voted President Colestein back into office. Had she been paying attention, she would have known it hadn't happened overnight, that it took a million tiny stabs to bleed democracy dry.

Pop Quiz:
Fill in the blanks:
Many people in the United States find it ____ to ____ about ____ until it ____ to them.

At the cove, the kid stands on a rock and closes her eyes. The wind tugs at her T-shirt.

"This is the universe," I say.

"Where has it been?" she asks. Her face looks very serious, as if she is focusing on taking in every single sound, first individually, then as a unit.

What will I say if the teacher asks about my shadow? About the kid's?

Balance this, motherfucker.

What I found in the Infinity Room: the universe sounded suspiciously like the interstate. Nothing was magic after that.

∎

Like so many in power before him, President Colestein is an expert at tapping into this country's shared anxiety, at using it to fuel mass delusion. That's why the term limit was scrapped after President Colestein's second, why he was voted back in for a fourth. *Do you want to pay for other people to think about what they've done? In nicer prisons than our apartments and condos and houses,* he'd said, not really asking—no, he already knew the answer, knew the economic crisis that plagued the country, knew that the masses needed a new scapegoat. He'd planted the seed of resentment, watered it with constant news coverage of prisoners going to college, learning trade skills, reading books, working out, doing the things they did with their time. And in the same breath, he could feign innocence whenever he received opposition, could hold his hands up and say, *Don't blame me for the cycle of violence. If anything, I've set everyone free.*

I don't know where he got his Shadester idea—perhaps it'd come to him in a dream—but the source didn't matter. Before long, Shadesters had lost access to fresh food and

timely health care. And we paid Shadester tax on everything. Of course, countless people lacked access to these
things long before the shadow policy went into effect—the
law just guaranteed it. Plus, the more shadows you had,
the harsher the restrictions and the worse people treated
you. Over the years, I've heard a few stories about multiple-
shadow Shadesters who, after one too many incidents, eventually stopped leaving the house altogether. They closed the
blinds, locked the doors, and retreated into themselves.

*We will take the money back from society's criminals and use
it for our schools and hospitals*, Colestein had said to a crowd of
hoots and hollers. *Because we deserve it. You deserve the balance.*

I remember losing a friend over my cousin's third prison
stint. I think he was in for grand theft auto, or maybe it
was drugs that time, I don't know—he wasn't well. You
and I had gone to a dinner party, one of those stuffy events
that marks the transition into real adulthood. The host,
our friend, was this rigid woman we kind of loved to hate.
When we told her we were trying to have a baby, she compared parenthood to prison. I said, *Much offense, but nothing
is like prison except actual prison*. We were never invited back,
but I didn't feel the conversation was over. I wanted to return to her house just to keep arguing, but you lied to me
and told me she'd moved.

Now, knowing what I know about the extremes some
Shadesters are pushed to, I'm glad my friend cut me off,

though she got the reason all wrong. I hadn't been using the creative part of my brain, the part reserved for conjuring up answers to the question *What's the worst that could happen?*

Before bed, the kid picks out her clothes for the first day of school: a black skull T-shirt and galaxy leggings with a rainbow tutu. Subtle, I think.

"Mom," she says, smoothing out her T-shirt.

"Yes?"

Tomorrow is a destination, not a date.

"I know we're different. Julian and Dune and Grandpa have just one shadow," she says. "Same with tons of strangers."

I don't know what to say so I unfold and re-fold some of her clothes. I want to uphold the honesty plan I made with you all those years ago, so long ago that the memory seems like a movie I once watched, not because I wanted to, but because everyone was telling me I just *had* to see it.

I've spent some time reading how-to-talk-to-your-child-about-Shadesters scripts posted online by NoShad parents. "They're just like us. Only different," said one.

"What else do you know?" I ask.

"I know Zig Zag didn't have to die," she frowns.

The kid looks at me for confirmation. I nod. It breaks my heart to nod. All our years together are stuffed inside that nod. I almost lost the kid once, and I am waiting, in quiet terror, for it to happen again.

■

"How do I look?" the kid asks, holding her arms out to the side, palms facing me, her morning hair a true sight to see. I've taken to calling her *wild, wild hairdo*, which she either likes a lot or doesn't like one bit, I can't tell.

"Like the moment an idea becomes an action," I say, snapping a few photos to send to your mom. I can hear you swimming around in my skull: *Why do you insist on talking to her like that? She has no idea what you're saying. Just say yes, you look beautiful, stinker, or whatever it is you're calling her these days.*

"Whatever," says the kid. "I'm going to be the coolest kid in class."

"I have no doubt about that."

Looking at the kid in that absurd outfit with her big book-stuffed backpack strapped to her—well, I start to feel emotional. What if she decides not to come home? I think she could probably survive two or three days on those books if she rationed them appropriately. I turn away to gather myself.

"Mom, are you being intense again?"

On the drive, the kid hums to herself, occasionally singing words I don't recognize. Since I am her parent, I can't trust my instinct that she is a lovely singer. As we pull into the parking lot, my chest tightens, my throat swells, I can barely swallow my saliva. I hadn't expected to have such a visceral reaction to this space all these years later.

Once I park, I take a moment. I press the back of my head against the seat and watch the wind hassle the palm trees lining the street, behind them, the sky a blend of yellow and black. When I unload the kid and set her down on the pavement, she surprises me by grabbing my hand. *Don't look at us*, I think, practically running, dragging the kid behind me. We see one other Shadester student, a few years older than the kid, walking alone, an eerie calm emanating from her, as if she's already accepted the fact that she'll probably accumulate a few more shadows by the time she graduates.

"Look, one of us," the kid whispers, poking me in the upper arm.

"This isn't the zoo," I say, trailing off as we are met by my old boss, Jamal, who twists his mouth into a hesitant smile. He hadn't wanted to fire me, he'd said; it had come from above him. I knew he felt bad about it. Although we'd worked in the school, we weren't employed by the school. We worked for an external behavioral health company, which caused some tension between teachers and the treatment team. Once a student was admitted to our program, the teachers suddenly treated them differently, as if upon admittance the student sprouted horns and developed the ability to breathe fire. I once witnessed a teacher, whose back was turned to the class as he wrote on the board, scream at one of my troubled kids to stop setting everyone off, even though the girl behind him was plucking his hair out. On my first day of work, Jamal had shoved me lightly and said, *Let's see what you're made of.* I am worried he can still see the answer: *Not much.*

"Look who it is," he smiles, leaning in for a sideways hug. His sideburns have grayed, but otherwise he looks exactly the same. He still walks like a lion, that slow assured gait I can't help but admire.

"You don't know me yet," says the kid, reaching out her hand. She ripples with confidence.

"No, I don't, but I'm sure I will," he says, giving me a wink. Even he, a mental health professional, sees an extra shadow and anticipates misbehavior. What awful things have I said or done that I am not aware of? What do I continue to do?

"She can see you, you know," I say. He shrugs and heads inside to my old office.

After Siegfried died, I was extra worried about the kid, so I tried sending her to therapy, but three different therapists broke up with her. The first said she was inscrutable, the second called her *disturbingly defiant*, and the most recent one said she was too old for this. I didn't ask what *this* was. As worried as I am, I'm also strangely proud.

If the kid had been on my caseload, I might have said, *It's okay to feel your feelings*, and she might have studied the You're a shooting star! poster in our office before ripping it off the wall.

We eventually find the kid's classroom, and the teacher, who I don't recognize, beams and welcomes us to Miss

Robinson's Learning Adventure. Her eyes focus in on the floor beside us, and she takes a quick step backward, swallowing hard.

The kid doesn't seem to notice the teacher's change in demeanor. She struts like a peacock over to a circle of kids who are engrossed in building something.

"Well, she's certainly brave, isn't she?" says the teacher, who I ignore.

One of the kids is picking his nose and rubbing it all over the bricks. Another sticks a block down the front of his pants, then the back. One boy, though, gives the kid a familiar look, one of reserved contempt, one that could be mistaken for annoyance if you weren't paying attention. I'm afraid of that look; I have nightmares about that look. But again, the kid doesn't appear to notice. She looks back at me and gives me the sweetest wave.

I should say something to Miss Robinson, I think, but I don't.

■

"Straight to the car, straight to the car," I chant, marching down the hallway past rooms 101, 102, 103, 104, 105. Then I pause outside 106. The teacher, who's writing on the board, is an older man I'd seen in passing a few times when I worked here. Kids are filing in with their parents. Smiling, dopey kids. Shy, fearful kids. A few parents look at me apprehensively—*what is this pervert doing here without a child?* The teacher hasn't decorated much. Perhaps he's succumbed to the big, dragged-down tired that takes almost everyone at some point. You would have never let this happen, Beau. Decorating your classroom, creating a beautiful oasis, was one of your favorite things. One year, after a gay student had been bullied quite a bit, you put a sign on your door that read THERE ARE NO CLOSETS IN HERE, LEAVE YOUR BELONGINGS ON THE SHELF.

I've heard it said that love is choosing to listen to how someone's day went at least thirty thousand times. Love is saying, *I am here, I am paying attention, and I care about that fight you had with your coworker.* Beau, sometimes listening to you scream *Fuck today, let's go on a date* was the only thing keeping me alive.

From now on, I will show the kid that I love her by listening to her explain how carpet squares work.

■

Alone with myself for the first time in five years, I decide to masturbate. When I pull my underwear down, crows emerge, squawking and carrying on, and dust flies everywhere, tickling my nose. I watch gay porn. A blindfolded sub is affixed to a Saint Andrew's cross by the wrists and ankles, facing his dom, who's thick and muscled in the way I like. At first, it's going well. I suck in air real hard when the dom begins to gently stroke his sub's penis, which grows harder and harder. I like watching porn with dicks because I like how visible the arousal is; I like to watch someone's desire come into being. I work myself slowly, nurturing my pleasure—I don't want to get off too quickly the first time around. You would enjoy this video, Beau. Climbing into bed with me, you'd sometimes get angry if I wasn't pre-pared: *Where's the porn?* you'd growl into my neck, reaching behind my head and gripping a handful of my hair, a slight yank, and I'd let out a moan, then a harder pull. (I act as if this were a regular thing, but it really wasn't. You often forgot the role I wanted you to play, forgot I wanted you to control and possess me, to objectify me. I had to use cues, face down, ass up, slowly swaying back and forth, as if to say, *Look, did you forget?* You had.)

I'm close to coming when the dom begins whipping the sub in the stomach and hips—high-risk zones. I wait for him to move elsewhere, somewhere safer, but he doesn't; he just keeps on whipping and whipping, the sub howling, his entire torso soon a sunburnt pink. I can't look away, I keep hoping the dom will stop but he doesn't, he's absorbed in his task, he sees no danger in it, or maybe he does, maybe he can only derive pleasure from actual harm, not simply the threat. If my clit were a dick, it would be soft by now. As I watch the man, I feel a rush of shame bubble in the back of my throat, near the place where my sadness typically orig-inates. The two aren't far from one another; they are inter-twined, irrevocably connected by my shadow.

———

To take my mind off my shame, I make a few cold calls. One older woman answers. Her voice raspy, soothing.

"I need something to help me cope," she says. I think I hear her shaking a drink in the background.

"With what, exactly?" I ask, scanning my mindcast files.

"I fucked up," she says, shyly. I haven't heard someone sound that way in a long time. Actually remorseful.

"Do you want to talk about it?" I ask, slipping into my social worker skin.

"I don't know," she says. It could be the connection, but she sounds far away, a dispatch from outer space. "What do you recommend?"

"Sounds like you need the starter set," I say, remembering my job. She sighs loudly, as if she can somehow transfer her exasperation from her body to mine.

When I tell Jackson about the call, that people are craving real human connection, he says, "No one keeps you alive except for you and your promise to yourself." Jackson has never lost himself. Jackson believes that you can self-talk yourself back to life.

Self-talk, there's where the mindcast money is. For instance, today I sell a man our largest box set after he spends an hour outlining all the ways a machine is better at his job than him.

"How often do you sit down and have a conversation with yourself?" I ask him.

"Never," he says.

"Now, is that any way to treat yourself?" I say.

After my sale, a singing telegram arrives at my door. The man sings *happy six-year work anniversary* to the tune of happy birthday.

Business is, as they say, booming. If people could inject themselves with mindcasts, they would.

■

At the end of the first day, I wait with the other parents outside. Children pour from the mouth of the school, and I hope the kid will find a way to blend in. We once had dreams of our spawn disrupting the Department, going full-blown anarchist, but now I only dream of her survival. A selfish wish, yes, but I've come to terms with my selfishness, its ordinary, comfortable shape. Once the kid spots me, she picks up speed and does a running leap into my arms like she hasn't done in years.

"How was your first day?" I ask, swinging her around.

"Put me down first and I'll tell you," she says, kicking the air.

"Okay, you're down, now spill."

"You're so annoying," she smirks, waiting to see how I will react. She fixes her tutu. "Why are you smiling? I said something rude!"

"It's nice, isn't it?"

"What is?"

"To love someone so much."

"So much what?"

"That you can love the annoyance, too," I say, giving her a light shove.

■

Pop Quiz:

Q: And how will you make your intentions known?

A: "Do you have enough light?" I ask the kid, who I catch reading in bed by flashlight way past her bedtime.

■

The kid comes home from school one day and wants to know what dignity means.

"I don't know. Like, self-respect," I say, boiling pasta. The water overflows and sizzles on the burner.

"I don't get it," she says, pacing.

"Get what?"

"The mom of this girl in my class asked me why you don't homeschool me. She said, 'Doesn't she have any dignity?'"

"I see," I say, rattling off exoskeletons in my head.

"In case you were wondering, I told her you had enough dignity to fill the whole universe," she says. "And I crossed my fingers it was a good thing."

■

I take the kid to a music shop to pick out a guitar. She spots the one she wants right away: an all-black electric. According to her, this is the best friend she's been waiting for. Her comment makes me more than a little depressed, but I maintain excitement because she's excited.

Twice a week, the kid and I go over to Julian and Dune's place after school, and Dune teaches the kid guitar and Julian and I drink beer and play video games. We play the cute games we can escape into, the cooking games and animal games, while we listen to good chord, bad chord, bad chord, bad chord, good chord, bad chord. It isn't long before it's mostly good chords, though.

Sometimes the kid demands we do a hybrid open mic/ improv session. She strums the guitar and invents lyrics on the spot, singing about rainbow clouds in love and blooming birds of paradise, her nod, I think, to Zig Zag. Once she feels satisfied, she passes it on to the next person. Dune and Julian are obvious cheaters. When it's my turn, I sing about a lonely pig that lives all alone in a mansion. The kid rips the guitar out of my hands before I can get to the part where the pig learns her lover has been sent to slaughter.

"Stop singing sad songs," bosses the kid.

"Hey, that song could have gone anywhere," I say.

"Now where were we?" she asks her fellow musicians.

On the video game, a tiny panda person herds us onto a rocket ship. We fly past the stars and satellites and space debris and land on a neon-blue planet that looks like its bottom half has been dipped in strawberry sauce.

"Welcome to _____," says the tiny panda person, head bobbing on its neck. "Congratulations on being pioneers!"

Our characters wiggle in excitement. I glance at Julian, who is smiling at the screen.

"Time to name your own planet!" says the tiny panda person.

"Oh no," I say. "This is way too much responsibility."

■

My dad and I take the kid to the park. It's a sweaty, sweaty day. We swing on the swings, we see and we saw, we play Shadesters and NoShads. And by we, I mean, the kid and me. My dad wanders around the park taking close-ups of insects. He shows them to me, his face proud.

After we exhaust ourselves, we sit on the roundabout and the kid looks stormy. My dad, shifting his position and wincing, his hips deteriorating at a rapid pace, looks at me as if to say, *I don't know this child, I just happened to stumble upon her.* Okay.

"Is everything okay?" I ask the kid, rubbing her back.

She traces imaginary drawings on her leggings for a bit and I don't press for details.

"I have a question for you both," she says.

"Great, Grandpa is awful at game shows," I say, my dad hmphing beside me. "Shoot."

"Well. How come everything that's important isn't good? And everything that's good isn't important?" she asks, eyes wide like tunnels.

"What do you mean?" I am appalled by her wisdom.

"Are you thinking of something specific?" asks my father.

"Power," she responds immediately, looking from me to my father.

"What about it?" he asks.

"It's like, it's so important to grown-ups to have power, but usually when they get it, they just do bad stuff with it," she says.

"Like—" I say, but she cuts me off and continues.

"Like my teacher gets to tell me what to do and I have to listen to her even though she just yells and yells. She doesn't want to know anything about me, just wants to yell."

No one says anything, but she's not waiting for a response.

"And then music is good, I really like to play guitar, but no one really cares," she continues.

"I do, I care," I say.

"I do, I care," she says, mimicking me and biting the inside of her cheek. "Doesn't make it important," she grumbles into her lap.

I decide that looking into a human mirror is not very fun. It's a wonder my mouth isn't constantly full of blood.

■

For the first time since the kid was born, I hire a babysitter: a deathly pale teen girl I found online with a chin piercing and a propensity for the phrase *No worries*. I take this to heart and drink a few beers before going to the only gay bar left in the city, Lucky's.

I sit in a booth by the window and drink beer after beer and try to imagine kissing every woman who walks through the door, but it's no use. I fear I'll never want to be with anyone ever again. Perhaps this is a good thing, a preventative strategy my brain has enacted without my body's consent. I fear you've ruined me forever, Beau. And it isn't that mouth-watering fear that accompanied the cool blade pressed against my collarbone the one time you agreed to knife play—it's not that orchestrated fear mixed with the divine comfort of knowing the blade had been dulled, that the edge of a student's paper was more likely to cut me. No, this is a true fear, one that pecks and pecks at my hands and face as I sit in the bar drinking, having a terrible and lonesome time.

Two men approach me, and I anticipate some sort of question. Maybe: *Could you move* or *Are you lost?* Possibly *Would you like a friend?* if they are feeling nice, but they don't address me at all. One points out the window and says, "Isn't it the prettiest?" and I want them to be talking about me, even if that makes me an it. When his friend agrees, the first guy presses a car key button and points, unlocking then locking his car, and for some reason, they hug, and it's touching in the stupidest way possible.

On the way to the bathroom, I spot a sign I've never seen anywhere else before. All it says is KNOW, accompanied by a symbol in which eight blue arrows, arranged in a circle, point outward. Know what? That going out had been a horrible idea? I never thought I'd have to set foot in another gay bar again, at least not without you there to grab my ass and bite that spot on my jaw that makes me sing and moan.

Hours later, I wake up sitting on the toilet, pants around my ankles. I decide that I must have just dozed off for a few minutes. I toss water on my face and exit the bathroom to find the bar deserted, all the doors locked. I check my phone. 5:00 a.m. I have twelve missed calls from the babysitter and a text that says, "Guess I'm staying the night. No worries. Better pay me for the extra hours, though."

Two cops are loitering on the sidewalk outside, sipping coffee. I duck behind the bar, so they won't see me, and then mix myself a screwdriver while I wait. I sit on the floor and chug my drink then pass out sitting up. In my dream, you are packing boxes and I am saying, *I don't want to move, I like it here*, but you can't see or hear me. You continue bustling around the house, stuffing our lives into various boxes.

Finally, I join you, but the coffee machine won't fit inside a sock.

A large, light-skinned bald man shakes me awake and says, "Is that you, Kris? What the hell happened?" It's Archie, my old friend from college. I squint at his name tag and see the word MANAGER under his name. He lifts me by the armpits, as if I'm a little kid, then sneaks me out the back.

I would have followed you anywhere, Beau. Maybe the problem is that I did.

When I arrive home, the kid runs from her room and squeezes my body. She looks up at me with these earnest eyes that just about kill me. I hand the babysitter a wad of cash and she nods and says, "I get it," then leaves to go do whatever it is teen girls with chin piercings do.

"Where were you?" the kid asks, not quite accusingly, not quite not. I consider making up an extravagant lie, but she's too old for that. Every lie I tell pushes her another inch away; what will happen when she slowly, finally, inches too far away from me to ever come back?

"I accidentally fell asleep somewhere," I say, trying to keep my cool.

"How do you accidentally fall asleep?" she says, narrowing her eyes.

"I'm sorry, stinker, I really am."

She shrugs then plops down on the couch and opens her Skys book, one she's been revisiting lately. The kid is taken by the moon, by its majesty and grace.

"Is the moon the same as Earth?" the kid asks, ignoring my apology.

"No, not really. People don't live on the moon."

"What is it then, if it's not the same as Earth?"

"The one place we all long to escape to," I say. My answer must stir something in her because she sticks her thumb in her mouth, something I haven't seen her do in a long time.

"I thought we'd kicked that habit," I say.

"And I thought you wanted to be here with me," she says around her thumb.

Later, I study the sleeping kid and think of all the people I've disappointed in my life. Ex-lovers, friends, parents, you, many times over. And now the kid. I keep wondering, when will the kid stop loving me unconditionally? When will loving me no longer be enough?

∎

After school, the kid and I swing by the grocery store. I want to get in and out as fast as possible.

"No imitations today, okay?" I say, wrapping my arm around the kid's shoulders. She gives me a close-mouthed smile then wiggles loose of my hold. She seems pensive, blanketed by an untouchable angst. She follows me around the store, staring off into space and whispering to herself, frowning. Every so often, she clears her throat and rubs her eyes with her shirt sleeve. I want to ask her what's up, but my lips won't move. I throw eggs, white bread, soup, chili, and frozen veggies into the cart, then get in line and stare at all the people around us. New couples grocery shopping together for the first time, an intimacy pulsating between them. Old couples grocery shopping together for the millionth time, an unspoken understanding connecting them. Shadester families trying not to draw attention to themselves. An elderly gay couple, not touching except for the sly brush of a hand on the cart's handle.

When it is our turn, I notice that the cashier is beautiful. Her beauty devastates me, steals my kneecaps. Black wavy hair, thoughtful eyes, and a full sleeve on each arm. I am stunned into stillness and silence. Thankfully, the kid climbs on the cart and tries to unload the groceries onto the conveyer belt, although she can't quite reach. She waves her hand in front of my face and says, "Hello, Earth to Mom? This nice woman doesn't have all day."

She shares a moment with the cashier, their eyes locking in a mutual question.

I smile a small, apologetical smile and begin to bag the groceries as the cashier rings them up. She pretends not to notice my shock, although I do catch her peeking at me a few times out of the corner of her eye, the ends of her mouth twitching upward.

"You just have the one shadow? Boring," says the kid to the cashier. I almost pass out on the spot. In fact, I consider pretending to pass out to emancipate myself from this horrid situation.

"I do, yeah, that's why I need these tattoos," says the cashier, not missing a beat. She holds her arms out and the kid studies them. Most of her tattoos are of trees: redwoods, sequoias, cacti, Joshua trees, and others I can't identify.

"What do you think?" the kid asks, consulting me.

"You're stunning," I hear my voice say. "Fuck, I'm sorry, do me a favor and ignore us both."

The woman smiles and holds up her left hand.

"That's really sweet, but I'm married," she says.

"That's okay, yeah, so am I, no worries."

The cashier glances at my ringless hand then nods. I usher the kid out of the grocery store and out of that poor woman's life. In the car the kid says, "Mom, do you think she'll be okay without an extra shadow?"

"Yeah, I think she'll be just fine," I say, thinking about the woman's lips. All week I can't shake the thought of her lips against mine, her tongue in my mouth. I want to grip that spot where her neck meets her skull and press further and further into her.

■

"Mommy?" says the kid. We are watching cartoons on the couch. A group of cats in suits scramble around trying to catch bad cats who won't stop blowing things up.

"Yeah, babe?"

"I miss Zig Zag."

"Yeah, me too."

"I have good news, though," she says.

"What's that?"

"I can see into other dimensions," she says, looking through me, possibly into one.

"Oh?"

"Yeah, and Zig Zag is in one of my favorite dimensions. It's full of monsters who eat up your sadness if you let them," she says. She's clutching Olly, her stuffed octopus, to her cheek.

"I'd like to go there," I say. I imagine handing a monster a framed photo of you and bowing out.

"If you're lucky, you'll wake up there one day," says the kid.

"Have you ever?" I ask, although I'm not sure I want to know the answer.

"No, not yet," she mumbles, brushing her hair out of her eyes.

■

It isn't long before I begin receiving phone calls from Miss Robinson throughout the day.

"Today, during quiet time, she drew a picture of the Department cameras then went up and showed the picture to the camera behind my desk. She was laughing hysterically," she says.

The next day, more news.

"I was reading the class a story on the carpet, and she

kept bursting into song when I got to a part she didn't seem to like."

"What was she singing?" I ask. I can hear kids wailing like sirens in the background. One boy yells "Fuck your mom!" Another says "Eat dicks!" And my kid is the problem.

"You're impossible," she says, hanging up.

The calls home remind me how the teachers used to rely on my treatment team to intervene the second our students did anything, no matter how benign, other than sit quietly in their chairs. Even you, Beau, irritated me at times. You were trigger happy, ready to call me about Randy if he so much as spoke out of turn. I tried to convince myself it was because you wanted an excuse to see me throughout the day, but I knew it was because the collective bias had seeped into your brain as well.

"Come take care of this," the teachers used to say.

In our office, we'd roll our eyes: "Be right down."

My mother hadn't found my teachers' calls home so amusing either. Once I'd gotten over my separation anxiety, the deviance began. In second grade, we'd been arranged in four-student pods, and after it became apparent that I wouldn't stop disrupting my group, my teacher moved me to an island by myself. I was so furious that the next day I stole my teacher's phone from her desk when she wasn't looking and changed her background to a picture of a hairy man mooning the camera.

"She's recruiting students to go on strike until we add an extra thirty minutes to their recess time," says Miss Robinson. She is frantic by the sound of it, which must mean the kid is succeeding. "Yesterday, they sat on the mulch in front of the seesaw and linked arms, refusing to come inside."

■

For the past few weeks, the kid has oscillated between two states: unnerving silence and giddy overconfidence. One day, when I pick her up from school, she's smiling like she's recently discovered she can turn carrots into cake.

"Should I be alarmed?" I ask, grabbing her hand.

"You shouldn't *be* anything," she says, looking up at me. "And if you have to be something, then you better be a unicorn." How, I wonder, has the obsession with unicorns spanned generations of children? Perhaps there is an unending enchantment associated with believing in unicorns, to saying, the hell with horses, give us a horse hopped up on magic.

"Did something happen today?" I ask. I have yet to let on that I know about her creative use of school hours. Mostly, I don't want her activities to stop. Her strong will is far better than the alternative. I don't want her to sit back and take whatever comes at her—I realize that urging her to blend in may be detrimental. I want her to venture out and secure what she wants from life. If that's taunting the Department, then so be it; they will live.

"Did you know unicorns can't talk?" says the kid.

"How pedestrian of them."

"Don't worry," she sighs. "I have at least ten more friends than everyone else."

When I was in kindergarten, I had a bowl cut—my own doing. At recess, this boy tried to kiss me and when I rejected him, he shoved me to the ground. *Stay down, you ugly boy.* I stood up, knees and palms bloody, ready to fight. When I went home, I told my parents I'd gotten hurt playing kickball with the popular kids. They ate it up.

My phone rings so often I have to put my clients on hold.

"It'll just be a minute, I have to go listen to how my child plans to ruin the world," I say.

"Mine, too," says my raspy-voiced woman. She's bought the starter kit, I think to shut me up, and now she calls me every morning. She needs someone to talk to, and I am, against all odds, a someone.

"I can't take this anymore," says Miss Robinson. "During a math quiz, she rounded up all the kids and told them they were all Shadesters and she was their Shadester king. She made them bow down to her on the carpet."

"King, huh?" I say, trying not to laugh as I imagine the kid in a royal mantle, crowning her court. It's clear to me this woman has no classroom management skills if the kid can usurp her role so easily. "Wait, did you say Shadester?" I ask, realizing I've never taught the kid that word.

"Yes, I did," she says. "She's certainly got a knack for influence, but I should tell you, there's a few kids who aren't so taken by her."

"What do you mean?"

"I think you should ask her."

■

I doubt you remember, but one evening, shortly after I'd been fired, you came home from work to find me scrolling through my phone and crying into a glass of wine. I was reading a story about a ten-year-old Shadester who killed herself after being bullied. She'd attempted suicide before, but no one knew. *I thought the marks on her neck were just hickeys*, said the dad in the news article. *I feel so stupid*, he said.

■

Instead of asking the kid, I decide to go straight to the source, to study her classroom microcosm. As soon as I enter the classroom, Miss Robinson pulls me aside.

"Perhaps you should consider homeschooling her," she says, clearing her throat.

I look at her as if she's just announced the class president will be the white boy currently yelling "Die, witch! Die!" while tugging on a girl's ponytail.

"Do I look like I know anything about the world?" I say.

"Look, I'm only trying to help," she sighs.

I make quotation marks with my fingers and mouth the word *help* in her direction.

"Check it out," the teacher says, nodding toward the kid and the new class president who have gathered near the coat closet, the boy leaning in close to the kid's face the way boys and men do. "That's Forrest—he's been stuck to her like glue," says the teacher.

The way they are positioned, the kid's extra shadow obscures Forrest's face. I inch my way over so I can eavesdrop on their conversation.

"You've got to do something *pretty* bad to become a Shadester," says Forrest.

The kid, bless her heart, says, "Oh, well, I do curse sometimes so that makes sense."

"No, that's wussy stuff. I'm talking like, you've got to make someone *really hurt.*"

The way he says the word *hurt* sounds like he's counting down the days until he can put someone in that kind of pain. He gives the kid a hug and vows to stick by her until the end of time. She looks confused but nods anyway.

■

The next time Randy came to school with bruises on his neck, he told me what happened. *My mom choked me*, he said, shrugging.

I thought of my hand on top of your hand, urging you to press harder. Of asking, *Do you want me to choke you, too?* Of you saying, *No, well, I don't know, well, maybe. Actually no, actually yes.* It went that way for a while. I didn't pretend to be a kink expert—I merely knew what desire entered my pelvis and séanced its way up my spine, calling upon spirits I wanted nothing more than to obey.

> Pop Quiz:
> Q: What do you want?
> A: I want to travel back in time and show that I can make decisions.
> Q: Aren't you forgetting something?
> A: What?
> Q: That living is time travel, too.

At dinner, the kid folds into herself—it occurs to me that she's suffering but I don't know how to access the suffering so that I can dismantle it. Instead, I try to fill the empty space with stories.

"Did I ever tell you about when I was in kindergarten? I was so afraid of being away from my mom that I cried and cried the second she dropped me off. This lasted for two weeks. Then she finally decided to delay kindergarten and send me the following year," I say.

The kid blinks through the tired wave of her day.

"You can't trick me," she says.

"Okay, so maybe my mother was my teacher's favorite person to call, too," I smile, standing up to clear our dishes. The kid seems to like that. She begins to imitate her teacher on the phone. She holds her right hand, thumb and pinky out, up to her ear and stiffens her posture, repeatedly curling her hair around her left ear.

"Hi, I'm Miss Robinson, and I smell like monkey poo," she says, her voice high-pitched, Valley-girl-esque. Perhaps it's a small thing, but in this moment, the kid reminds me that she is just a kid, that no matter her wisdom and intuition, she still needs space to let every wild inspiration enter and move through her without trepidation. Although, in order to stay alive, that very impulse needs to be exterminated, or so I believe, and if extermination isn't possible, then the impulse must be transformed into something more—what?—palatable? I don't know, I don't know anything.

"The smelliest monkey poo in the whole wide world," the kid continues, tugging on her soccer shorts, which, after one too many hard tugs, fall down around her ankles. She breaks character when she bends forward, hands on her knees and head between her legs while she wiggles her butt back and forth. Or maybe she knows something I don't about Miss Robinson's after-school activities.

———

I read the kid her three selected books and tuck her in then stand outside her bedroom door and listen to her ask Olly if it hurts when someone chops off one of its legs. The way she says the word *hurt* sounds like she can't tell the difference between love and pain.

I find myself thinking of Mischief. If she were here, I would ask her to hold my paw.

■

This morning, I wake up to a note left on the kitchen counter. It says "I'm guna wunaway frum home" in blue crayon, the *e* in *home* cramped along the right edge of the page. She had clearly run out of space and hadn't wanted to admit defeat by going to the next line. I check everywhere for her: her room, mine, the bathroom, the courtyard. There aren't too many places to look. I double back and search every closet. It doesn't occur to me that she might have actually run away. I figure the note is one of those plot devices children use to get attention.

The humming begins softly at first, then slowly gets louder and louder until I realize it's coming from the wooden chest in the living room. It's no small chest, it's large enough to fit a curled-up kid seeking solace from the world. Gently, I knock.

"Excuse me, I hate to bother you, but I'm looking for my

daughter. Have you seen her? She looks just like a goose," I say.

The door of the chest nearly whacks me in the face as the kid bursts out of it, all glamour and shine in a glittery T-shirt and sweatpants.

"Honk, honk," she says, flapping her wings.

"Love goose," I say. "Why did you fly away?"

"If I tell you, do you promise not to freak out?"

"What?"

"I'm not your daughter. I'm your Shadester," she says, waving for me to follow her into her room. "And you're my Shadester, right?" the kid asks, picking up her guitar and strumming idly. She looks so comfortable with that guitar in her hands, as if it had been made with her in mind.

"What do you mean by that?"

"Like, our matching shadows mean we're related, right? Someone at school said mom giraffes and baby giraffes have matching spots."

"No, we aren't. I've told you this before. You came from Beau-mom, remember? You're related to her."

"Yeah, but . . ." she trails off.

"Yeah, but what?"

"She's gone," she says, looking up from the strings. "Did Beau-mom have an extra shadow, too?" the kid asks.

"Why is this coming up? Did something happen at school?" I ask. She sniffles a little.

"This boy Shane won't stop," she gulps, "making fun of me."

"For what?"

It occurs to me that I've never seen the kid cry, at least not since she was a baby and her cries were the only language she possessed. Perhaps she cries at night, alone in bed, but I doubt it. She doesn't crumble the way I do.

"Shane says that I wasn't made by a mommy and a daddy. That since I'm a Shadester, I was made in a lab somewhere. Like an experiment," says the kid, whose face is scrunched in a last-ditch attempt to avoid tears. "I didn't even know what a Shadester was! Forrest had to tell me," she sobs.

She falls onto her back and places her forearm over her eyes so that I can't see her tears until they drip from her chin to the neck of her T-shirt. I want to comfort her with my touch, but I don't know if she wants me to. She isn't the type to be soothed by answerless gestures. The kid demands so much from me, including the ability to separate her from you, to see her blond curls and striking blue eyes and not think *Beau*, to look at her extra shadow, the mind warp it has on me, and not think, *Beau*, to listen to her matter-of-fact explanations for things and not say, *I know, Beau*. I know I need to give her words.

"Shadesters aren't lab experiments. We were born from mommies and daddies and mommies and mommies and daddies and daddies and people that don't fit either of those categories. Don't let that asshole fill your head with garbage."

My use of a curse word grabs her attention. She moves her forearm away from her eyes and peers at me.

"I don't understand where I came from," she whispers so quietly it slips into me like an odorless poison.

———

I can feel the kid's want. It tugs on every loose end of me—she's searching for relation, for blood, for history, for her reason for being. But I can't help but feel that her yearning is a bit nineteenth century, a bit when-will-my-lover-return-from-war.

I am reminded of what Siegfried once said: *Blood isn't what bonds people, it's what traps them.* Siegfried, my complicated moral compass.

You once said, *What if we never have a kid? Then my life will have been for nothing*, and I remember squeezing a wine glass so hard that it broke.

As I leave her room, I see her roll onto her side facing the wall and pull something, a paper, from her pocket and unfold it. I give her privacy. I'm not prepared for the day the kid finally asks me the source of her shadow, and with it, mine. She's old enough that I know she wonders; she just hasn't said the words out loud yet.

■

One night I wind up drinking too much rum and calling Shane's mother. Her voice is flat and detached when she answers.

"It's late," she says.

"You need to teach your offspring about right and wrong," I say.

"Who is this?"

"Mother of the lab experiment," I say.

She sighs. "He's just playing around. He doesn't mean any harm."

"Oh, by all means then, continue not meaning to harm."

She doesn't say anything. I can just see her standing in her robe looking at the clock.

"Listen, just make sure Shane never talks to my kid again," I say.

"Or else what?" she asks. I don't respond because I hadn't thought that far ahead. I clear my throat a few times and pour the remaining rum droplets down my throat.

"Hello? Are you still there?" she asks.

"Hello," I say, but what I mean is *help*.

Mrs. Shane's mom sighs then lowers her voice as if Mr. Shane's dad is listening in the next room.

"Don't you think I'm the one who should be calling in the middle of the night?"

"Fuck you, you fucking piece of shit fuckhead," I yell, hanging up before she can respond.

I find the kid in the hallway clutching Olly and rubbing her eyes.

"You woke me up," she says in her matter-of-fact voice. At first, it had irritated me when you spoke this way because I was all emotion and no logic, but after a while, I was able to interpret the subtext of your facts. Something like *It's raining* may have meant *I'd like to get rained in with you* or *I hope you're keeping warm tonight.*

"That is true," I say.

"Who were you yelling at?" she asks, joining me in the kitchen. I pull out a chair for her then take a seat.

"In a way, I think I was yelling at myself," I say. The kid waits for me to elaborate, her crystal eyes piercing through the dim. "I'm trying to be someone other than me."

"You *are* one of those crazy people Forrest told me about," says the kid, hitting me on the arm with Olly.

■

After guitar lessons with Dune, the kid comes home and practices for hours in her room. She continues to sing her scary songs.

"I have this, you have that, I have this, you have that and that and that," she sings, playing power chords and banging her head like a rock star.

"Can you play something a bit more hopeful?" I call from the other room.

"Why are you always up in my business?" the kid shouts back, switching to the song she'd written about the flaws of the education system.

Pop Quiz:
Q: What is a synonym for role model?
A: The kid, at school, disrupting power.

My dad calls. I haven't spoken to him in a while. Ever since Siegfried's death, it's been difficult for me to invest more than minimal effort into a relationship, knowing the person could leave at any moment, without so much as a whisper of a warning, even if that person is my dad. When we go over to Julian and Dune's, I try to turn off the part of me that craves closeness, but it's no use. I love them so much I can hardly speak.

"I'm worried about you, Kris," says my dad.

"What now?"

"Don't you think it's time you tried moving on? You know, date," he says. "It's been six years."

"I know how long it's been," I whisper. He makes a sort of hmph noise.

"I've been doing some research," he says. "People who remarry after their spouse dies report more buoyancy."

"More buoyancy," I say.

"Yeah, you know. Lighter. Less depressed." I hear him gulp down his drink, followed by a soft, sweet "Ahhh."

"And you, are you exempt from this advice?"

"My spouse didn't die."

"Semantics," I say.

"A date often involves a sit-down dinner, in case you forgot," he says.

"Are you done yet?"

"Humans were made to move," he says. I can hear the shrug, the fine-don't-listen-to-your-old-man in his voice.

I wouldn't know what to do on a date. How would I hold my body? What would I say? Was I supposed to laugh softly or loudly? How many questions was too many questions?

Was it better to be charming or vulnerable? How do I keep my human mask from peeling off?

The packages from your mother keep coming. She sends a framed photo of you and me. Your college soccer sweat-shirt. Your first edition books. Your elementary school re-port cards. Everywhere I look, there is evidence of you, piled all around the apartment, stuffed in drawers, stacked on my dresser and nightstand. The kid sometimes pauses and examines these items. She holds your sweatshirt on her open palms as if it's a drink-filled platter she doesn't want to spill.

"Can I keep this?" she asks.

"Of course, babe."

Then she scampers off to her room like a raccoon clutch-ing its trash-can treasure.

■

"Mom, here's some business for you," says the kid, emerging from her room, her guitar slung over her chest. I've been on my laptop trying to find a Shadester dating website, but it appears they don't want us to be able to find each other. It could fall under the category of *organizing*, even if the result is simply two people smashing their faces and bodies to-gether. The President has recently passed a new law: a group of five or more Shadesters is illegal and punishable by fines and additional shadows. Still doesn't explain the absence of a dating app.

"Oh no," I say.

"Forrest is coming over tomorrow after school."

"That's not the order this is supposed to go in," I say, shutting my laptop.

"He already said yes so it would be rude for you to say no," she says.

"And yet," I say. "I can and am saying no."

"What, why?" she says, crossing her arms across her chest.

"He's on my shit list, that's why."

"You don't even know him."

"So?"

The kid scoffs but doesn't respond.

"What?" I press.

"It's not like he's Shane. He tells the truth. You always tell me how important that is."

"He's a bad boy and not like the kind they try to make attractive on TV," I say.

The kid does something so unlike her it stills me. She looks me dead in the eye and growls, not quite like a bear or lion, more like a crocodile; it's the low, stretched-out growl of someone who's been hoarding their anger for centuries. I watch, curious what will come out of her next. Her eyes scan the floor of the living room until she finds it, a baseball she then picks up and throws out our living room window, glass scattering in and outside the house. The sound would have been beautiful had it been happening elsewhere.

"What the hell is your problem?" I ask the kid.

"I hate you. I wish you were the one that died instead

of Beau-mom," she says, slamming her bedroom door be-hind her.

"Don't we all!" I scream through the closed door.

Her words shake me, they rearrange my cells. I repeat the word *hate* several times, noting the lasting bite of it. You have to really sink your teeth into a word like hate or else it winds up sounding more like *hey*.

The kid sits in timeout in her room while I sweep up the glass. I've never given her a timeout before, so neither of us seems to be one hundred percent certain how it works. But after she stomped into her room, I hadn't wanted her to have the last word, so I knocked and said, "Timeout activated!"

An hour later, when I knock on the door again, the kid says, "Excuse me, your timeout isn't up yet, Mommy."

"It seems there's been some miscommunication," I say.

"You haven't had enough time to think about what you've done," she says, but as she says it, I can hear her creeping closer to the door, at first sniffling, choking, then the release.

■

I take the kid to see Tasty Cakes play at an underground pop-up that's allegedly safe for Shadesters; it's an aban-doned basement, no cameras. The bouncer works at the Department and for a price, keeps his boys away long enough for Julian and Dune to play a twelve-song set. Of course, no space is truly safe, someone could always snitch, but what other choice do we have? If you pay attention, you can sense a constant, nagging hum traveling through the crowd, from body to body—the hum of vigilance. But our friends have played at a similar show before and assured us it would be okay as long as we lie low and cling to the walls. *If you see anything suspicious, don't hesitate, get the fuck out,* Julian told us.

The kid watches our friends, mesmerized: "I can do this one day," she says.

I don't want to be one of those delusional parents who promises their child that they can do anything they set their mind to—I know the state of the world, how by the time the kid is a teen, the world will have swallowed her and spit her out several times already, but I also know change is possible. I'm not sure how, but history has proved it so. I just need to hold on and trust that the words I'm saying to the kid are dipped in more truth than fallacy.

"You sure can," I say, standing behind her and draping my arms across her chest.

As precarious as it is to attend a show in a basement full of Shadesters, it feels like our own miniature revolution. And despite my mounting anxiety—my brain has collaborated with my eyes to trick me into seeing Agent Brown everywhere—it has been worth it to witness Julian and Dune look at each other on stage as they play, like watching love unfurl in real time. For the first time since your death, I think I would like that again—as a real thing, not simply a beautiful notion. I think I would like to wake up every day and choose someone again, not yet realizing that's exactly what I'm doing with the kid, our fierce, unapologetic kid.

I have this, you have that.

∎

I invite Julian and Dune over for game night to try and cheer them up. Their dog died suddenly the other night—acute kidney failure. As many times as they've been over here, I've never allowed them in my room. But tonight, they want to see what I'm so embarrassed about. After a bit of protest on my part, we tour the tiny Beau museum I find myself in night after night. Julian studies your urn, careful not to touch it, while Dune narrows in on the abandoned house photograph above my bed.

"I can't tell if it's supposed to be hopeless or hopeful," they say, frowning.

"Maybe both," I say. The kid sneaks up behind me and spooks me, giggling when I jump. We've long since made up about Forrest, but what I refuse to accept is that eventually, the kid will win, and Forrest will come over after school one day. They will eat brownies, he will comment on their funny taste, they will play family and the kid will make Forrest play the role of a feral cat. "Your name is Mischief," she'll say, petting his head aggressively.

"You're looking at that same picture *again*," says the kid.

"Beau-mom gave it to me," I say. "Early on when we weren't sure if we'd make it."

"Make it where?" asks the kid. I think about it. Where were we trying to make it all those years ago? A decade ago now, and I can still feel the jagged rock beneath my butt, the side of my thigh barely kissing yours, the waves colliding with one another in what looked like a dispute but felt like a greeting. I can still feel the pleasurable prowl of your hand down my shorts when the sun went down and the people went home. I don't understand time, how it appears to fold in on itself.

"Home," says Julian, who's been quietly studying the stage photo across the room.

■

Bonus Question:
Q: How do you know when you've chosen someone?
A: How do you know when someone's chosen you?

■

Your mom calls. She tells me about the owner of the hardware store, his dreary face and dreary eyes.

"Kris, whenever I see him, he says things like, 'Why is the world like this?' Or 'The world is fucked sideways.' Yesterday I told him, 'It's the people, quit blaming the terrain.'"

I can hear squawking in the background.

"Seems the crows are getting on just fine despite the world," I say.

"They don't judge but they will memorize both you and your shadow's faces," she says.

As I tend to do whenever I speak to your mom, I try to picture our lives over there. The dogs barking their heads off chasing the crows in the yard. The crows holding a century-long grudge, shitting on our cars, on your mom's porch. Your mom tossing kibble into the yard as a lackluster offering. I decide I will be proactive and research how to repair a relationship with a crow. The people of the internet tell me that there is no repairing a relationship with a crow, and that one must move a significant distance away from the crow family, who will undoubtedly peck our faces off if the opportunity presents itself.

A few days later, it's my turn to call. She picks up but doesn't say anything. I put her on speaker phone and beckon for the kid to come talk to her Nonna. I've been telling her more and more about Nonna lately. We sit on the couch and listen to your mom talk to one of her many dogs.

"Tomorrow, you'll get rabbit. You can wait that long, I know it."

"Hello?" shouts the kid. "Can you hear us?"

"Oh yes, sorry, love, I was talking to Connie."

"Spoiled rotten," I say.

"You, too, could be spoiled rotten," she says. "I don't pick favorites."

"Spoil us, spoil us!" chants the kid.

"I'll spoil you by teaching you life skills," says your mom.

This time, I imagine your mom teaching the kid to fish in the river. The kid catches a trout and holds it up, proud for the camera, our camera, not the Department's. She declares that she has caught us all dinner. That night, we each enjoy our single bite of fish.

If you researched the pathway to change, you'd notice the graph looks eerily similar to the pathway of grief. Both more or less begin with denial and end with acceptance. *According to whom?* I want to ask.

That night, I tell the kid we're going to make wind chimes. I am surrounded by cutlery and string.

"Why?" she asks.

"No special reason," I say, chewing on the inside of my cheek. She raises her eyebrows at me. "Okay, Nonna happens to be best friends with about fifty of these. She showed me and Beau-mom how to make them once."

I see her calculating the math in her head, like, how do Nonna and Beau-mom know each other?

"You know Nonna is Beau-mom's mom, right?"

"Pffff, yes, I know," she says. She picks up a spoon, breathes on it, then sticks it to her nose.

We follow directions I found online and, soon enough, we have a passable product. I hang it on a coatrack in the living room.

"Doesn't it need wind?" she says, staring at its pathetic quiet.

"That's why we'll make our own," I say.

We count to three and then we huff and we puff and yet the spoons are uninspired.

■

One morning after I drop the kid at school, my father comes over unannounced, grabs me by the hand, and drags me to his car.

"Get in," he barks, and I do. He drives us into town and parks outside of Lucky's.

"You're taking me to a closed gay bar," I say.

"I know what I'm doing," he scoffs in reply, taking off his seat belt and exiting the car. I follow him, curious. He heads around back, where he knocks four times. My old friend Archie opens the door and moves aside for us to come in.

"They're about to get started," he says. Seeing Archie is like slipping into a warm bath at the end of a long day. His presence, his lack of reaction to my extra shadow, reminds me that I existed long before Darlene, that I will continue to exist with it and maybe even after both of us are gone.

Archie leads us downstairs to the basement bar, near the bathroom I'd recently taken a nap in. I stop when I see Shadesters sitting in a circle sipping coffee and water. An attractive Latinx woman, who appears to be the leader, shuffles papers around, smiling an easy smile.

"Siegfreid would have wanted you to go," my dad murmurs in my ear, giving me a little shove. That gets me. I blink away my tears then take a seat. There are about twenty people here, well over the new five-person Shadester limit. Instinctually, I search the room for Department cameras, quickly spotting one in the upper right-hand corner behind the DJ booth. I'm not so sure about this.

"Help yourself to some coffee," the facilitator says, turning her gorgeous smile on me. Oh no, is it too late to form some type of personality?

I look around. The group is mostly white—some queer, some not—except for an East Asian woman, a Black straight couple, their hands intertwined on the woman's lap, and the Latinx facilitator, whose name I learn is Michelle.

Once, on a walk into town, I witnessed a white Shadester man approach an older Black woman outside a bar. She had an extra shadow, too. When she asked what he wanted, he said, *I just love meeting people who are like me.* When she didn't respond, he said, *We're all in this together!*

Someone, for the love of god, please take away his copy of *The Three Musketeers*, I thought.

The meeting begins. People smile at me. I think I smile back. It's blurry in the way that forced intimate spaces tend to be. I don't speak up, but I do listen. When the white people talk, it sounds like the oppression Olympics. Gold medal goes to the guy named Dave or Doug or Donald, who can no longer afford his vacation home. I drink five cups of coffee to keep my hands and mouth busy. Near the end, Michelle addresses the group.

"Raise your hand if you think you don't deserve happiness," she says.

Everyone raises their hands, including the Black couple, who raise their interwoven hands together as one.

"We can rewrite the narrative," says Michelle.

After class, Michelle pulls me aside and gives me her phone number. She says it would be nice to hang out sometime. She emphasizes the word *nice* as if it's a new word, one I've never heard before but would very much like to know more about. I accidentally step on her foot as I'm leaving.

Back outside, I am dazed. My father sneaks up behind me and grabs my shoulders.

"Booyah!" he says.

"What the fuck are you still doing here?"

"You didn't expect me to trust you in there, did you?" he says, smiling. "So how was it? Does anyone need medical attention?"

"Why would you bring me here? It's not safe, I saw the camera," I say. He rolls his eyes dramatically then leans in, beckoning for me to lean in, too—he has a secret to tell me.

"Archie works with some hackers to get around the camera issue."

"How?"

"I'm sixty years old, you tell me," he says. When he begins to twirl his mustache, he slaps his twirling hand away with his free hand. "Most of the time I don't even realize I'm doing it," he says.

"Oh my god, you met someone," I say. He stiffens, then tucks in his already tucked-in shirt and hikes up his pants.

"You say it like I'm not a total tomcat."

———

Within five minutes of meeting Michelle, I knew I wanted to keep being around her. She did that thing few people have done to me—she made me want to ask questions and actually stay long enough to learn the answers. Which is why, when I get home, I place her number on the bathroom mirror, where I ignore it for several days.

"Did you know you can store numbers in your phone?" the kid says, brushing her teeth before bed. She says goodnight then stays up until some ungodly hour writing song lyrics in her notebook, Olly the octopus perched on her back.

My dreams tonight are haunted. I set our apartment on fire then try to put it out with a watering pot. *I knew you were impractical, but I didn't realize you were this impractical*, you say, standing outside with your arms crossed over your chest, observing the flames. Then you transform into the kid.

■

At the next meeting, Michelle leads us in some visualization exercises. We imagine ourselves in our peaceful places, free of judgment and fear and pain. A place where we can be exactly who we are and exactly who we want to be at the same time. After, I try to slip out the door, but Michelle grabs me and says, "This wasn't an entirely unselfish exercise," and I almost knock over an entire row of chairs.

Later, I tell Dune and Julian that I'm going to do something I haven't done since you died, and Julian turns to Dune and says, "I knew this day would come."

"They're going to run away and become desert people without us," says Dune, shaking their head.

"Real funny," I say, imagining the freedom of open space, a sky bigger than the ground. "Actually, I'm going to text someone several words, more or less in the correct order."

"No," says Julian, raising his hands to his cheeks.

"She's beautiful, but you already knew that. I feel guilty, but you already knew that, too," I say.

Reality Testing:
My brain: Everyone will hate me for moving on.
Beau, the kid, Beau's mom.
Reality:

If I were a social worker assigned to myself, I might say, "Beau is sick of explaining to all the other dead people at weekly poker why her wife finds a certain nobility in moping."

∎

My first text to Michelle: "I am thinking of a number between one and one thousand."

"Let's grab some drinks," she responds.

I meet Michelle at Lucky's, where we slide into a corner booth with our drinks. Beer for me, spiced rum and Coke for her—her long-time favorite, and no, she never developed an aversion to spiced rum, not even after all the college parties and toilet-bowl mornings.

"Sometimes I have dreams I'm being assassinated," says Michelle, her voice casual. She's dressed in a navy suit tailored so perfectly it's like a second skin. I look down at my joggers and Henley T-shirt and consider pulling the fire alarm to save me from my humiliation.

"Are you some type of prominent person I should know about?" I ask, immediately regretting it, but she smiles, even if it is a pitying smile. There's something unwavering about her; her deep brown eyes lend themselves to inviting trust without tangible reason.

"I'm so important you've never heard of me," she says. I can't tell if we're joking or not, so I finish my beer. "Tell me about you," she says, sipping her drink.

"That sentence," I say, "nearly counts as assault."

She reaches across the table and traces the veins in my hand that branch off from my wrist like a tree. When she touches me, I gasp. I feel like one giant exposed nerve. I know she notices but we both pretend she doesn't.

———

The next time we hang out:

Michelle: "I like people who are complex."

Me: "So, am I just a collector's item to you?"

Tonight, she's wearing a V-neck white tee under her gray blazer, and I want to die.

Michelle: "You don't have to talk to me if you don't want to."

Me: "But I do, that's the problem."

Michelle: "Do you have to talk to me or do want to talk to me? There's a big difference."

Me: "I'm here, aren't I?"

Michelle: "Arguably my favorite thing about you."

She laughs, touching my hand again. My body is just as confused as I am. It doesn't seem to know if it's terrified or turned on or both. We haven't progressed to kissing yet. At the rate we're going, I'm worried I'll come before she can slip me some tongue.

I go home and talk to your urn. I want you to hear it from me.

"You'll be pleased to know you could beat her in arm wrestling," I say. "Come on, laugh," I urge you. "I'm not going anywhere, you know that."

Underneath your urn is a poem you printed for your class. You wanted to know if I thought you should teach it. The first two lines: "Don't believe the body that turns away from itself / don't believe the body that claims to love its absence."

■

"What is your birth story?" I ask Michelle, thinking of your mother. I behave as if I am her ambassador. If she were here, after she got the not-Beau tantrum out of her system, she'd probably word it differently. She'd say, "So, are you going to tell me your birth story, or what?" as if Michelle were purposely holding out on her.

Michelle isn't expecting this question. She chugs down her cocktail, an attractive move on her part. We are at Lucky's. The kid's with Grandpa. I've weaseled my way into an old button-down of yours, but the collar won't cooperate.

"Believe it or not, that's not the first time I've been on the receiving end of that question," she says, reaching out to fix my collar. Then she gives me the highlights—her mother was induced then induced again then induced again and no one popped out. "As I understand it, I was having a perfectly nice time at the spa," she says. "So, they did the old slice and dice."

■

"The best way to love someone is to start with asking them how they'd like to be loved," says Michelle at the next meeting. Everyone nods, some people smile shyly at each other. Michelle briefly catches my eye then looks away. "This starts with yourself," she adds, and most people examine crumbs on the ground.

When Michelle meets the kid for the first time, she's prepared—she knows the kid's a Shadester like us. Together, we draw outside with sidewalk chalk. We are illustrating the other dimension the kid is always carrying on about. The sadness-eating monsters are orange and furry with blue hearts covering their bodies.

"This is the most important project I've ever been trusted with," says Michelle. She's very serious, and she knows how to entice the kid. The kid attaches herself to Michelle immediately.

"She gets it," says the kid, nodding.

Like catharsis in reverse, I feel like I am finally gathering all the emotions I've dropped since your death. And it feels nice.

∎

Despite my body's pleas, I avoid having sex with Michelle for weeks. I'm scared I'm going to forget how to have sex, specifically that I won't know how to have sex with someone who isn't you, someone with different nerve endings and pleasure points, someone whose body doesn't know mine the way yours did. I'm worried that sex is absolutely nothing like riding a bike, but when Michelle and I finally fall into bed, we peel each other's clothes off, and I remember that all I need to do is listen with my body, with my hands that search and scavenge. I'm excited, it's been so long, my hips buck at first touch.

"Relax your body, relax your body," she whispers. My excitement embarrasses me, I feel compelled to justify my body's unfettered response.

"In my defense, this has been the longest foreplay session of my life."

"Fair," she laughs, biting my collarbone, my stomach, the inside of my thighs, and despite her hunger, she goes slow, her movements smooth and sure, full of attention that nears worship. Once we get going, I begin to doubt that this was the right decision, and yet her touch feels so good. I hope she can't sense my dueling desires—I both want and don't want her, both need and don't need her, both forgive and don't forgive myself. We struggle to stay quiet, so the kid won't hear.

At the second kink class, our teacher said, *Sex is a conversation between two or more people.* If that is true, then Michelle's body is saying, *Give me all of you,* and mine is saying, *I want to keep what little I have left.*

Mine is lying.

When I slowly pull my fingers out of her, she grabs my wrist and pulls my hand to her lips, slipping my fingers into her mouth and sucking them clean.

I've never been the type to grow attached after sex—sex itself doesn't hold any particular meaning for me, but sex with Michelle has cracked me open and spilled me all over the street.

Pop Quiz:
Q: You are walking when you stumble upon a sign.
It says YOU ARE HERE with a red arrow pointing to
paradise. What do you do?
A: Spin in circles until I fall over.

Once the post-sex haze has lifted, I begin to feel sad
about the possibility of losing her—a possibility that exists between all humans at all times, which makes it so
painfully ordinary that I can't imagine acknowledging
its presence out loud. I'm a stupid, stupid woman with
stupid, stupid nerves. And I've fallen in love. For a long
time, I thought love was merely something that lasted
a long time before it got sad, but lying in bed next to
Michelle, watching her eyes watch me, it occurs to me
that the more in love with someone you are, the sooner
the sadness settles in.

If I were a social worker assigned to my case, I would say,
"Kris, if you're feeling compelled to destroy something, that
means it is good. It is really good."

■

Michelle climbs out of bed to go to the bathroom. When
she gets back, she gives herself the grand tour. She examines the framed photos of you and me on the dresser, in the
living room. She flips through your books, studies your urn.

"I'm really sorry," she says, climbing back into bed. The corners of her eyes are bubbling.

"I'm not sure whether you would have loved her or hated her," I say.

"I have a feeling . . ." begins Michelle, smiling a little. Then she changes course. "Shhh, do you hear her snoring? It's so adorable." She holds a finger to my lips. Even a room away, we can hear the kid.

■

"If you're going to join this family, I have one condition," says the kid.

"What's that?" asks Michelle. I can see she's trying not to laugh.

"You have to listen to us teach you about Siegfried."

"About what?"

"Not what. Who!"

Michelle looks at me. I smile weakly. There is enough space between us and Siegfried's death that most days I forget about what he did, how I feel all mixed up about it.

"Our old friend," I say.

"He could paint you the prettiest pictures in all the land," says the kid. "And he was so smart, like the smartest person I've ever met."

"Hey," I say.

"Hey," she says, waving as if she's greeting me.

"He sounds lovely," says Michelle.

"Someone murdered him, I know they did," says the kid.

"Seriously?" asks Michelle, looking at me.

"I mean, yeah," I say. I pull the kid in for a hug and tell her, "It's okay, don't fight them." After a few more choked-up moments, she releases her tears, letting out a distressed yelp.

■

Michelle officially moves in, and it's clear there isn't much space for her. I've done very little to consolidate your things, but she doesn't complain. She squeezes her dresser into the corner, she swaps out my embarrassing pots and pans for her normal pots and pans. I catch her organizing your papers and stacking your books against the wall.

Beetles, spiders, ticks.

■

Now that Michelle lives here, the kid informs me that I can't cook.

"Well, of course, I can't," I say. "I thought that was apparent."

"I always thought food was supposed to taste bland until I tried Michelle's cooking," she says. "Spices are our friend."

"Yes, there is salt and then there is pepper, and then . . ." I trail off, unable to name any others.

One night, Michelle makes us mofongo with rice and beans.

"It's not nearly as good as my mother's, but it will do," she says. "I went to the store as soon as it opened to get plantains and garlic. Had to square up with some guy and his parrot."

■

A few nights later, the kid requests Michelle's presence during our bedtime ritual. My initial reaction is to say, *What about Beau-mom?* But I keep quiet. I understand that the kid has the capacity to fall in love, too. Rubbing her cheek against Olly, the kid's eyelids bungee as we read. When Michelle closes the last book, the kid's eyes spring open.

"You're not finished yet," she says. "One more book," she says, digging around in her nightstand. She pulls out her notebook and hands it to me.

"What's this?" I ask.

"The last book," she says, lying back onto her pillow.

I open it to the first page where she has drawn a picture of us three, the kid between us holding both our hands, everyone's shadows present and accounted for. Underneath the picture she's written, "Nobuddy noes ware the shaddos come from. Its owr seecrit."

"Babe, why did you write this?" I ask, panicking. Michelle and I haven't talked about what the kid knows, how we handle her extra shadow. The kid shrugs, avoiding my eyes. She studies her comforter, her dim shadows. "Is everything okay?"

No answer. I look at Michelle who grabs the notebook and examines it, smiling to herself.

"The story isn't real," says the kid. "It's not real life."

She pulls the covers up to her neck then rolls over to face

the wall. I kiss the top of her head, holding my mouth there for a beat longer than usual. I feel like I am losing her, that I am always in the middle of losing her. We exit her room, leaving the kid's door cracked open how she likes it. She's funny that way, always wanting one eye on the action.

"We're really doing this, huh," I whisper in the hallway. Michelle raises her eyebrows, pulling a stray blond hair from my chin.

"My guess is you haven't told a single person why you have your extra shadow," she says. "That's exactly what they want."

"What is?" I say, wondering if the animals with exoskeletons know how lucky they are.

"To isolate and shame you," she says, lowering her voice so the cameras can't hear. "You're safe here," says Michelle and leads me into the bedroom. She sits on the edge of the bed and pats the spot next to her. It's so strange, I feel as if I've entered an alternate reality in which this is Michelle's room, apartment, child, life, and I'm a visitor who assures everyone that I am just passing through each day.

"Do you promise?" I ask, toeing my shadow.

"I've got my stories, too," she says, resting her head on my shoulder.

"You mean, my self-loathing isn't increasing my sex appeal?"

"Stop stalling."

I begin to tell her the story. When I say your name, she twitches but doesn't interrupt or stop me.

We'd come home from bar hopping one night, both lit up and horny. Earlier that day, you'd taken a pregnancy test; it had been negative. I think you'd wanted me to fuck the sadness out of you. I pinned you against the wall in the living room and kissed your neck and nibbled on your earlobes while you pressed your hips to mine. My clit was throbbing, I wanted you in a rushed, greedy way, I wanted to hold your head to my clit as you sucked and sucked. You struggled to unbutton my pants, so I took them off myself, almost toppling over and elbowing you in the jaw. A part of me was still wishing I could impregnate you. I wanted to fuck you good and hard and shoot twenty-five million sperm into you as I came. We were both bitter about biology and all of its limitations, about the sameness of our bodies and how nature forbid us from reveling in that sameness.

The details are blurry, but I know we fell into a human tangle on the bed—the lights were off, but the moon shone in through the window, dappling you in light, and you were mine, I remember that much. You were mine.

Alcohol inspired a dominance in me that wasn't typically present when I was with you; you'd always refused to be submissive, even for me, so I'd pushed that part of me down, like one pushes on the top of an overflowing trash can in order to make room, only for the bag to split when you lift it. Now, aggression poured out of me. I gripped your neck, just for a second, then your jaw. I pressed my hand over your mouth, again, just for a second. I was testing you, determining what you would allow and what you wouldn't. My hand circumnavigated your throat but never stopped moving. *Do it, I know you want to*, you said. *Are you sure?* I said. *Don't do it for me*, I said, still wandering and testing. *I want you to, I want to make you happy.* And for the first time, you grabbed my free hand and wrapped it around your throat.

I should have said no.

I should have said, *There's a reason you're supposed to do these things sober.*

I can think of a thousand things I could have done other than comply.

But I'd been waiting for you to want this.

And now you finally did.

Is this good? I said, pressing hard on each side of your throat. You nodded, thrusting your hips faster and faster, bucking like a wild, vicious thing. I watched the muscles under your skin undulate, your parted mouth as you moaned. Then you came, your back arching toward the ceiling, your blood vessels popping out of your neck, your face flushed.

The next thing I knew, you were unconscious. I didn't know if you were breathing or not. I heard myself cry-yelling, *Please don't be dead, please don't be dead.* People always say that you immediately sober up in these situations, but the truth is, you fucking don't. My vision was blurred, and I couldn't remember what I'd learned in CPR training. I lowered my ear to your mouth and thought I felt wisps of air, but I couldn't be sure. I grabbed my phone from the floor and called 911. When they arrived, one of the young paramedics said, *What the fuck did you do?* as he shoved me out of the way.

You woke up shortly after they confirmed you were

breathing, and I started to cry again, or I remember noticing my tears again. I ran over to kiss your forehead, but they intercepted before I could reach you. I didn't understand what was happening. They turned me around and put me in handcuffs then walked me out to their truck and drove me to the Department. Within hours, I had a hangover, a new shiny shadow, and the knowledge that I'd hurt the one person who trusted me more than anything in this faithless world.

You've stamped me forever, like a library card.

> Reality Testing:
> My brain: I forced you to indulge in my kinks. If it had been up to you, we would have had vanilla sex, everything would have been okay. If it were up to you, you'd have gotten a refund on that *How to Train Your Sub* book.
> My brain: If I hadn't choked you, you wouldn't have thrown a clot.

"Do you feel better now?" Michelle asks.

I collapse onto the bed, so I don't have to make eye contact with her. I'm sobbing, half-choking on my spit. And now she knows I'm an ugly crier.

"Not really, no," I say, clearing my throat. "What happens when the kid asks how I got my shadow? I can't tell her the truth."

"For starters, stop thinking about the truth as a series of words," she says. I don't know what the fuck she's talking about, but I like listening to her. "There are a million ways to show your child that sometimes the people we love most are the ones we wind up accidentally hurting."

Michelle is good with feelings and with talking about said feelings. She's the type of person I wished I was when I let the troubled kids kick me in the shins and tell me they wanted out of this bitch school.

What are my troubled kids up to? Randy would be nineteen or twenty by now, probably a Shadester several times over. If one wanted to catalogue my toxic traits, one might start with my inability to understand how people's lives keep going, even when I am not looking.

Michelle shares her shadow story with me. When Colestein implemented the new Shadester policy, she quit the Department and they gave her an extra shadow on the spot. When she challenged their decision, things got ugly; they slandered her name, threatened her family. She had to move her parents somewhere safe and then she disappeared for a while. Michelle reckons the Department was terrified of her sharing classified information.

"They told me I was a danger to the balance," she says, rolling her eyes.

"Classic," I say.

"That feels like a lifetime ago. Now I'm a freelance copy-writer. Shadesters," she laughs. "The great remote workers of the country."

"I can't believe you worked at the Department," I say.

"Social workers aren't all they're cracked up to be, you know. It's like how-to-spot-a-white-savior 101."

"Okay, yes, then we're even."

"Yes, I suppose we are."

"Great use of strategic stabilization, Agent Gomez," I say, and she shoves me.

■

I didn't speak for a week after I got my extra shadow. You cried. You bought me a new TV, you made me steak and crab legs, you didn't say a word when I poured whiskey in my coffee. You cried.

That first time, post-shadow, when you straddled me on the couch and kissed my neck, something in me recoiled. *I'm not ready*, I said, peeling your hands off my chest. You didn't initiate again, until one night in bed, a goodnight kiss escalated into something more. I pulled back, swallowing hard. I wanted it, wanted you, but I was afraid. Traumatized is the word, although I didn't want to reckon with what it meant to be traumatized in a world that would not hold me. You grabbed my hand and slowly guided it down your boxers, watching me to gauge my comfort. You showed me how to be gentle again. What you didn't show me was how to forgive myself.

I only resumed speaking because something within me had mutated, not that I realized it at the time. My anger didn't always behave like anger—sometimes it acted like resignation, other times like a disappearance. I could tell by the way you looked at me that you saw the change. You did your best to keep me out of trouble. I ran my mouth, tried to provoke fights with strangers. You always stopped them before they got out of hand. But you weren't always good— no, you couldn't be. *Great, a gay Shadester parent, that's going to go over well*, you once said in the middle of a fight about I don't even know what.

Our fights made me think of blue jays in the mountains. Gorgeous but vicious. Blue jays are for admiring only from a safe distance away. I often thought you and I should have stopped there: a few feet away from each other, looking.

■

Pop Quiz:
Q: Which is more important: the object or the light that illuminates the object?
A: I know that I've spent my entire life convinced I wasn't real unless I was loving someone with everything I had.

■

It's been a week since we swapped shadow stories, and Michelle has something she wants to say. I can tell by the way she's on her third coffee of the morning. She stands at the kitchen counter, reading the back of the half-and-half container, tapping her foot.

"Out with it then," I say, hugging her from behind and kissing her on the neck.

"What?" she says. Now she's examining the olive oil spray bottle.

"Quite the reading material."

"There is something I want to tell you," she says, slowly turning around to face me.

"I promise to listen even if the topic is a non-preferred topic."

"Well, back before—"

Just then my dad barges in the house. He wants to know why strangers don't appreciate him photographing them at the beach.

"It's not my fault they look happy," he says.

■

I take Michelle to see Julian and Dune play at another pop-up. On the walk there, I tell her about Agent Brown and what I'd done. I want to know if she knew him, or knew of him, if he is someone I should be worried about all these years later or if my paranoia is showing. I tell her

I suspect he killed Siegfried, but that will have to be one thing we never get closure on.

"Not all gays know each other, gosh, Kris, get with the times," Michelle says, smirking at me. I grab her hand and we walk like that, hand in hand, our shoulders rubbing because we want to be close to each other.

"When we first met, I thought you'd kill me with seriousness," I say.

"And now? What's your read?"

"Being with you feels like wearing an old fuzzy sweatshirt. When I take it off, pieces of you stick to me."

"Lint, you're calling me lint," she laughs, and I laugh, too. But then my anxiety returns.

"So, you really don't know this agent?"

"No, I haven't heard of him. But I can ask my old Department friend. Mitch is the only one who still talks to me."

"Assholes."

"Assholes," she agrees.

"I don't want to sound paranoid but . . ." I say, cutting myself off.

"What you did was very stupid but very necessary," says Michelle.

I know it's a weird desire, but I'm feeling so good and warm, and I want you to share that goodness with us, I want you to walk down the street on my other arm, laughing with Michelle and me. Oh, to be in love and want to practice polyamory with a ghost.

About a block from the pop-up, I spot Mischief prowling the alley with an orange striped cat and a fluffy gray one.

"Hey, that's my cat," I say, pointing at her. I feel as if I've just spotted a celebrity.

"Which one?"

"The one that looks like a movie star."

"What's she doing out here?"

"She lives . . . out here," I say, gesturing vaguely. "She sought emancipation when she was just four years old."

"This might be splitting hairs, but do you really think it's right to call her *your* cat?"

At the concert, a big, burly man with an unkempt beard stamps our hands and says that if there's a raid we'll be on our own. After my friends play a few songs, they stop to drink from their plastic cups and charm the crowd. Dune bends down and whispers in the ear of someone in the front row, then addresses everyone: "Tasty Cakes says pass it on." The crowd whispers down the alley. Hands over ears, eyes smiling. By the time it gets to me, I hear "Touch nose fly paper sales." Michelle cups her hand to her ear, and I pause, taking a deep breath to steady my heart. I lean in and whisper, "You look like the rest of my life."

∎

"We like her," says Julian.

"Which means we'll have to learn to be okay with saying goodbye to her," finishes Dune. I don't know why they
say that; they've never seen me with a partner before. But it
feels accurate, nonetheless.

"I'm not going to let that happen," I say. "I'm no longer
avoiding my own avoidance," I say, thinking of Siegfried.

■

When I pick the kid up from school, she's imitating the
teacher—her back to the teacher, flipping her hair from
shoulder to shoulder every few seconds, one hand parked on
her jutted-out hip—and Miss Robinson looks uncomfortable but not necessarily self-aware enough to realize she's
the subject of this comedy show.

"Thank god you're here," says the teacher.

"I could do Forrest, instead, if you want," says the kid,
smiling. She switches to a wide power stance, a smug look
creeping across her face. She seriously needs a new hobby.
"Or I could do the entire class at once," she offers. I mouth
I'm sorry over the kid's head. "Why does everything have to
be about Shadesters with you?" she mimics, rolling her eyes.
I feel my hand automatically form a fist.

The kid gives Michelle the same special attention, studying
her mannerisms and movements. We three sit on the couch
together and watch cartoons, we color pictures, we listen to

the kid play songs on her guitar, we play board games and video games, we bicker and make up. I worry I will lose it all at any moment, but I keep my exoskeletons to myself.

"Finally, I've perfected my performance," announces the kid.

"Michelle, brace yourself," I say, gripping her thigh.

The kid fixes her hair into a ponytail then kneels on the ground in front of us, something Michelle does when she's trying to get through to the kid. Her eyes are a perfect imitation of Michelle's right now: soft and sweet, yet focused. I don't understand how the kid has access to everyone's inner world the way she does. Michelle and I lean in closer, eager for her insight.

"Baby, baby, baby, it's okay to feel what you feel," she says in a soothing voice. She rubs her chin against her clavicle the way Michelle does when she wants to feel close to herself.

"I didn't realize how frequently I do that," whispers Michelle, looking sheepish.

I consider what Michelle said about the Department wanting to isolate and shame us. I can't help but think that if this is isolation, then it is beautiful.

■

"What was it you wanted to tell me the other day?" I ask.

"What? Oh," she says. She swallows hard. I've stressed her out.

"Actually, hold that thought," I say, promptly forgetting my question. The oven timer is going off. Michelle's birthday cake is done. "Oh, it appears I've made you a drippy sandcastle," I say, examining its sagging body.

"I love drippy sandcastles," she says.

The kid walks into the kitchen. "Can't bake either," she mumbles under her breath.

■

"You're probably wondering why I asked you to meet with me today," says Miss Robinson.

"Yes, that is a thing I am wondering," I say, playing my part. I'm seated in a chair made for miniature humans. "Her grades are perfect."

"Yes, they are," she says. "There was a brief period of time in which she was somewhat tolerable but she's back to not listening. She walks around and talks to all the other kids while I'm trying to teach. She'll stand up during the middle of my lesson and go over to other students' desks and poke them or tell a joke," she says. "The students, of course, love it. Me? Not so much."

I laugh.

"Seriously? That's it?"

She uncrosses then recrosses her legs and straightens her spine as if making herself taller will communicate the grave importance of the kid's misbehavior.

"That's it? I can't get anything done. I've tried timeouts, no recess, sending her to the principal. Nothing works. She smiles and takes the punishment like it's a reward."

"Man, I love that kid," I say. Miss Robinson glares at me so hard I feel compelled to check the edges of my T-shirt for singes.

"She also started a petition to remove Charlie from the classroom."

"Who the fuck is Charlie?"

Miss Robinson nods toward the Department security guard pacing the hallway outside the door. He's dressed in black pants and a black jacket. He carries a gun. There are security guards all over the school. They say things like *Oh, hey, pretty ladies* and wink at the kid and me.

"I'm on her side with this one," I say, fumbling with my hands in my lap.

"Does she listen at home?"

"Yeah, of course."

That gets her riled up. She even uncrosses her legs and leaves them uncrossed, then leans forward, resting her elbows on her knees in the standard dyke position.

"Does she understand what's going to happen to her if she keeps acting out this way?"

"You stay out of my business, and I'll stay out of yours," I say.

For the first time this meeting, Miss Robinson looks like she pities me, the kid, us, our lives together. She looks down at her legs and shakes her head, trying to gather her thoughts, or perhaps trying to dispel them.

"I'm not prejudiced, I'm just stating facts," she says, avoiding my eyes.

"And what fact is that?"

"She's not going to stay young and cute and innocent forever."

"You haven't seen my late wife," I say. Miss Robinson sighs audibly.

"Protecting her is the right thing to do," she says. "And you protect her by taming her."

Find and circle the following words in the word search:
Right
Wrong

R	I	G	H	G	Z	L	A
I	B	E	F	A	M	I	H
G	I	N	R	A	S	G	O
M	U	R	W	R	I	N	O
H	D	F	K	R	I	T	T
T	T	T	O	R	O	Q	P
W	R	O	G	N	X	B	L
H	E	L	P	A	Y	C	M

I swoop by Forrest's house to pick up the kid. Forrest's dad makes sure to tell me how much they enjoy having the kid around. He says it with such tenderness, I can tell he's putting in a lot of effort to prove they're an accepting family.

"She's such a pleasure," he says, several times over. I've

met this type before. His kindness is nearly intolerable, although I suppose it's better than the alternative. The kid seems happy enough. In the car, she babbles about Forrest's video game system, which of course, neither of us have ever seen before. When I tell her the teacher isn't thrilled by her behavior, she acts shocked, taken aback. She cries out, "Oh, the horror! Let me write a song about it."

"This is why you should have let me come along," says Michelle when I tell her about the meeting. "We could have bad-cop-bad-copped her."

■

Michelle, the kid, and I go to the movies to see some new superhero flick. The kid holds my hand while we wait in line to buy tickets. Some little white girl, all lip and teeth, exits the theater with her father and taps his arm before pointing right at us.

"Look, Daddy. That's the girl from school I was telling you about."

Her father, who looks uncomfortable, says something to her, but they're too far away for me to hear. I assume he's taking care of the situation, but then the girl giggles. Instinctually, I move my body in front of the kid's. I shout at the girl to beat it and find something better to do with her time than be a dick. Michelle grabs my arm and murmurs, "Let it go, Kris."

The father mumbles something else to his daughter,

holds out his hand as if to say, *Stay here*, then strides over to us, a stupid smirk forming at the corners of his lips.

"Listen, you're not going to talk to my daughter that way, okay? Give her a break, she's never seen a child with a second shadow before."

I laugh a small, mean laugh in his face. I consider sucker-punching him right where he stands. Michelle steps forward, but before she can speak, the kid shoves both of us out of the way, and steps toward the man, her chest puffed out.

"It's not like seeing a bear at the zoo, mister. Move along," she says, shooing him with her hand. The man looks dumbly from adult to adult as if to confirm that really just happened—he had been told off by a Shadester child. Then he stuffs his hands in his coat pockets and stomps off to join his asshole daughter.

"That was the coolest thing I've ever seen," says Michelle, high-fiving the kid. The kid shrugs, not easily impressed. She has the luxury of spending every day and every night with herself.

In the bathroom before the movie, the kid examines herself in the full-length mirror. She does several runway poses. She blows herself a kiss in the mirror.

"So, who did I hurt?" the kid asks so casually she could have been asking what size popcorn I want.

"Excuse me?"

"I've spent hours staring at my shadow trying to find a clue, but I can't figure it out. They both look the same to me."

"Oh, boy," says Michelle, washing her hands and looking at me in the mirror.

"I know how it all works now. Forrest explained it to me," she says with a shrug of her left shoulder. The kid's acting okay, but she doesn't seem okay; I can sense a forced steadiness in her voice.

"Forrest needs some of his trees chopped down," I say. The kid ignores my joke and persists.

"Was it that time I kicked you in the face when I was a baby? When you were changing me? Remember, you told me that story."

I gulp. I feel all the heat travel from my body to my face. I feel my forehead with the back of my hand, then splash some water on my face, hoping for relief. When relief doesn't come, I consider my options: I could easily say yes and leave it at that—that's the story and we're sticking to it. No one has to know besides my father, Michelle, and me, and the kid could continue to look in the mirror every day and brush her teeth and comb her hair and flash an uncomplicated smile. She could look at herself and like what she sees, she wouldn't have to feel guilty—accidents happen—and my face is fine from the kick, we're all fine.

"Well," I say.

"That was it, wasn't it?" she says. I get the sense she's baiting me. "Michelle, you weren't here yet," she says, turning to my girlfriend. "You didn't get to know me as a baby."

"Is Shane still messing with you at school?" I ask.

"I'll trade you answers," says the kid, her arms folded

across her chest. I look at Michelle. She nods at me. *Go on,* she mouths.

"In here? Right now?" I say. A woman is standing at the sink, slurping the boogers out of her baby's nose with a straw. "Mommmmmmmmm," her toddler whines.

"I'm sick of all the hiding," says the kid. I open my mouth several times, but no words come out. I feel defective, trapped. My chest fills with the knowledge that I don't know how to answer her one burning question. I think about what Michelle said about truth.

"It wasn't your fault," I say. "I don't know much, but I do know that. It wasn't your fault, babe."

"What wasn't?" she says, squinting her eyes. Michelle slips out of the bathroom to give us some privacy. The woman helps her toddler wash and dry his hands. They don't so much as glance at us.

"Beau died giving birth to you," I say, blinking at the ceiling. The kid spins around so her back is to me, but she's studying me in the mirror.

"So, I killed her?" she asks.

Shrimp, grasshoppers, cockroaches. Shrimp, grasshoppers, cockroaches.

"Babe, no. No, you didn't kill her," I say, letting the tears do what they do.

"But why would I have a shadow if I didn't?" she says, tilting her head. "There's a reason I have a shadow. I did something bad to someone."

"She died, but you didn't kill her."

"How do you know? You can't know for sure."

"Because I just know, okay?"

"How soon did I get my shadow after Beau-mom died?" the kid asks.

"I tried to fight it, I swear. I almost got another shadow that very same day down at the Department."

I lean in and give her a kiss on the cheek, and she wipes it off with a dramatic gesture. Then: the world's quietest wrecking ball.

"Do you wish I'd died instead of Beau-mom?" she asks.

I approach the kid and before I can open my arms, she wraps her arms around my waist and presses her head to my stomach, my arms pinned to my sides.

"No, I don't," I say. "You're where I want to be."

The kid pulls away and rubs her eyes dry.

"Sometimes," says the kid.

"Sometimes what?"

"Sometimes Shane and his friends still mess with me, but me and Forrest take care of them," she says, examining something, maybe a food stain, on her leggings. I don't ask the obvious question because I don't want to know what taking care of them entails.

During the movie, Michelle holds my hand, which is clammy. In the middle of a fight scene, I can't keep my dinner down any longer—I run out of the theater and puke and puke until the toilet bowl turns green. Someone walks in on me and says, "Oh, I didn't know anyone was in here."

———

Toward the end, when the superhero saves the city from an evil mutant, the kid whispers, "So, I'm a Shadester?" in my ear. I nod, thinking we'd gone over this already. "And you're a Shadester?" I nod again. "And Michelle's a Shadester?" Yes. She leans forward and smiles at Michelle on the other side of me then sits back in her seat. "I'm proud of who I am," she says, fighting back tears. I wrap my arm around her shoulders and pull her close to me. Her small body bends awkwardly over the armrest, but she doesn't complain or move. She smells like sour candy and butter.

"Remember this," I whisper. "They named us Shadesters forgetting that shade protects people, too."

"Funny—it's shade when you need to escape the sun, like under a tree. But a shadow when they hate us," she says.

■

By the time the movie ends, it's dark outside. I take her hand and point to the ground around her. No shadows—it's the same darkness that obscures everyone else. I want to show her that she's a kid, a musician, a troublemaker, a friend, a math whiz, a million other things before she is a Shadester.

"No one would know you're a Shadester right now," I say. "You're free."

"But *I* know I'm a Shadester," she says.

"I think what your mom is trying to say is, she wants you to remember who you are without your shadow," says Michelle.

"Were you both born with your shadows?" the kid asks.

We shake our heads no.

"Then you don't understand," she says, stomping to the car.

In the back seat, she scowls at me in the rearview mirror. But when I pretend to look away, she's smiling to herself.

"You could use some acting lessons," I point out. Michelle shoves me in the arm. "What?"

"So could the Shadester in *Slime Man*," she says, referring to the movie we'd just seen.

"What Shadester?"

"Exactly," says the kid. "No one even noticed him."

The next day, I take the kid to see the stage. I want her to see what most Shadesters have to go through, that there is a ceremony involved. There's been an uptick in NoShad onlookers lately, most likely because it's an election year and they want to show where they stand. There are signs with banal insults everywhere. Voices full of contempt. A few people with guns on their hips. Department employees manning the line of Shadesters, ignoring the crowd.

"No, no, no," whispers the kid, shaking her head hard.

I look at her, waiting for more.

"The wrong people have all the power," she says.

■

"One of my personal favorite lessons from this new program," I tell my raspy-voiced customer, "is to wake up every day and do visualization exercises."

I say visualization exercises in a soothing voice.

"I don't know why I keep calling," she says.

"It took some getting used to, but now I can achieve whatever I set out to do," I say. She sounds like she's mulling it over.

"But is it really all that different from the other ten I've bought?" she asks.

"Yes, it's got all new strategies to help you get out of your own way."

"How did it do that for you?"

"Me? Me? Me?" I say, pretending as if I've only just discovered that I am a person. "Today, I actually went inside of a bank."

"Wow," she says. "I'll take it."

■

One thing Michelle does that I can't decide if I like or dislike: she talks about you a lot, in the hypothetical. What you would have done in certain situations, whether you would have approved of us or not.

"Your Beau, your Beau," she says, as if she's hiding her own Beau somewhere.

"I'm not nearly as possessive as you think I am," I say.

"Today you got mad because you found out we aren't the only ones the mailwoman leaves a holiday card for."

"I love you, too."

———

At two in the morning, the kid wakes me with a bloodcurdling scream. I bring her tea and rub her back a little. She sniffles, nestling her face in my shoulder.

"I dreamt I was a whale that shrunk to the size of a ladybug," she says.

"Well, that doesn't sound so scary."

"It was!" she declares. "No one could see me. Not you, not Grandpa, not Michelle, not Forrest, not Nonna, not anybody. I was stuck on my back on your hand," she says, holding her hand palm-up and poking the center of it. "I tried to wiggle off but couldn't."

"Impossible. Sweaty palms," I say, holding my hands up as evidence. "You'd slip and slide right off."

The kid gives me a gratuitous laugh, but I know she doesn't see any humor in the situation.

"You want to know what I think?" she says, wrapping her blankie around her head.

"What?"

"I think you don't know what scary really means."

"I have nightmares, too, you know."

"What happens in them?"

"You leave me every time. You get on a train, a flight, into a stranger's cars. You leave me because you want to. Do you know what I mean by that?" I ask.

She nods.

"I think I'd better start sleeping with Beau-mom from now on," she says. "She'll keep me safe."

My first thought? *No, she's mine.*

For a moment, I consider hiding your urn from the kid. What does that make me?

Pop Quiz:
Q: What is Velcro made of? Do you know?
A: I know that it took over eight years of research to create it.
Q: How many tiny hooks is too many tiny hooks?

■

First day of first grade. I take photos and text them to your mom. Shane is in the kid's class and so is another Shadester—a trans girl, Eve, who the kid immediately buddies up with. The kid's teacher is a lonely looking white man with a terrible hairline. His name is Mr. Donnelly. When I drop the kid off on her first day, Shane says, "Your hairline's showing" to the teacher. I don't know what else a hairline is supposed to do, but nevertheless, when we go over to Julian and Dune's that evening, and Dune beats the kid in checkers, she says, "Well, at least my hairline's not showing."

And here I am thinking I'd taught her to be original with her insults.

The next day the kid brags about how she'd been "caught being good" at school, undoubtedly a first for her. She says that she shared her crayons with some doofus named Bait, only she doesn't call her a doofus; I do, in my head, like an adult.

"Do you know what *caught* means?" I ask, confused.

"You can come to school with me if you need practice with your vocab," she offers, twirling her imaginary mustache.

"Have you been hanging out with Grandpa without me again?" I ask, and she shakes her head, then says, "Do *you* know what caught means? Like a bunny in a trap."

"Who taught you that? That's cruel."

She waves her hand in front of my face and says, "Now you see me, now you don't!" then runs to her room and picks up her guitar. She is at least as good as the men who play by the pier for spare change.

Your mom likes the pictures of the kid. She says the kid looks just like you. I like talking to your mom because she's the only person who seems to understand that time doesn't exist, and that it's just as hard today as it was that day in the hospital. On the phone, her voice is older, a bit quivery. I'd forgotten how aging works. She must be able to hear the surprise in my voice.

"Don't worry, I'm as strong as an ox," she says.

"Is that so?"

"In fact, I am part ox. I've always been good at outdoor work."

"When was the last time you encountered a human?"

"Let me see here. Depends on if we are counting you or not."

"That mouth of yours is going to get you into trouble," I say. "Here, I'm passing you off." I hand the phone to the kid, who rips it out of my hand and starts talking a mile a minute.

"When are you going to visit, Nonna? Did you know we are next to the ocean? How cool is that? We can look at the water whenever we want. You could, too. Mom says you love outside. I love outside, too. It's so much better than being inside, don't you think? I don't like walls, they make me feel boxed in, but outside is good, outside the breeze gives you small kisses all over your face."

Then she listens for a while, pacing around the house, mmhmming.

■

The kid's good behavior was a fluke. Within a week, I am receiving calls from dear old Mr. Donnelly. The kid has superglued Shane's seat and now his pants have a hole in the butt.

"I'm sorry, the number you are trying to reach has been disconnected."

Then she steals Shane's phone and programs it to call him Shitstain, as in *Shitstain, Mom is calling.*

"Ah, humiliation—one of the many torture techniques approved by the Department," says Michelle.

When the kid comes home, we don't tell her that we know, since her trial-and-error experiment is not yet complete.

"She can't be working alone," I say.

Most recently, the kid played the substitute for a fool. All day, Shane collected everyone's papers, dished out crayons, cleaned up the rug, and erased the whiteboard, because the kid convinced the substitute Shane was the classroom assistant.

"Important job," she told the sub. "Highest in the ranks under you."

This one I do mention while I clean out her lunch box.

"You have brought great dishonor to this family," I say.

"What? How?" she asks. She thinks I am serious.

"Why didn't you make Shane go grocery shopping for us?" I say.

She smiles. She's with me now.

"I'm still learning."

She flops down on the couch and turns on the TV, but she's not really watching. She's studying her hands in her lap.

"He deserves a lot worse, you know," she says, not looking up.

"Oh, I know," I tell her.

■

When you were seven months pregnant, we went to visit your mom at her cabin. The second she set eyes on your round belly, she burst into tears. Up until then, I'd never seen her anything but furious or delighted, and I suppose she was delighted, but other emotions were present, just beyond my reach. Maybe she was thinking of when she'd been pregnant with you, how she'd been so lonely doing it all on her own that she brought you into the world early. I knew she thought that way because any time she had a few beers in her, she started talking like a turnstile. After hiking all day, we'd stay up late watching reality TV about people who wanted love or pretended to want love and she'd tell us it was all her fault you'd been born premature. *I just couldn't wait any longer*, she'd say.

"What is the shape of a mother?" I ask Michelle.
  "In my case, long and narrow," she says.
  "Like an arrow?"
  "More like a passageway."

A passageway would be nice. I imagine you and me as two water slides that begin separately but dump into the same pool.

∎

My father insists that he take the three of us out to lunch to meet his new girlfriend. What I know so far: her name is

Audrey, they've dated for six months, she likes online shopping and romantic comedies, and she is at least twenty years younger than him.

"I'm not sure what this has to do with me," says the kid on the way there.

"Pretending to be happy for someone you love is a key life skill," I lecture.

"Or we could *actually* be happy for him," says Michelle.

"You make a point. Not a particularly good one, but a point."

"I don't know why you're in a huff about this. All you do is complain about how he won't get over your mom."

"I don't do that. I'm going to need to see some citations."

"Personally, I'm glad he's found someone," says Michelle.

"He better buy me stuffed French toast," says the kid.

Once we've been served our meals, Audrey places her hand over my father's and announces that they are planning to have a baby, that she's begun to track her ovulation. I accidentally spit my first bite of BLT onto my father's face.

"I feel ready, you know?" she says. "I've lived enough life, done enough crazy things."

"The thing is, I'm mostly shooting blanks at this point," says my father very solemnly. "We'll have to do that lesbian thing you did."

"Great, cool, thanks a lot, Dad."

"Shooting what?" asks the kid, making a finger gun. I grab the kid's hand.

"No, no, put that down."

"This is going to be fun, isn't it?" says Michelle. She smiles like a maniac into her burger.

"What's ovulating?" asks the kid.

"Well, sweetie," says Audrey, leaning forward onto the table and speaking in a baby voice. "It's the best time to try to get pregnant."

"She's not a baby," I say to Audrey, squinting at her. I have to actively refrain from hissing.

"Why are there good times and bad times?" asks the kid. I make a hybrid smile-frown face that I'm sure makes me look constipated.

"Well, the ingredient from the man can be finicky sometimes," says Audrey.

"What the fuck," I say.

"What the fuck!" repeats the kid, grinning.

"We don't say fuck."

"But you just said fuck."

"Oh my god, this is amazing," says my father, holding up his beer in salute. The kid gives my father a harsh look as if to say, *Hush, the grown-ups are talking.*

"What ingredient? What man?" she asks. "Two moms made me!" I brush her long hair out of her face and try to remain calm.

"Remember how I said Beau-mom gave birth to you? Well, I couldn't give her a special, uh, ingredient, so we asked a very nice man to do that, and guess what! He did! And then they mixed together to make you."

At this point, the kid is freaking out.

"Is the man okay? Is he missing a part of him? Does he need it back? Will he live?" I laugh so fucking hard I snort, but then quickly regather myself because there is true panic in the kid's eyes. I don't know what she's picturing,

254 · MARISA CRANE

but I assure her he's perfectly intact, wherever he is, doing whatever he is doing. All his vital organs are present and accounted for.

"Phew, okay," she says, wiping her brow in an exaggerated way she only could have seen in a cartoon.

"Like I was saying," my father begins. "We may need an ingredient man."

"Do I ever get to meet my ingredient man?" the kid asks.

"I—"

"We'll talk about it, won't we?" says Michelle, meeting my eyes.

"Fine, just make it all about you guys," says my father, raising his hands in defeat.

■

"It finally happened," says Dune over the phone. They sound as if they've been pushed through a million compartments.

"We'll be right over," I say, then hang up. When I look at Michelle, she knows. She nods and grabs the kid's guitar and tells her we are going next door. "You two head over there now, I'm going to run out for a second," I say.

I'm lucky it's a Monday. I run to the store and grab some beer, a few party horns, a sheet cake, and a couple tubes of icing. In the car, I use the icing to write a message on the cake then carry it to their door and knock. When Julian answers, I hold up his cake.

"Congrats, it's your shadow party!" I announce, passing out the party horns. Julian looks weepy, his eyes a sick, sad world I know all too well. Even so, he smiles through his tears, some of which I hope are happy. Dune comes up behind him and wraps their arms around his waist and he places his hands over their hands. He glances back at them over his shoulder, sniffling then laughing at his sniffles. Everyone blows their horns while the kid runs around the room, blowing hers so hard she breaks it. It's okay, I got extras.

"Oh my god, I can't believe I didn't know we were having a party," says the kid.

"It certainly wasn't planned," says Dune, smiling at the kid. "But that's okay."

I pass out the beers and juice while Michelle slices the cake, which reads "Happy Shadow Day! Congrats on a new lifelong friend!"

"Can I have the word *Happy*?" says Julian, studying the cake.

"I want *friend*!" demands the kid, practically climbing Julian's body.

We go around the room and take turns telling Julian the things we love about him that have nothing to do with his extra shadow. There are so many. Julian beams and beams, he never lets go of Dune's hand. We spend the rest of the night drinking and dancing in their living room. The kid stays up way past her bedtime—there are no rules tonight, there is only celebrating something the Department doesn't want us to celebrate, and maybe it isn't much, but our bodies, dipping and diving like currents of energy throughout the room, feel like small sparks of resistance, our miniature revolution. These moments of joy belong to us and no one else.

When I think of the word *family*, I picture a surprise party, everyone floating toward the ceiling like balloons.

∎

Pop Quiz:
Q: How will you control the future?
A: I might consider the utility of puppets, of tying strings to the corners of my mouth and tugging upward on them whenever the Department tugs down.

∎

"You need to behave better than the NoShad kids, not worse," I lecture the kid.

"Better, worse, what's the difference?" she philosophizes. I sigh. With that brain, she's bound for a solitary life.

"I'm scared for your social life, I really am."

"First of all," she begins, gesturing wildly in her booster seat, "Forrest is my best friend, and first of all, this girl Kylie who's in Shane's little crew thinks that Forrest is her best friend, and first of all, he doesn't even like her, he just asks her to play with us sometimes when we need someone to be the agent when we play Agents and Shadesters, and obviously me and Eve can't be the Agents because of our shadows, and first of all, that's another story because Kylie tells us that people like us shouldn't be allowed in the classroom, and first of all, I know she got that from Shane, it's like no one can think for themselves, you know, and first of all, you're probably going to get a call from the principal saying I kicked Kylie, which is true but only because she was mean to us, and first of all, you can't punish me because I'm telling you about it first, which has got to count for something, and first of all, if you want me to keep on being honest when I kick some jerk-face then I should get a free pass on this because she deserved it, and first of all, you always tell me not to take anyone's shit so that's what I said when I was kicking her, I said, first of all, you have no idea what you're talking about, and then I said, first of all, seriously? We invited you to play so you should be nicer to us, and anyway, Mom, I'm sorry that she went home walking with a limp, but I'm not sorry I did what I did."

The kid pauses and takes a deep breath while I adjust to everything she has said. She exhales then looks at me, a deflated balloon of a child. She softens her voice.

"First of all, if I'm being honest, Mom, I know I'm acting all tough, but it's just my tough mask."

■

"What would your Beau have done in this situation?" asks Michelle, rubbing her chin against her collarbone.

"She would get the kid boxing lessons."

"Huh," she says, smiling.

"We're only joking," I shout at the living room camera as I plug in the vacuum cleaner. I have the urge to text my dad and ask if he plans on vacuuming in order to help his new kid fall asleep.

Will the new kid attach to his body as I did?

Will my dad still twirl his mustache to soothe his nerves, or will he shave its bristly gray and begin again?

Will the new kid find a way to detach? Will they even entertain the idea?

Will my dad become someone I no longer recognize?

"Vacuuming can wait," says Michelle, coming up behind me and kissing my neck, the feel of her cold hands against my pelvis, my thighs, and back again, her middle finger circling my clit for a moment or two before moving on.

"Oh, I see what you're getting at," I say.

"What's for dinner?" she asks once we've moved to the bedroom. She rips off her shirt and shorts then climbs on top of me. The blinds are up, and our neighbor is running in place in his living room. I alternate between wanting to pull the blinds down and liking that he can see us.

"I don't know, what do you want?" I say, tilting my head back, welcoming little bites to the jaw.

"I don't know."

"We have those weird hot dogs."

"What weird hot dogs?"

She's found that spot on my neck that makes me go *oooooh*.

"The weird ones," I breathe. I'm both turned on and hungry.

"Oh, of course," she says. "Is there such a thing as normal hot dogs?" She sits back on her haunches and removes my pants, one leg at a time. They're tight, it isn't easy, and while trying to help her, I accidentally kick her in the boob.

"Watch it, they're huge like . . ."

"Pomegranates?" I offer.

"No," she says, sliding my shirt up so she can bite my hip. "Like . . ."

"A bee's nest?" I try, quickly losing the ability to think. "Wait, that doesn't sound right. Do bees have nests?"

"Hives, they have hives."

"Yeah, they're hanging there like beehives," I say, while she removes my shirt. I tug on her sports bra. Off with it. I want her and I want her now. No more nips and bites and slow burning down my body.

There was certainly a time when such mundane conversation would have turned me off. I wanted to delay reality a little while longer. But now, it's that very realness, a reminder that we are extremely boring creatures who must do a myriad of boring things each and every day, that grounds me in our sex, makes me trust her even more.

I push her head down and hold it there, my fingers digging into her hair. That first lick. The shudder and recoil. The surprise in the expected. I close my eyes and pretend I have a cock, a hard, throbbing cock she wants to take care of for me. Although we haven't discussed it previously, I'm feeling inspired—I bring her head up and tell her to wait, then grab the strap-on and harness from under the bed. She watches me slip on the harness then slip the dildo in, transfixed but also curious. I think she can tell my intention isn't to fuck her. I lie back down on the bed and stroke my dick a few times, my clit throbbing.

"Suck my cock," I say, running my tongue over my front teeth.

"Yes, ma'am," she says. She takes her job very seriously. While she works, I grab any part of her I can reach, I scratch her upper back, grip the base of her neck, pull her hair. I press on her jaw with my thumb, I like to feel it move, the cycle of flexing and relaxing, I squeeze her biceps so hard she jumps a little. When I come, it is an earthquake.

■

Now I am in the principal's office. The principal is a leather-skinned woman with the deepest frown line I've ever seen. She doesn't remember me from when I worked here, but I remember her. Per my coworkers' advice, I spent most of my time avoiding her. She got off on singling out our kids for punishment. The kid is in the chair next to me, an ice pack on her lip.

"Two-day suspension," says the principal, shuffling her papers. "Naturally, she'll be referred to the behavioral pro-gram upstairs."

"Kids fight every day."

"Well," she says.

"What about Shane? He's been bullying her for over a year."

"He's, well, he's low-risk," she says, answering a phone that hadn't been ringing.

Back at home, I switch the kid's ice pack out and set her up on the couch with blankets and pillows.

"It's not like I have the flu," she says.

"So, what happened?"

"Shane and his friends were threatening me and Eve on the playground. He got up in my face, so I clocked him. Only reason I even got hit was because his stupid friend sucker-punched me while I was hitting Shane."

She smirks. She's resisting telling me that I should see the other guy.

"This is the part where I'm supposed to say no fighting," I say robotically.

"But, instead, you say . . ."

"I'm happy you defended yourself and Eve."

She smiles. "I don't think he'll be messing with us anymore."

■

Jamal calls to tell me the kid has been admitted to the behavioral health program after several assessment attempts. "Several, several," he says, sounding tired.

"And why's that?" I ask.

"She knocked all the bookshelves in the office over."

"I'm sure she had a good reason."

I hear him exhale into the phone.

"When the assessor asked her why she did that, she said only certain people deserve her attention then left the room."

The assessment is what's known as a biopsychosocial assessment, intended to take the whole person into account when evaluating problems. Psychological symptoms, living situation, family history, medical history, education, financial status, all that. When I ask to see the kid's assessment, Jamal sighs and says, "Kris, don't you think you're a little too close to this?"

"I used to sit where you're sitting," I say.

"Yeah, used to."

"I have every right," I say.

He relents. The next day at school he hands me a packet of papers. Under stressors, the assessor has written "Shadester identity" and "Shadester mother."

If I were a social worker assigned to myself, I might say, *Kris, is this a big deal or a little deal?*

And I might respond: *There is no deal.*

∎

After the kid's first day in the behavioral program, she comes home looking like she'd been caught in a tornado. Hair a mess. Dirt on her face.

"That Miss Claire is slippery," she says. "But don't worry, I dodged her."

"Tell me that's your worker," I say, covering my mouth with my hand. Michelle hides her face in a marketing book.

"Worker, schmorker," she says. "She didn't know what hit her."

She brings her guitar out to the living room, plugs it

in, and enlightens us with a lovely head-banging tale about Miss Claire, the fun-killer.

"Today," the kid says, "Forrest and Eve asked if they could be in the program, too, but Jamal said no."

"It really doesn't work like that," I say.

"But I never get to see them anymore," she whines.

"You'll find a way, I'm sure."

"Today, Miss Claire snuck out at lunch and took a nap in her car," says the kid.

"How do you know?" asks Michelle before I can get to it.

"Well, because I snuck out, too," says the kid, studying us for a reaction.

"Where exactly?"

"Just to second recess. Her window was all fogged up."

"Second recess," I say.

"I have straight A's," she reminds us.

What to say?

"So, you're telling me you were like Miss Claire?" asks the kid when I explain what I used to do, that I didn't always call sad people over the telephone, that I used to see them in person, I used to catch them when they were much younger.

"My car naps were only on Fridays," I say. She laughs.

"Did the kids like you?"

264 • MARISA CRANE

"Of course not."

"In group, Mr. Jamal makes us go around in a circle and say one bad thing we did that day and then how we think we could have made a better decision," she says. "I can never pick just one."

"Has Shane stopped messing with you?"

"Sure, sure," she says, waving me off. "But there's a new NoShad in town. Everyone calls him Donkey. He says his dad always votes Colestein. He spit on my shadow the other day. The good one!" she laughs. "Awful aim."

"Great, a mini fascist," I say.

"School mostly feels like an obstacle course," she says. "Dodge Miss Claire, avoid Donkey, meet Forrest and Eve under the stairs."

■

One night when we're getting ready for bed, Michelle pulls me into the closet where the camera can't see us. I've never been in here before. It's not the type of closet one refers to as a walk-in—really, it's barely a *look-in*, but somehow, we fit. She says she's finally gotten ahold of her old Department buddy Mitch, who is head of the tech team.

"So, what did he say?" I whisper. She is clutching my arms.

"Nothing good, Kris."

"I'm going to bleep someone."

"Brown's basically untouchable," she says. "He has a history of orchestrating raids on known Shadester spots."

"And?"

"He appears to have no qualms about killing Shadesters and covering it up."

"Jesus fucking fuck," I whisper. "Any chance your tech guy can turn off these cameras so I can properly curse the Department out?"

"Hmm," she says, raising her eyebrows.

■

We've helped your mother enter the twenty-first century by gifting her a phone that has the ability to video call. A whole new concept for her. The kid and her wave back and forth at each other with big dumb grins on their faces.

"This is dog one through seven," she says, moving the camera in such a way that we can't see any of the dogs. "The other four are out back being amateur detectives."

The kid shows Nonna our homemade wind chime, still hanging pathetically in the living room.

"Very good for your first go at it," she says. "The secret is to eat your favorite food with the forks and spoons before converting them."

"That's where we went wrong!" says the kid. "Here, say hi to Michelle," the kid says, moving the camera so your mom can see Michelle in the kitchen pulling a quiche from the oven.

"No, no, I look gross," says Michelle, covering her face.

Later, your mom sends me a text: "Who was that in the kitchen? I couldn't see her."

"Just a friend," I say.

"It's okay," she writes.

■

Second grade is, as they say, a delight.

"What now?" I say into the phone.

The kid's teacher, whose name is evading me at the moment, says that the kid has disrespected her for the last time.

"I'll make her tell you what she did," she says.

"Hello, hi," says the kid. "So, well, I said, 'Fuck this shit' to the teacher."

"What for?"

"Mom, it wasn't fair, it really wasn't. Forrest and I wrote basically the exact same answer on a quiz and the teacher gave Forrest full credit and me only half credit."

In the background, I hear the teacher yell, "That's not how it happened."

"Hmm, three guesses as to why she did that," says the kid. Click.

The kid gets after-school detention for a week. The principal thinks that will talk some sense into her. Every day, Michelle and I pick her up at 5:30 p.m. and try to feed her small bits of wisdom.

"This, too, shall pass."

"Your teacher represents a large portion of the population."

"Use this time for reflection."

"French fries can fix anything."

We order a mountain of fries at the drive-through. The kid asks for "one hundred and six ketchup packets, please."

Little do we know, the kid doesn't want this time to pass. Eve is in detention with her. Detention is where they come up with the idea for a secret society called The Shadow Puppets. Their plan is to teach NoShads the truth about Shadesters, about who the Department is targeting with their legislation. The first lesson plan: Colestein can't be trusted. When I learn of this, I kick myself for teaching the kid to read.

"What do you two think about this?" I ask Julian and Dune, who are on the couch clutching their glasses of wine.

"I think it's not very secret if we all know about it," says Dune.

"I worry about her," I say. "She has the influential skills of a dictator and the organizational skills of a wedding planner. A terrifying combination."

"I'll join," says Julian, toeing his extra shadow on the rug.

"She is drawing attention to this household," says Michelle. Julian glances at the camera.

Michelle and I decide to stage an intervention. We ask the kid if she can please sit down on the lounger in our living room. I've taped a sign to the back that says HOTSEAT. She has the calm of a sociopath taking a lie detector test.

"I don't want to stifle your creativity, but I will intervene when I think something is unsafe," I say.

"Like right now," says Michelle.

"Right now?" asks the kid.

"Not literally right now," I say.

"We mean your secret society. It's not safe for you," says Michelle. "We don't think you realize how powerful the Department is."

"That's exactly why we created the group, people!"

"Okay, I don't want to scare you, but they could make you disappear without a trace. Like you never existed," I say.

"They don't scare me."

"They should," says Michelle. "I used to work with those people."

"Whose fault is that?" snaps the kid.

We stare at her, hoping for a mind control miracle. I cross my arms, Michelle moves her hands to her hips. The kid exhales sharply, making sure we notice her sigh.

"Fine, I won't do it anymore," she says. I squint my eyes at her; it can't have been that easy.

■

Your mother's decreasing tolerance for her cameras seems to be synced up with mine. She calls and tells me how she's begun hiding in the out-of-view spots throughout her house. One-foot-by-one-foot squares. She slouches onto the floor with her back to the wall, closes her eyes, and reminds

herself that there was once a time in which we could mis-
behave in peace.

"The only audience I had to worry about was my guilty
conscience," she says.

"I don't understand," I say. "Your grandchild acts like
the cameras aren't here."

"Youthful arrogance," she says. "They all believe they're
invincible."

"Oh, let me fill you in on our most recent adventures."

Although I grew used to the surveillance cameras years
ago, the kid's plans have brought about a renewed sense of
fear, of hypervigilance. I cannot blink even if I want to.

■

Despite the kid's propensity for trouble, life goes rather
smoothly for a while. The kid makes it to third grade in one
piece. Donkey and his best friend, Titus, aren't in her class.
Michelle is Michelle, my person, my love, my best friend.
Julian and Dune practically live with us except for when it's
time to go to bed and we say our goodnights and they walk
the ten feet to their apartment. Of course, all this goodness
makes me suspicious.

We go out to dinner with my dad and Audrey. They have
something they want to tell us, and I pretend I have no idea
what it could be. My dad talks of blueberries, don't I just
love blueberries?

"Are you having a stroke?" I ask him. Audrey laughs,

rubs his shoulder. He begins twirling his mustache and Audrey gently pulls on his forearm.

"I'll just say it," says Audrey, pushing her hair out of her face. "Twins!"

"The size of blueberries," adds my father.

"What are you going to do with twins?" I ask.

"Make blueberry pie," says my father, shrugging. He looks pleased with himself.

"Just to be clear, you're not going to mash the twins up and eat them, right?"

Audrey clears her throat and wipes her mouth with her napkin.

"Thank god I'm having two more," he says. "Hopefully one will have a chance at not being so morbid."

"Can I name them?" asks the kid, smiling.

"I think they probably want to name their own children, babe," says Michelle, always the heartbreaker.

"Ugh, why, though?"

"How about this? You can choose the middle names from a carefully curated list of approved middle names?" says Audrey. I turn to the kid.

"The most exciting opportunity of the year, by far," I say.

When we get home, my dad has sent me the link to their registry in seven separate emails. The registry consists of a lot of bird-themed clothing. I guess Audrey likes birds, and I think that sounds good as long as she's okay with me calling the twins Goose One and Goose Two.

———

I don't know what's wrong with me, but I can't shake this feeling of impending doom.

What I'm trying to say is—I've never been afraid of anything more than I've been afraid of my own happiness. But I want it, oh I want it. Something tells me it isn't happiness without fear. This small fact keeps me breathing and sleeping.

∎

"Excuse me," I say to the couch you picked out, your mugs I drink from every morning, your ugly lamp I loved to hate.

"Excuse me," Michelle says to your books, your bedside bin, your sweatshirts, your cologne bottles.

At night, I watch the kid try to cuddle your urn in bed, but it pokes her in the chest, in the belly. I watch her grab a marker and write "Beau-mom" across the top of it.

∎

When I pick the kid up from school, I scoop her in my arms and hold her horizontally, pretending she's an airplane, but she's a bit old for this poor excuse for entertainment, plus Forrest and Eve are watching nearby, so she screams for me to put her down, which I do, after announcing that the engines are failing, we're going down! She tugs her shirt down to cover her belly and furrows her brow at me.

"Where's Grandpa?" she says.

"He's probably trying to figure out how he's going to chase two toddlers around given his current anatomy."

She pulls a phone out of her pocket, a phone which I have not given her, and says, "It's okay, I'll give him a call." I am many things—confused, alarmed, amused, etc. "Yeah, hi, she's right here. She says you need new bones," says the kid, wearing her, and your, business face. She has her hand on her hip and she's tapping her foot like a middle-aged mom in the suburbs. "Oh, is that soooo?" Now she's raising her eyebrow at me.

"What?" I squawk.

"Here," she says, shoving the alien phone at me.

"What?" I squawk into the phone.

"Kris, where the hell have you been? Have you seen our baby registry? You haven't answered my texts. It's like you're you or something," says my dad. He actually sounds concerned.

"Did you gift her this phone?" I ask.

"Of course. You think I'm going to let you dictate when I talk to my granddaughter? She's a fast texter. Eve seems like a good kid. I'm learning to make kale smoothies. Audrey is very into extending my life span."

"Audrey and I are on the same team," I say. "Listen, Dad. I'm happy you're happy."

"Do you have a program for new Shadesters?" the woman on the phone asks me. I'm leaning on the kitchen counter, face in my hands.

"Of course. I've found it really helpful," I say.

"Does that mean you're a Shadester, too?" she whispers.

"Yes, it does."

"Can you tell me something to make this easier?"

I consider making a joke, but then I remember how helpless I felt when I got my shadow, how I would've given anything for someone to tell me that everything was going to be okay, even if they were lying. She deserves the luxury of hope.

"I can think of at least five people who love me, shadow or no shadow," I say.

"But how can you be so sure?" she sniffles.

When I hang up, Michelle puts down her laptop and makes her way over to me, laying her head on my shoulder. She'd been writing ads for a cat raincoat company. She is good at copywriting because she understands people, what makes them tick, how a single moment can transform a desire into a need. Right now, she understands that I need her reassurance, that what I said on the phone was, in fact, true. She searches for my hand then grabs it and kisses the back of it, making her way up my arm to my clavicle and then neck. Michelle is very different from you. She often communicates with her body, her hands, her mouth. We kiss a slow, deep kiss, then break apart. She presses her palm to my chest and rubs in small, rhythmic circles.

Throughout this quiet period, I begin spooking easily. Every time the kid or Michelle comes around the corner, I jump out of my skin. I don't know what has gotten into me, exactly, but I can't say that it's entirely unfounded.

A new thing: Michelle has begun going out for drinks with Mitch, her old Department friend, about once a month. Whenever I ask her how it went, she waves her hand and says, "Oh, you know."

"No, I don't know. What do you talk about?"

"People, places, and things, mostly," she says, laughing.

"Whatever you're doing, please be careful, if not for me then for the tiny cats in raincoats," I say.

"I'll think about it," she says, heading into the bedroom to undress. I follow her and do the same, our extra shadows overlapping so it looks like her head is my head, her arms my arms.

■

The kid and I are watching home videos again, despite my concerns that Michelle may get upset that I can't, or won't, let you go, but when she sees what we're doing, she sits down and watches with us, laughing and smiling along. She is what one might call well-adjusted—I wonder what that is like.

On the TV, you're playing soccer in the backyard with one of your many uncles. Steve? Or is it Chance? I never did get them all straight. You look to be around the kid's age, seven or so, and very nearly identical. Jack-o'-lantern mouth, long blond mane, strong calves, take-no-shit face. You kick your uncle in the shin while going for a fifty-fifty ball and he wails, "Fucking fuck fuck fuck shit motherfucker" while grabbing his lower leg and jumping up and down. Whoever was filming—your mom?—laughs at the string of curses, the camera shaking up and down.

"I was obsessed with watching videos of myself when I was a kid," says Michelle. "I'll have to dig some up."

"I'd love to see baby Michelle running around, putting everyone else's emotional intelligence to shame," I say, kissing her on the cheek, the jaw, the neck. That is typical—once lip meets skin, I don't want to stop. I cover her face with kisses before remembering the kid.

She has a curious look on her face, softer than I've seen on her in a while.

"Look, it's me," she says, pointing at the screen.

"Not quite," I say, drinking my beer.

"God, would it kill you to play pretend just once?" she whines.

"What do you want from me? What do you want me to pretend?" I ask. She recoils a bit, biting the skin around her cuticles like you and your mother and her mother before her.

"I don't know," she says. "Just stuff."

"I'm sorry," I say, seeing that I've hurt her. The words are lumpy on my tongue, I don't have much practice. I think of my parents, the lack of practice they'd had in the art of apologizing. I don't want to carry on that particular family tradition.

"Can I sit on your lap?" I say. At first, she clenches her jaw and ignores me, then softens and moves her blankie out of the way to show that there's room for both her blankie and me. I almost break down at this simple, beautiful gesture. I move from Michelle's side and pretend to sit on the kid's lap. She pretends I'm not very heavy, and we both pretend we know what the hell we're doing.

After we watch your home videos, Michelle joins me in the shower, something she hasn't done in a while. It makes me wonder if maybe she does have the capacity for jealousy, if she's looking to reassert her dominance. She isn't interested in shower sex—the shower is too small, there's no room to maneuver, plus we have both suffered the cruelty of giving head while the water burned our eyes, got in our mouths, half choking us until we're convinced this was the way we would die, devoting ourselves to another's pleasure.

She grabs a bar of soap and makes a lather in her hands before spinning me around so my back is facing her. She doesn't say anything. The water is warm against my chest. I study my boobs, my large nipples, my outie belly button. I am me, I am inside my body, she is her, she is inside her body. She is using her body to communicate with my body, to remind it who is in charge. She brings both hands to my back and scrubs in circles, starting out light and gradually increasing the pressure until she is not so much cleaning me as she is digging to the center of me, and I have to hold on to the shower rod for support. I smile to myself. I am powerful in my powerlessness.

But it's not long before we are disrupted by the kid barging into the bathroom and pulling aside the shower curtain. Michelle quickly pulls her hands away, though I still feel the memory of them on my back.

"I need to show you something," the kid announces, running out of the bathroom.

"Well, that was nice while it lasted," I say. I give Michelle a quick kiss then climb out of the shower and towel off.

"Nice wasn't exactly what I was going for," says Michelle, following me out of the shower.

"I know," I say.

"What do you think she wants to show us?"

"Probably her plans to beep beep beeeeeeeep," I say, censoring myself for the bathroom camera.

I think this will get a laugh out of Michelle, but she doesn't respond. I watch her dry off, admiring each exposed area as she moves the towel up and down her body. It is a simple thing, but I want to hold on to every detail in case those details were to suddenly disappear.

We find the kid sitting on the edge of her bed, clutching a piece of paper, a question mark on her face. I can tell she's trying to make sense of the paper. Michelle and I pause at her bedroom door then proceed forth with caution.

"I found this when I was a baby," she says, handing it to me.

"You didn't find anything when you were a baby except for a bottle and poop," I correct her.

"Whatever, I was really young," she says, waving me off as she does. "I think I know what it is."

I look down at it. It's the first page of our sperm donor's paperwork. It has his first name, occupation, education, carrier status, and a paragraph about him and his charms, written by one of the sperm bank employees.

"What do you think it is?" I ask, biting my cheek. Michelle peers over my shoulder at the paper and then excuses herself from the room. I hear her making a drink in the kitchen.

"This is my ingredient man, right?" says the kid. I can tell she isn't the slightest bit certain her assessment is correct.

"Yes, that's your ingredient man, stinker, or as we adults call him, the sperm donor," I say, putting my arm around her.

"Does he love music, too?"

"I'm not sure, babe. Maybe. We both heard Beau-mom's attempts at playing on that home movie."

She laughs.

"So . . . does that make him my dad?" she asks, twisting her face into the expression she reserves for when my farts smell particularly awful.

"I don't know about that," I say, trailing off.

"Why not?"

"I just, I don't know, I don't know."

"One day hopefully I can meet him," she says wistfully.

I text your mom: "I could really use your goddamn help over here."

The kid, seeing my phone, says, "Hey wait, where's *my* phone?" then scrambles around the house before finding it in the refrigerator next to the fruit punch. Just like that, it's as if she's forgotten about the twenty-three mystery chromosomes. Not that I can count on that lasting.

■

At first, there had been a father and a mother, and then there was only a father. When you and I decided we wanted to have a family, I thought, there will be a mother and a mother and that's the end of that.

■

On the other end of the phone there is yet again someone who is not calling to say I've won a million dollars. At least it's not Mrs. So-and-So, the teacher.

"She graffitied the side of the school building," says Jamal.

"Where was Claire?" I ask, just to be a jerk. As I've said, I really don't want to be that parent, but I must admit, it does have a certain appeal, getting to blame someone else for once. I can see why the other parents did it. The transference of energy.

"She has a whole caseload to attend to, Kris."

"I wasn't really asking, Jamal."

"Okay."

"What did she graffiti?"

"It says 'How can you live with yourself?' with yourself spelled wrong and a huge black shadow over the words."

"A valid question," I say.

"Where did she get the spray paint?"

"Your guess is as good as mine. I'm just the child-rearer here."

In the principal's office, the kid's sitting in a chair against the wall under a sign that says, EVERYONE IS A WINNER! I open my arms and she runs into them like she's a child getting away with childhood.

"Are you okay?" the principal asks, pointing to my chest. I look down to see that my sweatshirt is on backward.

"No, it appears I've woken up well-rested," I say, and she nods as if the kid's behavior makes sense now.

"Well, she's suspended for a week this time," the principal says, looking me in the eyes as if eye contact were the one solution we hadn't tried yet.

"Sure thing," I say. "I'll, of course, have to make her a nest of blankets." And the kid, who, I realize, will not be a kid forever, laughs, quickly covering her mouth with her hand.

"Principal Carson, Donkey's been threatening me again," says the kid.

"Is that so?" says the principal.

"You people don't take it seriously. You think he's just a kid, but he's not. He's a monster."

"And what does this have to do with your graffiti, young lady?"

The kid turns to me and rolls her eyes.

"Let's get out of here," she says.

"I know there must be a right way to address this," I say to Michelle.

"Well, do you want her to stop?"

"I don't know."

"Well," she says, raising her eyebrows.

I go into the kid's room. She's talking to your urn the way I used to.

"In four words or less, tell me why you graffitied the school," I say. She thinks on this.

"Siegfried," she says, raising her thumb from a closed fist. "Lives," she says, raising her pointer finger. "On," she says, raising her middle finger.

"You and I are going to learn self-defense," I say. Then I confiscate all of her graffiti paraphernalia: her notebook, stencils, X-Acto knife, spray paint, and gloves.

There was that time I asked Siegfried what we should give criminals instead of shadows. I didn't necessarily think we needed to bring back prisons, but I didn't know what we were supposed to do with the people who'd committed serious crimes. Real crimes, not Kris crimes, not the kid's crimes. Not Siegfried crimes, or so I'd thought at the time.

"Forgiveness," he said.

"And what if they don't deserve it?"

"What is this talk of deserve? What does that word even mean?" he said.

■

I'm not feeling so cute when I realize that a week of suspension means one very long week of the kid asking me to revisit the whole dad issue.

"I'm old enough to know," she whines.

"I wasn't aware there was an age qualification for talking to a man neither of us have ever met," I say. "He's literally an ingredient. Like a cake."

She giggles a little in spite of herself.

"I am pretty yummy," she says, raising her eyebrows and smirking.

"Yes, you are," I say, tackling her to the ground and pretending to nibble on her arms and legs, and soon she is squirming and cackling.

"Stopppppppppp," she yells through her laughing tears.

"Okay, okay," I roll off her and she sits up and looks me square in the eye.

"Don't you think I should have a choice in the matter?" she asks.

"Don't you have other children-things to complain about?"

Another day, more questioning.

"What will knowing your sperm donor change for you?" I ask the kid.

"Everything," she says.

"I'd hate for you to be disappointed," I say.

And that's how it goes, back and forth for a week. The truth is, I no longer remember if the sperm donor was an open identity donor, meaning the kid can contact him when she turns eighteen, or anonymous, meaning she can never contact him or know his identity. I know you and I must have changed our minds dozens of times. We had queer friends who had done both. No matter what we chose, we felt we were making the wrong decision. I know that I need to check the paperwork, but a part of me is afraid of learning the answer. One possibility makes me feel jealous; the other makes me terrified. I don't want to disappoint her, to squash her last bit of hope. As long as she believes I am the one withholding, then there is someone for her to direct her anger at.

"I remember when having to navigate being gay at a young age was my biggest problem," I tell Michelle one night after the kid and I have been in a fight. A small one, but a fight, nonetheless. The subtle kind that makes the hair on your arms stand tall. We listen to her playing sad chords in her bedroom.

"I didn't tell anyone until I went to college. It was easy then because all of my field hockey teammates were gay," she says. "I was spoiled—my team was like this super gay microcosm."

"I wish we could pluck the kid's shadow off and stuff it in our pockets."

"And what would that do? She'd still want to find her father."

"Ew, don't call him that."

"Forgive me, ingredient man is a bit hard on the psyche," she says, laughing. I laugh, too, as I imagine dancing around the kitchen with you while we follow the instructions to a recipe: one cup of jizz, one egg, twelve doses of hormones. I imagine putting a glass pan in the oven—forty-five minutes later, the kid!

■

The kid and I watch video tutorials that show us how to protect ourselves from assailants. We learn to focus on the vulnerable areas, emphasis on the groin. We practice groin kicks on each other, and soon, I am on the couch icing my hoo-ha while the kid shows Michelle how to escape a headlock.

■

A crucial part of me hasn't changed—I still get horny whenever I am feeling unsettled. Fucking feels like proof that I am in control. No, that isn't right—it's more like proof that I can handle the disorderly condition of my life. Ravenous and reaching, I seek out Michelle. In bed, I feel as if I am performing, not in a feigning pleasure way—believe me, I am buzzing—but in an out-of-body way. I'm keenly aware of the Department cameras, of the men or women watching the slap slap slap of our naked, sweaty bodies. I wonder about the women watching, if they like what they see or shy away from it. When I ride Michelle's dick, I feel like I am performing for everyone—me, Michelle, you, the Department. Even Siegfried, wherever he is. I want everyone to see the stage I've crafted for myself. I'm keenly aware of your things still scattered throughout the room—they serve as evidence that you'd once been real enough to consume. I sit back and watch myself in the closet mirror, I watch the swim of my hips, the muscle and strength of Michelle's thighs as she moves beneath me. At one point, I press down hard on her thighs, and growl, "Stop," and she does, biting down on her bottom lip. I don't want to come, I want to exist in that liminal space forever, on top of Michelle, in control of my own passion and power, as much the provider of my pleasure as the taker. Michelle, I know, can tell something is going on with me, but she doesn't question it.

"Are you going to come for me?" she asks, chin up, a serious look on her face that says she isn't fucking around and that I better remember who my audience really is. What have I done to deserve this woman? Deserve, there's that word again.

"No," I resist, playing. She brings her hand to my cheek and pats it a few times, each pat a little harder than the last, as if testing the waters, as if seeking permission—*Can I, without asking, can I?* I don't want to give her that satisfaction, to say *yes, hit me.* I want her pleasure cut short at the very moment when things could escalate. I want to feel like a god when I smile and remove her hand from my cheek.

I climb off Michelle and tell her not to move. I pull the dildo from the harness then slip the leather straps down her muscled thighs. I watch myself in the mirror as I throw them aside. There's something ceremonial about my movements, as if I am trying to deepen history.

"This watching yourself is new," she says, grinning.

"Shut up," I growl, pulling her legs apart.

I feel between her thighs—she's soaking wet. Without meaning to, I gasp, both moved by and in awe of her wetness. The mask comes down. I can't breathe. I start at the balls of her feet, kissing every inch of them, then her ankles, her calves and shins. I move back and forth, right to left, making sure each side is completely covered. I pull her legs into my lips, so that she is the one acting on me, I am the lips, the object that Michelle happens to. By the time I reach her cunt, she's quivering, every kiss like a skipped stone causing little ripples throughout her body. I begin to tease her, dipping the tip of my finger into her then pulling it out to explore elsewhere, to circle her lips, to trace the crease of her hip. When she can't take it anymore, she grabs my hand and jams my fingers inside her, a tempered scream emerging from her mouth. I start slowly, but she won't let me, she bucks wildly and keeps begging for me to go faster, I've become object, no, a tool, yes, a tool to satisfy her. I do as I am told, and when she comes, she squirts all over me, drenching my stomach and thigh and forearm.

"Holy fuck," I say.

"Holy fuck," she agrees.

"I'm keeping you on me forever," I say, collapsing beside her. I examine her cum, smeared on my skin like paint, clearer and thinner than the cum on my fingers. It's evidence of—of, what exactly, I don't know. Of love and its multiplying truth.

"Please be careful with yourself," says Michelle, staring at the ceiling, her one leg flopped over mine.

"What do you mean?"

"What I mean is, don't do anything you don't want to do or aren't ready to do again. You know?"

"I'm fine," I say, gritting my teeth. "It was a long time ago."

"I know you bury that shit deep, but it's still there, whether you like it or not."

I feel the familiar rise of shame in me. I feel it self-ignite then surge through my body, heating then numbing the tips of my fingers and toes, collapsing my chest, rounding my shoulders. When my mind attempts to rip itself from my body, I resist. Crabs, centipedes, mites. I want to stay, I want to see.

"I know I don't say this enough, or I guess ever, but I appreciate how honest you are with me. Even when it's something I don't want to hear," I say, kicking her leg off so I can turn and face her. I feel out of my mind with fear. What if she dies just like you, just like Siegfried? What would be the point? This beautiful, beautiful person. I hate to admit it, but I need her.

"Speaking of which," she says, clearing her throat. She isn't looking at me, she isn't moving.

"What?" I say, sitting up on my elbow.

"I have to tell you something."

"Oh, no, are you dying?"

"What? No."

"Then what?"

"It's something I've been wanting to tell you ever since I met you, but I didn't know how. I mean, I tried early on, but we kept getting interrupted. And then after a while, it felt like it'd been too long, like the window had passed. So, then I just kept"—she pauses, shaking her head a little—"justifying not telling you by telling myself it's not a big deal, it was a long, long time ago."

"Michelle, I may explode if you don't just say it."

She doesn't respond. She kisses my face, my neck, my chest, rubbing her hands everywhere, all over me. I think she's priming me to respond well. Consider me primed.

"Out with it," I say, growing dizzy.

"Well, okay. I, well, I did date someone who died?" she says. It sounds like a question.

"Okay, who? Better be someone famous," I say.

"Beau. I dated Beau," she says, searching for my eyes. "Dark and stormy, that was me."

She reaches out to grab my hand, but I rip it away, charging out into the living room, half blinded by my hot tears. She follows me, trying to explain, trying to make it all make sense, but I don't want her words.

"I'm sorry, I should have told you. It was a really long time ago. We only dated for like six months. It hardly mattered," she says, but I'm already shoving her out the door, jaw clenched so tight I nearly crack my teeth—I'm not sure if I'm clenching because I want to keep my words in or keep Michelle out of my mouth.

"Leave me the hell alone," I say, sobbing uncontrollably,

my chest heaving. I feel violated, stupid, the subject of the world's longest-running joke.

The kid bursts out of her room, sees the scene, sees our tears, sees that they are tears of separation.

After Michelle leaves, begging for me to forgive her, I realize I'm still covered in her cum under my sweats and T-shirt. In the bathroom, I strip but I can't bring myself to wash her off me.

■

I retreat to the kid's room where your urn now lives. It has been so long since I held you in my arms. *You're going to leave me, aren't you?* I once said. *No, never,* you said.

"I'm never going to see Michelle again, am I?" asks the kid, curling into the fetal position.

Later, I find her sleeping on the floor with her blankie, her face pressed against the air vent. She finds the flowing air soothing. I have three missed calls from my dad, followed by a text: "Heard the news. You doing okay?"

My response: "There was Beau, and then there was everybody else."

For a moment, I consider *accidentally* sending that text to Michelle instead of my dad so that she will know how much she's hurt me. But the thing is, I'm not sure if I feel more jealous, furious, or violated.

There are no instructions that came with my body that said, *Press here to access your feelings.*

■

"Today Donkey and Titus followed me all over the playground," says the kid. "They didn't say or do anything. They just watched me." She shivers when she says it. "It's worse than the cameras because I can see their faces. I can see how much they don't like me."

Without Michelle, I resort to telling my dad about the kid's stalkers. He gets hung up on their names.

"What kind of names are Donkey and Titus?" he asks.

"I know in your day they only had four names, but times have changed."

"That's what Audrey tells me. The other day, I thought she was reading me a list of crystals," he says. "I'm getting nervous. Only three months left to decide."

"Tell me, when you've been kicked in the groin, how long are you down for?"

"Never more than a few minutes," he says.

■

Dad comes over while the kid's at school, getting some version of an education.

"Don't you think you should get a safe for that?" he asks, pointing at the kid's birth certificate, which I store in a basket on the coffee table, along with all of my other important documents—THANK YOU cards I never sent and a coupon for a free Shadester self-defense class.

"People are welcome to steal that, if they're so inclined," I say.

"As much as I want to believe otherwise, you don't strike me as a real person," he says. He scrunches his face up at his laptop and leans forward until his nose nearly grazes the screen. He looks at me then starts punching it with his finger, trying to show me something. I've never seen a laptop this advanced. It comes with a little censor you stick to your temple, then you control the mouse with your mind.

"I paid extra for this component," he says. "This might help with the Donkey situation. Shadesters can't even get this capability, so you're welcome."

"You could be saying anything."

"Look with your eyes," he says.

That's how it goes for several minutes before he grabs my finger and points to the words *Built-In GPS*, and then he smiles at me like the proudest grandfather to ever give his granddaughter a phone and use it to stalk her. It isn't a bad idea, to be honest. I'm mostly mad I hadn't thought of it first.

"You can check it," he says, clicking, moving the mouse, clicking, clicking, growling. "Aha! Here," he says, pointing again. I feel my legs give out.

"That's not the school," I say.

■

We run to the car, panicking, my dad's run athletic despite his arthritic joints. I can't feel my body. My head fills with gruesome inventions—kidnapped by the Department, beat up by Donkey and deposited in a ditch. I'm tired of fearing Agent Brown, I'm tired of never feeling truly safe, I'm tired of biting my cheek raw.

When we get to the car, my dad leans against it, his head pressed to his forearm, panting. I cry so hard I vomit in the grass.

"I'm sure she's fine," he gasps.

"What makes you so sure? Is it her extra shadow?" I ask. He doesn't answer. We follow the beeping dot, my beeping dot of a daughter.

Jackson calls while I'm driving, and I ignore him, but he keeps on trying so eventually I answer.

"What?"

He chatters into the phone: *new tapes, new mantras, out soon, be on the lookout, pump up your clients, cold calls, the coldest of calls, practically frozen, drink some tea with honey, you sound awful, get in the spirit, Kris, I'm not convinced you want to become an expert in this field, prove to me you've got it in you.*

I hang up on him and risk a glance at my dad, who's gripping the passenger side door handle, his knuckles white and bulging, and I realize I've been driving ninety-five in a fifty-five miles per hour zone as well as on the wrong side of the road.

I toss my phone at him and tell him to call Michelle, temporarily forgetting what happened between us.

When she doesn't answer, he leaves a message filling her in. Beau, what were you like in a crisis? I'm beginning to lose the sharp of your detail, you're growing blurry around the edges. What do you call that? The remembrance of love superseding the specific details of that love? I don't know, all I know is that I miss Michelle.

"Keep your eyes peeled," I say, as we approach my blinking dot. We're about a mile from the kid's school. Where is she and why? Then, we spot her, sitting under the shadow of a tree in the park. Luckily, no officers or agents are around. She's in the grass hunched over a bunch of papers, brow furrowed, scribbling furiously with what looks like a joint between the fingers of her other hand. She isn't alone. Eve and Forrest are sitting on either side of her, peering over her shoulders. Eve reaches over her and grabs the joint and sucks hard on it, collapsing into a coughing-dissolved-into-laughing fit.

"What in the hell do you think you're doing?" I shout, slamming the car door and stomping toward her. My dad stays in the car, for once understanding his place in the world. When she sits up, she reminds me of a nutcracker, stiff and attentive.

"Shitfuckshitfuckfuck," she explains. I plop down on the grass next to the truants.

"Ummm, umm, ummm," says Eve, standing up to leave and tugging on the back of Forrest's T-shirt.

"We were just, well, you see, uh, it's a lovely day for homework," says Forrest.

"That's the best you've got?" I resist smiling. I have to admit, it's fun to watch three stoned kids squirm, especially Forrest, given his tough-guy attitude.

"We should get going," says Eve, grabbing Forrest's shirt again, her eyes bloodshot and dreamy.

"Not so fast. You can't go back to school like that," I say.

"Don't leave me alone with her!" begs the kid in mock-terror. I catch her gauging my response out of the side of her eye, and then she giggles.

"Real funny, stinker."

She sniffs underneath both arms then looks at me and shrugs. An age-old joke between us.

"School? Ever heard of it?" I ask.

"I know, I know, I'm sorry," says the kid, shuffling her papers around. We both know she isn't sorry, but neither of us care.

"Me, too, Miss," offers Eve. "Are you going to tell my parents?"

I shake my head and pat the grass next to me, where Eve reluctantly plops down.

"Forrest, anything to say for yourself?"

"I think they covered it," he says, grinning, challenging me.

"Wait, how did you find us?" the kid asks. I nod at the phone in her lap. "Grandpa," she growls, twisting her invisible mustache.

I pluck the joint from Eve's hand and take a hit.

"I'm just glad you're safe."

"Whoa, hey, wait a second," says the kid.

"What, you want three dollars for this?" I laugh. I don't

even bother asking where they got their shitty weed. If a kid was determined to find weed, a kid would find weed.

"Your mom's right," says Eve.

"Ah, the three most beautiful words in the world."

The kid rolls her eyes, which is the signal that I've done my job.

"What are you three up to anyway?" I ask, pointing to the stack of papers, which are covered in sketches and cross-outs and arrows.

The kid looks at Eve, nods, looks to Forrest, nods, then turns to me.

"Um, well, we were having a Shadow Puppets meeting."

"Oh no," I say.

"What?" says the kid, looking around the way paranoid high people do.

"You said you would disband the Shadow Puppets society," I say.

"Oh," she says.

"Oh is right," I say. "You lied to me."

"I'm sorry, Mom." She looks like she really means it. My anger immediately dissolves. "But now we're even, because you lied to me, too, about the GPS in my phone."

"Okay, well what are the Shadow Puppets doing today?" I ask.

"We're starting a petition to get the Shadester stage torn down," says the kid.

Oh, their sweetness and naivete, I could gobble it up.

"Eve had to go there when she got her extra shadow," explains the kid.

"It was the worst thing ever, Miss," says Eve, hugging

her legs to her chest. None of us say anything, then Eve speaks again. "Ever." It sounds so final, I get goose bumps.

"I had to go there, too," I say. The kid looks at me with wide eyes. She's only known me with an extra shadow; perhaps it had never occurred to her that I had a different life before Darlene. Or, as is customary of children, she's forgotten that I'm a fully realized person with history as opposed to a mother-machine dispensing food and drinks and irreplaceable wisdom.

"What was it like?" asks Forrest, inching closer to me.

"Watch it with your potato-chip breath," I say.

"But what was it like?" asks the kid. A shiver goes through Eve's body.

"They put you on display and invite the public to watch. They turn your shame into a spectator sport. They want the NoShads to participate in disgracing you," I say, meeting Eve's eyes. "They make sure you never forget. Ever."

"Fuck a petition," says Forrest.

"Yeah, let's go bigger," says the kid.

I want to hug her. Also, to restrain her.

■

Shame hadn't been something you and I spoke about, although I knew you'd felt it, you must have. You told me about growing up, how you watched everyone around you make Father's Day cards at school while you drew pictures of you and your mother. You told me about your friends missing school on take-your-daughter-to-work day. You said these things factually, as was your way. You didn't act ashamed. For some reason, that made me even more upset. I could picture a young you, punching a wall and then asking the wall if it was okay.

■

After the kids sober up, after my dad and I deposit them back at school, after my dad brags to the kid about out-smarting her, after the kid demands we never track her again, after I picture Eve on that stage one too many times, after I burn our breakfast for dinner and try to hide the burnt French toast under icing and sprinkles, the kid finally asks the question she's been sitting on.

"How did you get your shadow, Mom? You never told me. Whatever it is, I can handle it."

I crack my neck a few times, trying to buy some think-ing time.

"That's new," the kid says, imitating me.

"You don't need to know all the details. All you need to know is that I accidentally hurt Beau," I say, swallowing my sad. She seems unmoved. I fear that the soft part of her has been swapped out for stone.

"That's it?" she says.

"What did you expect? A three-act play? Sometimes the story isn't even a story. Just a single moment."

"Something more, I don't know, riveting," she says.

"Sorry to disappoint," I say, reorienting to the reality be-fore me. I have imagined this conversation so many times over the years and never once had it gone like this. I, too, am suffering from disappointment.

"It's cool," says the kid. Our kid.

"The Department is just waiting to give people more shadows. Especially someone like me or you. You know that, right?" I say.

"Of course, I know that," she says, scoffing, but she doesn't look so sure. "Have you ever known anyone else who was born a Shadester?"

"No."

She nods, brushing the hair out of her face.

"The other day I was walking to Forrest's and some creep on the street winked at me and called me a freak. Then, he said he wanted me to hurt him, that I looked like the type that knows how to hurt someone just right. Someone who knows how to make it feel good and bad at the same time," she says, twisting up her face.

I scoot my chair around the table and put my arm around her, pulling her close.

"I'm sorry that happened to you. Are you okay?" I ask.

"Yeah, but only because you asked," she says, burying her face in my shoulder.

"I love you," I say.

"I love you, too, Mom."

What does it mean when you say *I love you* because you so desperately want to hear it back?

"Wait, where's Michelle?" asks the kid, looking around.

"I'm figuring out how to set aside our differences," I say, feeling lonely.

■

Pop Quiz:

Q: What do you think of when you hear *dark and stormy*?

Circle the answer that is most correct.

    A. A cocktail

    B. An excuse to soak to the bone

    C. Your late wife's face framed by her raincoat

    D. A shadowless night

    E. A betrayal

■

When I open the door and see Michelle standing there, all sweetness and beauty and apology, my fury melts into craving. I kiss her hard on the mouth, with life-or-death urgency.

"I wasn't expecting that," she whispers, holding my face in her warm hands.

"Me neither," I say. "Now, tell me everything."

Michelle tells me so many stories, Beau. We spend all night drinking and talking and laughing. We bring your urn out into the living room so you can listen. Hearing all the stories I didn't know is like getting to live a second life with you. All the Beau memories she gifts me.

"On our drive across the country, we camped in the mountains and met a black bear. He visited our campsite every night. Beau fell in love with that bear. She named him Gelato. I swear she would have tried to take him with us if I'd had a bigger truck," says Michelle.

"She was a bear. Looked tough on the outside but she was so soft."

"That's why I gave her that nickname."

"She never knew if you were praising or insulting her."

"It meant I'd take her in any weather," she says. We are holding hands. It feels strange but healing to connect over you. She leans in and kisses me, and I peer at your urn out of the corner of my eye.

Finally, I think I've got it all figured out: there is space for all of us here.

■

You are all we speak about for weeks. Michelle tells me Beau stories and I listen and smile and fill to the brim. I nuzzle my face against her face. I want to live in the bothness of love forever.

She tells me about the time you punched a guy in the face for hitting on her. I try to stifle my jealousy.

She tells me about the hound dog you used to have named Gus, the flop of his ears as he pranced through the woods. I wish I'd gotten the chance to meet him.

She tells me about your winning goal in the championship and the after-party that lasted all night and into the next day.

She tells me about the hole you made in the wall at that after-party, how you attempted to fill it in with a pizza.

These stories burrow their way into my cells and make a nest. It feels like coming home, over and over again, the bedroom light on, your body silhouetted at the window.

I know I am growing obsessive, but I don't know any other way to grow.

The kid is often present for these stories. Sometimes she en- joys them, but other times she looks ripped in two. Gnawed on. I want to know what's going on inside of her, if there's anything I can do to settle her inherited storm.

Pop Quiz:
Q: How do you know when someone's chosen you?
A: When the kid falls asleep on the floor next to the air conditioner, I imagine she's dreaming of driving down the open road with the top down, the wind pulling her cheeks back into a grin.

■

Finally, I call your mom and tell her about Michelle. I'd been keeping them from each other, afraid of what it would mean to combine my two worlds, which, if I'm being honest, I realize is a bit rich of me considering they aren't my worlds anyway—you and Michelle had molded a world together long before I'd ever met you, and you two spent many nights drinking beers with your mom around a bonfire, imagining what it would be like to live out in the woods where sometimes the birds were the only people you talked to all day.

"Huh," she says. "I always liked her."

"Good," I say.

"Well, you know what they say," she says. I can hear her wind chimes going crazy in the background.

"No, what do they say?" I ask, hoping for some wisdom.

"If you can't resurrect them, you might as well date their favorite ex."

"Huh, haven't heard that one before."

"Everyone is too far away from me," she sighs. I can barely hear her. It sounds as if she's set the phone down and wandered into the river.

■

"Do you have any Beau stories left?" I ask Michelle one morning while flipping through one of your old teaching folders in bed.

"I've been meaning to talk to you about that," she says, examining her hands. "I think I've run out, Kris."

"What do you mean? I'm sure there are tons of little things you haven't told me yet," I say, blinking back my stupid tears. It feels like the day I lost you all over again.

"Look around you, Kris. You live in a Beau museum. You're like the caretaker in a low-budget horror film," she says, gesturing around the bedroom.

"No, I absolutely am not," I say.

"That's exactly what a caretaker in a low-budget horror film would say." She gets up to investigate your succulent plant—it's dying, at last.

There are whispers of you all around us. Your antique film camera that still kind of works sits on the dresser next to my ever-growing pile of clothes. A stack of your favorite books on the floor next to the bed. Every morning, I wake and topple them over, then find peace in restacking them.

Things and things and more things, adding up to a life once lived.

I don't know how to respond so I pull her on top of me and bite her trap muscle. I start to take off her shirt, but she stops and pushes me away.

"If I wanted to be in a throuple, I'd at least want both my partners to be alive," she says, a new determination in her eyes.

"So, what are you saying?" I ask.

"I'm not sure."

"Are you breaking up with me?" I say, panicking.

"I'm not sure," she says. "I think I need to go think for a while. I'd suggest you do the same."

And just like that, Michelle stands up and leaves, taking her few items from the apartment. A few minutes later, I receive a text from Dune: "Should we come over?"

"You two make me understand why people in movies smell each other's armpits and like it," I say.

This seems to please them. Dune smells their pits then signals for Julian to take a good, long whiff, which he does.

"Ahhh, like chocolate chip muffins," he says.

"Does it pair well with the lager?" laughs Dune.

After some consideration, I say, "I think I would like to smell Michelle's armpits."

"We'll help you get rid of Beau's stuff," says Julian.

"The urn stays," I say, standing up.

And then we get rid of your things. The kid watches in silent awe; I can't tell if she's amazed or appalled. It's the most awful thing I've ever had to do. Afterward, I text Michelle a photo of the clean apartment. When I say clean, what I mean is empty.

Beau, I don't feel you anymore.

■

I meet Michelle at a late-night diner.

"You deserve better," I say, and then, unlike all the times I failed partners in the past, when I was too young to understand just how malleable I was, I become better.

I do what she suggested in our support group, when we first met: I ask her how she wants to be loved, then I listen.

We decide we need a date night. My dad comes over because I want him and the kid to spend more time together. She's been asking about her donor again, and I want her to see that one man in our lives is plenty, that we don't need a man we don't even know, a man who very well might hate us if he knew about our shadows.

Michelle and I wait until the sun retires for the evening, then we go to a nice steak restaurant, a place we chose mostly for its dim interior. She wears a white button-down and a burgundy vest and pants. I have managed to slither my way into a dress. I like the way Michelle looks at me in this dress. Like she might devour me before we sit down. After dinner, we go to a cocktail bar and drink expensive cocktails we can't afford and steal kisses in the booth. We pretend we are tourists.

"What a wonderful way to end our trip," I say, raising my glass.

"Do you think you'll want to visit again?" Michelle asks, tilting her head. I'm not very good at this game, but I love it and love her for playing along.

"Oh, absolutely," I say. "Everyone seems so happy here."

"It's because of all that sun they're getting."

"Maybe that's it."

"Even the Shadesters are friendly," Michelle laughs, breaking character.

"We are pretty damn friendly, aren't we?"

"Except when there wasn't enough whiskey in your drink."

"We won't talk about that."

We pass *I love you*s back and forth all night then go home to what seems like a ghost-less apartment until the next morning when the kid says, "Where is my dad? I want to meet my dad."

"What about your granddad? He's like a dad but more grand," offers Michelle.

"Knowing your biological parents isn't all it's cracked up to be," I say.

"Look at me, I'm Mom," she says, lowering her voice, "and I make jokes when my daughter is trying to be serious." She bites the inside of her cheeks for extra effect. She doesn't have the guts to mock Michelle so I'm the proud recipient of all the criticism.

The kid is trying to show me who I am, one imitation at a time, if only I'd listen.

"Good to see you haven't lost your talents," I say, trying to settle my heart rate to somewhere below 180 beats per minute.

"Is it so terrible that I want to know someone who's actually related to me?" the kid asks, stomping into her bedroom.

It's impossible for the kid to meet her sperm donor, this I now know; I triple-checked all the paperwork in case I'd missed something. Later, I confide in Michelle that we chose an anonymous donor.

"In a way, isn't this a little easier? We have a solid reason why she can't meet him," says Michelle.

"I feel like we failed her," I say.

"You couldn't have known."

We wanted to give our child freedom, but we'd also wanted the word *parent* to mean more than just biology. Maybe it was selfish, but we wanted two mothers to be enough.

■

"Do we even own anything?" the kid asks, looking around our apartment. Earlier, she'd run laps around the newly clean living room floor.

"We own that couch," I say.

"Grandpa bought us that last year," she says.

"It's called a gift."

"I wouldn't know," says the kid, raising her eyebrows at me.

"What do you call your electric guitar?"

"Another limb," she says, shrugging, losing interest in the conversation. The kid has gotten so good at guitar that Dune wants her to play with Tasty Cakes tomorrow, even though Julian has said he cannot, in good faith, put the kid in that type of dangerous position—not that I told the kid any of this. She would freak out and demand she be allowed to play. I'm inclined to agree with Julian's assessment, but how long can the kid possibly live this compromised existence? Whenever I start thinking too hard about it, I open a beer.

Find and circle the following words in the word search:
Freedom
Safety

S	A	F	D	F	Z	L	A
I	B	E	F	A	R	I	S
G	I	N	R	A	S	E	A
M	U	R	W	R	I	N	F
H	D	F	K	R	I	T	E
T	F	R	E	E	Q	M	T
W	R	O	G	N	X	B	L
H	E	L	A	A	Y	C	M

"It feels like our time here is running out," I say to no one.

■

Here's the thing: when an insect grows too big for its exo-skeleton, it sheds it, a process known as molting. This may sound benign, but insects cannot breathe while molting. They must stop eating and lie very still. Completely inca-pacitated, they are vulnerable to a predator attack.

■

Outside the school, waiting to pick the kid up. The air is the type of hot that swallows you whole. I stand under a tree, grateful for its shade. Before the school bell rings,

Agent Brown and one of his colleagues, a young guy that looks like a pop star, coked-out eyes and all, exit the front doors. Brown blinks rapidly into the sun before slipping on his sunglasses, his head already glistening with sweat. He's more muscular than I remember, some bulk in his shoulders and back. He pauses and looks around, smoothing out the front of his suit. I turn sideways, burying my face in my phone, and watch them out of the corner of my eye. After they survey the area, they climb in their car and drive away.

Not long after, the kid exits the school flanked by Forrest and Eve, Jamal trailing a few feet behind them. I wave to the kid from under the tree and she does a little handshake with her friends then strolls over to me, Jamal still in hot pursuit. I can tell he's trying to maintain his cool, but his lion swagger is off.

"Why the hell was that Department agent here?" I ask, cocooning her in a hug, which she slips out of.

"Oh, he came to talk to my class about, um, how to identify radicals at school," she says, unfazed. I wait for her to continue. "Like, he taught us signs to look out for, you know, so that we can report the student right away."

"Can I talk to you alone?" Jamal says, grabbing my elbow. "Start your homework," he tells the kid, who flops down on the grass and does exactly as he says.

I let Jamal drag me away, but I refuse to take my eyes off the kid. I recall several years ago when she asked my father and me why everything that's important isn't good, and she cited power as an example. What I didn't point out was that she was only thinking of what society found important. I hope now she can see that if it's important to her, then it is good. That her tireless rebellion, although not particularly smart or safe, is both important and good. The kid is not like me—I never wanted to be an activist, I only ever wanted to survive. No, survive isn't quite the right word. I just wanted to make it through without too much pain. I didn't think I was asking too much.

"This agent, man," says Jamal, shaking his head. "He might as well have been describing her."

"He's trying to turn everyone against her, isn't he?" I ask, watching the kid press the end of a pencil to her lips, deep in thought.

"It sure seems that way."

"Jamal."

"Yes?"

"Thank you," I say. "For everything."

Have they added subjects since I was last in school? This Department-approved homeschooling guide seems to think the kid requires knowledge in the field of ethics. But the sample lesson plan fails to mention ethics whatsoever—it is more concerned with law and order, the infallibility of lawmakers. I burn the guide in the courtyard then begin work on my first lesson plan about the animal kingdom: many animals can recognize and even utilize their own shadows. For example, the black heron positions its wings around its head like an umbrella, creating a shadow that attracts prey. Once a fish swims close enough, the heron stabs it with its beak.

Today, Michelle teaches philosophy class. I sit in on it with a stack of pancakes. The kid swipes one from my stack and folds it up like a sandwich, dripping syrup all over her lap, while Michelle writes on our new whiteboard: "What is a fact? Do facts actually exist? Why or why not?"

"My teacher said it's a fact that the shadow law keeps our country safe," says the kid. "So, no, facts don't exist."

"We're your teachers now," I say.

"This pancake needs chocolate chips, Miss Teacher," says the kid. "I don't see how homeschooling is any safer. Brown is probably watching us right now."

■

My dad wants me in the labor and delivery room when Audrey gives birth. Good thing, because when Goose One is born, Dad passes out and I catch him before he hits the floor. Audrey takes a selfie with me and Dad's limp body then soldiers on. The kid sits in the corner, reading from a printout of approved middle names, groaning conspicuously. Audrey releases a deep guttural scream and Goose Two pops out while my dad sits on a chair, taking small sips of water. The geese are covered in womb cheese, but I can still make out their fiery red hair. At least I know what their birth story will be.

A week later, we are allowed on the premises. We bring my dad and Audrey takeout. I hold one twin while Michelle shows the kid how to hold the other. "Carefully," she says. "Support her neck." I can tell Michelle's got baby fever by the way she keeps getting them to grab her fingers. Maybe, maybe. Let's figure out the nine-year-old beast first.

"Sperm donor has red hair," says my dad, dark circles under his eyes. "But it's okay. He's a literal rocket scientist."

"I've seen pictures. You had red hair before it went gray," says Audrey.

"Mine was strawberry blond, thank you very much."

The kid looks up from Goose One, or maybe it's Goose Two. I do not know their given names.

"Don't you want them to meet their real dad?" asks the kid. My dad looks at me.

"I'm sorry, I never realized what a pain this must have been for you." He turns back to the kid. "I am their real dad, end of story."

■

I call your mom and cry into the phone.

"It's everything," I say. "Everything adding up."

"What are you holding on to over there, kid?" she asks.

"The twins need me," I say.

"Don't kid yourself, honey."

"I know, Mom," I whisper.

■

For weeks, the kid resorts to asking Michelle what she knows about the kid's so-called father. Michelle tells her she has nothing to report, that she'd tell her if she did. "I wish you wouldn't lie to me," says the kid on more than one occasion.

Then during a morning math lesson, the sperm bank calls. I motion for the kid to take a break in her room, which she gladly does. A shy woman treads lightly on the other end.

"I just wanted to let you know, well, that we received a call from your daughter yesterday," she says. "She was looking for her sperm donor's name and address. I thought you should know."

When I hang up, I turn around to find Michelle standing behind me, rubbing her cheek against her collarbone.

"What now?" she asks.

"Look out, this isn't going to be pretty," I say, heading for the kid's room. Michelle intercepts me, wrapping her arms around my waist. "Today is the day she's going to learn the difference between a dad and a father," I say.

"Sometimes you still call your dad your father."

"That's when he's misbehaving," I say. "Like how your mom calls you by your full name when you've been caught smoking weed out of an apple with the neighbor, Daniel."

"That's an oddly specific example," says Michelle.

We find the kid holding your urn in her arms. She examines it from every angle, as if she is an archaeologist and she's just discovered a career-making artifact. Frankly, I hate the way she's handling you.

"It's strange, isn't it?" she says, without looking up.

"What is, babe?"

"How you'd rather me be raised by a glass vase than a live human."

"I can count two live humans right in front of you," I say, crossing my arms and leaning against the doorway.

"Honey," says Michelle. "What I think your mom is trying to say is she and Beau never intended for you to know your sperm donor. I know it's hard to accept but he was never part of the plan."

"Then why did he do it? Why did he help make me?" she asks, still staring at your remains. Michelle looks at me and raises her eyebrows. I don't know what to say, I'm too outside of myself to do any good. Shrimp, cicadas, crabs.

"He just, I don't know, wanted to help out people who needed it. People who couldn't make babies on their own," I say.

"So, you really won't let me meet him?" she asks.

"Okay, here's the thing," I say, inching toward her. I want to hold my kid, but she sees me coming and moves back a step. Michelle clears her throat in the doorway.

"I looked back in our records, and well, we got an anonymous donor," I say.

"Anonymous," repeats the kid, dead-eyed.

"It means that none of us can find out who or where he is," I say. "I tried, I swear."

"You can't be serious," says the kid. She's speaking slowly, or maybe it's me that's hearing the words slowly, as if we're underwater and the sound is taking longer to travel between us. The kid takes a few deep breaths, and it seems like she's on the verge of calming herself, but then she begins pacing around the room, snorting like a bull ready to charge, your urn still clutched between her hands. I don't know where to focus my attention.

"I can't fucking believe this," she says. "Were you in on this, too?" she asks Michelle, who says, "No, of course not. No one was *in* on anything. Your moms made the decision they thought was right at the time."

"At the time?" I say, shooting Michelle a look.

"I should have done this a long fucking time ago," says the kid.

"Bleeping," I say, correcting her language.

The kid stops for a second and stares at the urn in her arms and then I realize what she is about to do but I'm powerless to stop it. She looks at me to check that I'm watching then she winds up like a baseball pitcher and throws your urn against the wall, smashing it to pieces.

"I'm sick of being raised by a fucking dead person," screams the kid, gesturing wildly.

"You're a monster," I say. "An absolute fucking monster."

"So maybe I am."

Your ashes fly everywhere, like a dust storm, and when the dust finally settles, the kid is gone.

Part III

■

. . . Sometimes, parents & children

become the most common strangers. Eventually,
a street appears where they can meet again.

CHEN CHEN

Michelle and I wait, but the kid doesn't come home. I check out the GPS tracker, even though I know she left her phone behind. We grab flashlights and our phones and head out to look for her. I have only a few ideas of where she might be. We check the park, the beach, the graffiti alley, the stage. We call Forrest's and Eve's parents. Nobody has seen or heard from her.

We head downtown, hoping to find her smoking or philosophizing with friends. Nearby, a newscaster is reporting something or other and a girl in a moose onesie hops up and down in the background, waving her arms and saying, "I have something to say!"

The newscaster, this disgruntled middle-aged dude, finally stops talking, turns around and says, "No, thanks, I think we've got all we need here," and she says, "I used to be a model. Your loss," then scampers away, and I feel proud of her for no real reason.

We return home and throw beer down our throats. I call the Department to report a missing person, but they tell me it's too early, I have to wait twenty-four hours.

"What is your actual function?" I scream into the phone before hanging up, my face a wet, salty mess.

I sweep up your ashes and put them in a plastic bag. I cry so hard that I throw up and burst a blood vessel in my eye, the white part now a galaxy of dark red.

"Do you think she hates me?" I ask Michelle.

"You did call her a monster," she says, putting a hand on my leg.

"I did, didn't I?"

"She a little bit deserved it."

"I think I a lot a bit deserved it," I say, setting you on the kitchen table.

When I look at your ashes in that baggy, I feel an ever-lasting appreciation for having had the privilege of loving you and being loved by you. But I feel no grief—my grief is gone; it's a horrible, beautiful realization. I'm now grieving the loss of my grief. And, more importantly, the distance I've put between me and the kid, who every day feels less and less like a kid.

■

Pop Quiz:

Q: What is the story you've told yourself about yourself?

A: That I'm not a capable person.

Q: Have you ever considered taking a red pen to your life?

■

Can't sleep so I'm concocting the beginnings of a plan for when the kid returns, assuming she does. A plan that concerns your mother. I've always been simultaneously afraid of and drawn to your mom. She has what one might call a churning presence. I'd walk into her house feeling one way and leave feeling smoothed in all my rough spots. It was the in-between that disturbed me. I couldn't remember how I ended up on the sidewalk, walking to the car, smiling into your cheek.

The last time I saw your mom before you died, you were pregnant, and she was tracing the MOM tattoo on your bicep. She didn't even mention my shadow. I couldn't decide if that enraged or charmed me.

"This is the only type of tattoo I approve of," said your mother, then she took us to the tattoo parlor where she got MY BEAU tattooed on her shoulder. "Have you two settled on a name yet?" she asked. We glanced at each other, silently consulting, then shook our heads no. "While you're at it, add another *my* with adequate space after it," she said to the tattoo artist, who nodded.

Entranced by the buzzing of the tattoo gun, I'd examined you and your mom, a pair, a tag team, two atoms bonded—I never had and never would have that with my mother. You held her hand while she grimaced. Had I already met the kid, I might have adopted her phrasing: *I have this, you have that.*

I remember I excused myself and threw a tantrum in the tattoo parlor bathroom. I kicked and kicked my extra shadow, who I hadn't yet named, who I hadn't yet accepted, who I still considered a what.

■

Around 5:00 a.m. your mom's time, I give her a call, knowing she'll be up with the crows.

"The only kink in the plan is that I've misplaced her," I sob. She's silent for a moment.

"You know, when Beau was around her age, she told me she was running away forever, then she marched across the street and rang Larry's doorbell. I think he thought she was selling him something because he let her in."

"Deb," I say, wiping my nose.

"Yes, Kris."

"Why are they always running away from us?"

"They aren't, kid. They're running toward something."

"And what's that?"

She thinks on this. I hear a few dogs demand their breakfast in the background.

"Something . . . something philosophical," she says.

After we hang up, Michelle wanders into the kitchen, bleary-eyed. Without speaking, she makes a pot of coffee even though it's 2:30 a.m. We both know there's no point in trying to sleep. Once the coffee is brewing, she comes to me and wraps her arms around my neck. Instinctually, I place my hands on her waist like we're at a middle school dance, and that's what we do—we sway back and forth. At the end of the imaginary song, I kiss her softly. My atoms are buzzing. All we need to do is track down the kid, the one who may or may not hate me. Michelle slips out of my arms and pours us each a mug, extra cream for me.

"I'm glad you finally caught up to me," says Michelle.

"What do you mean?" I ask.

"I've been thinking we should go for a while now. I just, well, I didn't know how to bring it up to you," she says.

"I sense an accusation about my personality," I laugh.

"I'd been looking into some small towns, out in the desert or mountains, but Deb's would be lovely if she'll have us."

"It'll be like we're at nature camp all the time," I say. She nods, then raises an eyebrow at me.

"So, do you love me, or do you love me?"

"What's the good news?"

She digs a Post-it out of the kitchen drawer and writes a quick note and hands it to me: "Been talking to Mitch about surveillance—he can reroute Beau's mom's cameras to an empty house nearby."

"What?" I say.

"Yeah," she whispers. "We're home free."

I don't respond. I can feel the tears coming on strong like a drunk man at the bar.

"Don't worry," she says. "We'll find her, okay? We have to."

■

The next day, the kid who is no longer a kid still doesn't come home. On the phone, a Department agent does a nice song and dance about how they're doing their best to find her. Michelle and I recruit Julian and Dune and my dad to join our search party. My dad comes over and asks what I did to her.

"Nothing, nothing," I say, flailing around the room.

"Hmph," he says.

He goes to twirl his mustache, but it's gone. I've never seen the skin above his lips before. I feel claustrophobic. There's a stranger inside my house. It's the sign of something ending, but I don't know what.

I send the search party to check the normal places while I peek in people's windows, per your mother's story. Who knows, maybe the kid has decided to take after Mischief. Maybe she's found a nice window to jump through. A new family who has been assembled correctly.

Twice I get screamed at, told to leave their property immediately *or else*. Okay, okay, away I scurry. No one else catches me creeping.

Nice windowpane. Dig the rustic look. Ugly children, though. I can see the slobber from here.

None of the kids are mine.

Not the one eating mac and cheese on the couch.

Not the one licking the brownie batter spatula.

Not the one working on homework or pretending to work on homework at their desk.

Not the one taking photos of themself holding up a peace sign.

Not the one punching their sibling in the arm.
Not the one crying on their bed.

Oh, who is that grabbing me around the waist and lifting me into the air? It appears a Department agent is carting me away and to his vehicle. "Guess peeping toms can be women now," he says. His friend turns around in the passenger seat and scans my face with his tablet, which I promptly spit on. "Seems we've caught a live one," he says to the driver. He bares his teeth at me. I ask him to turn down the radio, I have sensitive mom ears. He turns it up and up. Soon we're speeding through the streets while a woman on a commercial says, "You can try Shadow Dimmer today, just eighty-six easy payments of $79.99."

"You hear that?" says driver guy. "Just eighty-six easy payments."

Front seat guy slaps driver guy on the shoulder, and they have a nice laugh at his ability to repeat information. I close my eyes and wait for the exoskeletons to come. The mollusks and the mites. But they don't.

■

The next thing I know, I'm being handled like a box out for delivery. The men rip me out of the car and toss me to the ground. They leave me there for a moment or two, then pick me back up and shove me into the stage line. The sun starts dropping, and my shadow dims the old-fashioned way.

"Busy day," says driver guy, or maybe it's front seat guy. I don't know who is who, now that they're out of their designated seats. They admire the crowd, fighting over a young woman they've apparently set their sights on. ("Hot, nice ass, *and* knows how to write a damn good sign.")

Finally, they grow bored and leave. I turn around and face the stage for the first time.

Ahead of me in line, a small person with a perfect widow's peak. Bear. Well, at least I've located her.

■

"Excuse me, don't I know you?" I say, tapping the kid who's no longer a kid on the shoulder. I'm not sure where we stand, if she'll forgive me or not. She turns around and looks at me, her sleepless eyes slow to take me in. She looks wind-blown. At first, I think she's going to turn around and ignore me, but then her eyes soften.

"You," she says. I can tell she's happy to see me, but she also wants to stay mad at me, and I don't blame her. Her mouth does that twitchy thing at the corners.

"Bear," I say, softly. She looks at the stage, blinking away evidence of emotion. "I'm sorry," I say.

She returns her attention to me and wraps her arms around my waist.

"What are you doing here?" she asks.

"No touching!" yells a guard, who pokes me in the back with a rifle. The kid releases her death grip on me. He continues down the line to harass some other people.

"What are *you* doing here?" I ask, examining her for

injuries. There's some dirt smudged on her face and hands but no signs of blood loss.

"A man in a fancy suit tried to force me into his car. I did what you taught me. Swift kick to the groin," she says, showing me her best kick.

"No swift kicks to the groin!" yells a new guard. He approaches us and decides to stick to our side as we make our way through the line.

"I've never been more proud," I say.

"Hopefully, I kicked him hard enough so he can't ever be an ingredient man," she says.

I look at her, surprised by what she knows about male gonads.

"What? I've been doing some light reading," she says.

The guard clears his throat and adjusts his grip on the rifle. We quit talking and look at the stage. Right now, an East Asian woman, around fifty or so, is taking a verbal beating. But there is one person cheering her on. At the very front, her husband holds up a sign: WILL YOU MARRY ME AGAIN?

When it's Bear's turn, she sticks her head in the air and marches on stage. She stands on the designated X and folds her arms across her chest. An armed guard is standing too close to her; I don't like it. She doesn't seem to notice or mind, though. She squints her eyes and sends laser looks throughout the crowd.

"Bear Rosen-Allen," says the guard. "Assault on an innocent man."

"Child psychopath!" people scream.

"She belongs in an institution!"

"Who raised this demon?"

Bear files off the stage, her new shadow in tow. She takes a few steps, enough for me to doubt whether she's going to turn around, but then she stops, wipes the sweat off her brow, and turns toward the stage, toward me. They announce my name. My crimes: trespassing, invasion of privacy, insubordination, harm to the family's psyche.

"Kill the creep!" someone shouts. The armed guard chuckles a little, as if to say, *You know we can't do that in broad daylight.*

"I feel dirty just looking at you!"

"Fucking monster!"

■

When we get home, everyone is waiting for us, including Audrey and the geese. Bear kisses the twins then pretends to eat their toes. She waits for them to laugh, but they're not there yet.

"I promise you they like it," says Audrey.

Bear moves down the line, giving everyone a huge hug. Once she releases Julian, she turns to the group and begins to regale everyone with her heroic groin-kicking tale. According to her, the man was a giant. "At *least* five foot ten," she says. He wanted to show her something in his car, a brand-new scooter, top of the line, you don't want to miss it. She told him no, thank you, and if he liked it so much, then he should bring it out and ride it. When he grabbed her, she reacted, in her words, "faster than lightning." Everyone *ooo*s and *ahh*s at the appropriate parts. No one asks about the aftermath.

■

Later that night, after everyone's headed home and Michelle's gone out to buy some road trip things, Bear and I sit at the kitchen table, examining each other's extra shadows.

"What will you name this one?" Bear asks.

"I'm partial to the name Gladice."

"Why do you always pick old lady names?"

"I don't know. Maybe because it makes them seem harmless?"

"Colestein's right-hand man is an *old lady*," Bear reminds me.

She presses her hand against the wall, but she can't seem to line her hand up with any of her shadows' hands. Every time she raises her hand to the wall, her shadows seem to jump to the side.

"I'm going to name mine Zig and Zag," says the kid, smiling. "What are you waiting for? Shake their hands."

I attempt to shake Zig's and Zag's hands. Then we sit in silence. I get up and grab a beer, make the kid tea, busy myself.

After I sit back down, Bear tilts her head back and looks at me through the bottom of her eyes.

"You know, I thought I would feel different about this shadow," she says.

"How so?"

"I don't know, this one I earned or whatever, even though it was self-defense."

I don't say anything, just sip my beer. She continues.

"It feels just the same, only I can remember getting this one."

"Are you happy or sad about that?" I ask.

"Neither. I'm nothing about it," she says, shrugging. "I don't care what people think of me, but I know the stage hurts other people. Did it hurt you?"

"Yes," I say.

"I don't want you to hurt," she says. "But deep down, a tiny part of me was happy someone called you a monster. So that you'd know how it feels."

"That stranger, he was easy, babe. I don't know how it feels to be called a monster by someone you love, someone who loves you. You didn't deserve that."

"Well, what are we supposed to do now that your daughter is a monster?" Bear asks, giving me a look. I hate that look. It's the one you used to give me when you'd suggest we do something reckless like take a trip with money we didn't have. It's the look that says, *Your move.* I know I shouldn't be, but every day I'm still shocked at the similarities between you two. Are mannerisms and facial expressions heritable? Do we pass on the way in which we move throughout the world?

"You're not a monster, I didn't mean that, I could never mean that."

I decide I will inch my hand toward her on the table and see if she inches her hand back. I move my hand forward. At first, she stares at it as if it's a foreign being, then she swallows hard and slides her hand a few inches toward me.

"How do I know that?" she demands.

"I wish I had better words than I'm sorry, but I don't," I say. "I'm sorry." I can barely breathe, my chest is wound so tight. I move my hand closer to her then study her face. Her dimples are showing even though she isn't smiling. Her lips are pursed like a woman asking to see the manager, but her eyes are soft, eager even; I hope she's looking for reunion. She looks both young and old, new to this lifetime but old to so many others she left behind.

She slides her hand closer to me. I mirror her. Then, our fingers are touching. I cover her not so small hand with mine.

"Me, too," she whispers, her eyes drifting to your bag of ashes. Her shadows billow out from either side of her, two on one side, one on the other, like a pair of uneven wings.

Unlike me, she was born a crowd.

"I want you to know that if I had the chance to do it all over again, I'd choose you twice," I say, hoping the door connecting us will stay open forever, hoping that if given the chance, she will make the decision to stay. "Fuck that, I'd choose you three, four, twenty, one hundred times over."

Her bottom lip is quivering, her eyes pooling.

She gets up from her chair and I take her in my arms. When we cry, our bodies shake as one.

Once we calm, she says, "I love when you say fuck," at first fighting her smile then letting it break across her face.

"Do you want to go on a road trip?" I ask.

"Really?" Bear asks, the life surging back into her face.

"A really long road trip. Like we-don't-know-when-we're-coming-back road trip."

"*Finally*," she says.

"How quickly can you pack?" I ask but she is already tearing apart her room.

A text from your mom: "Beau would be proud of you."

■

The next day, Michelle and I are in the bedroom, triple-checking our suitcases. Michelle flits about the room like a hummingbird. I wrap my arms around her stomach and hug her from behind, burying my face in her back, inhaling her delicious scent.

"I can't believe we're really doing this," she says.

"I can," I say, kissing her hard on the mouth.

I guess we're making a lot of commotion because Julian and Dune come over to investigate. When they ask where we're going, I invite them along on impulse. Good thing we have a truck.

I text your mom and tell her the family unit just got bigger by two.

Her reply: "Will June and Dulian and Bear require a separate band practice space?" she asks. I laugh, not bothering to correct her on the names.

We all go for a walk so we can chat.

"It's safer for us there," says Michelle. "She lives on ten acres of land. We can explore and be free. We'll continue homeschooling that one," she says, nodding toward Bear. "Plus, the Department won't know we're there."

"Pays to have been on the inside," says Julian. He's trying to keep his cool but he's bubbling with excitement.

"But before we go," says the kid, holding up her pointer finger. "We're going to make a statement."

That perks everyone's ears right up.

■

I grab Bear's confiscated graffiti materials from my closet and bring them out into the courtyard, away from any cameras. We go dumpster-diving and secure a few large cardboard boxes from TVs and bookshelves and fridges. Once we have enough practice canvasses, Bear and I argue about what the message should say.

"No, they won't get it."

"Who is they?'

"You know, they. The Department."

"That sounds like it's about a fish."

"You sound like you're about a fish."

"This isn't where my activism exactly thrives," I say.

"What activism?" laughs Bear.

"My, well, my being alive activism."

"I think I know what we should write."

We get to work on the different letters. I help Bear draw each stencil then I cut them out with an X-Acto knife, despite her insistence that she has a steady hand. I only draw blood twice. The stencils don't exactly look professional, but they'll get the job done. I can't help but think of Siegfried. I wish he were here stirring up trouble with us. I can hear his voice now: *Graffiti is a beautiful way to say fuck you.* After his death, I didn't want to believe what the cops said about him because I wanted to continue believing the lessons he taught me while he was alive—in the friendship we shared. It's taken me this long to realize how foolish my logic was. As if his bad parts could ever cancel out his good parts.

Once we've finished making the stencils, Bear lays them out and hmms at them.

"Something isn't right," she says. "I think we need to change our audience."

"What? This isn't marketing," I say, thinking of Michelle.

"Just trust me. I have an idea."

She picks up the electric-blue spray paint, shaking it, then freehands a message across the largest piece of cardboard. She stands back and looks at it, smiling that dimply smile.

Without looking at me, she holds up her hand for me to slap it.

"It's a hug for the Shadesters," says Bear. "Or a parachute? I don't know, it can be many things."

"I think that is probably the biggest middle finger to the Department there is," I say.

"Hey, you're right," she says, smiling.

When we go to bed, Bear asks me to tell her more about Nonna. Is she smart? Can she play the guitar? Is she anything like Beau? I tell her about the woman who made the woman she came from, the woman who'd relished raising her daughter without the help of a man.

"Her name is Deb," I tell her. "She is like Beau in so many ways. They have the same tough outsides and mushy insides. They are both fiercely loyal. Once you've earned your place in their lives, they'll never let you go. Deb will take us on hikes and identify every type of plant. She collects stray dogs. You will be happy and dirty just like the dogs. You will probably look like a polar bear covered in all that fur. In the morning, you will listen to the wind chimes transport you anywhere and everywhere. At night, Deb will cook steaks for us. She will burn them. After dinner, we will sit on the porch with some drinks and watch the fireflies dance. She's going to love you more than any one person ought to love another. She will make you crazy. We will let her."

■

Then there is the business of alerting my father of our departure. I text him in the middle of the night when I think
he might be awake with the geese. Ask him what's up, how
parenthood's treating him. He texts me back immediately:
"Kris, I don't remember you being this bad."

When I call, he answers in a hushed voice.

"You were much younger when I was a baby," I say.

"Even so," he says.

"Dad, I have to tell you something."

"Okay."

"Michelle, Bear, and I are moving in with Beau's mom.
Julian and Dune are coming, too."

He takes a deep breath then exhales slowly.

"You sure know how to break an old guy's heart," he says.

"We have to do this," I say. "The decision has been
made." I pause. "No, I mean, I—we—made the decision."

"Velcro, Velcro," he says. I can hear him smiling into the
phone. "You have unstuck yourself."

■

It's our second-to-last night here, and Michelle is in bed
beside me, map in hand.

"I wasn't aware people could still read maps," I say. Instinctually, my eyes travel to the place on the wall where
the abandoned house photo once was. Earlier, with a few
not so gentle nudges from Michelle and Bear, I'd thrown
it out. I no longer need reassurance that you're with me. I
know you are.

"Not people. Just me," says Michelle. "I've mapped it all

out. We could get to Deb's in as few as five days if we drive nine hours a day."

"Where can we stay?"

"I've found a bunch of first-come, first-served camp-grounds along the way. Julian and Dune have two tents we can use."

"Oh, the ground," I say, feigning squeamishness so she won't detect my real squeamishness. "I'm used to luxury," I say.

"Guess we'll have to leave you behind then."

Reality Testing:
My brain: We are about to embark upon a new forever.
Reality: We are about to embark upon a new forever.

■

The next day, we pack up the truck. We move the couch into the alley. I write several drafts of an email to my land-lord until everyone agrees on the best version. I leave him an envelope with two months' rent on the kitchen counter. Bear draws hearts on the envelope. We wave goodbye to the Department cameras. Nothing illegal about moving. Bear sticks her tongue out at the cameras. Outside, when I ask her about it, she says, "I still want them to think of me as a little kid. Like I'm not capable of what we're about to do."

I grab her hand, marveling at my child, my human rea-son for survival. For the very first time, I consider that there is some of me in her as well. How can there not be? She has my passion, my unfortunate handwriting. My attraction to trouble.

I am reminded of what you once said, when you were eight months pregnant and we were trying to imagine what the kid might look like. *Who knows, maybe she'll have your curly hair*, you said. Such an offhand comment, but it warmed me, nonetheless. Already, you'd forgotten the sperm donor's role in the equation. And you were right—we did it, we made this child. You and me.

By the time the moon is high in the sky, the three of us are vibrating. It reminds me of the pre-drug jitters I used to get. All that adrenaline.

"Now, does everyone remember the plan?" I ask, buckling my seat belt.

"Yes, yes," say my two best friends, grinning at each other on the sidewalk. Once we accomplish our mission, we will pick up Julian and Dune at the designated location and hit the road.

■

I drive to the center of town, where the stage is located. I park behind an abandoned building and slip on my beanie and sunglasses. Bear does the same. Michelle stays behind as the lookout. Bear and I observe the stage from behind the building. It's 1:00 a.m. so the building and the square around it is empty; the stage only operates between 7:00 a.m. and 7:00 p.m. since our shadows are most visible during these times. That, and shaming someone is a collaborative process. If you get a shadow late at night, you must wait until the morning to be humiliated. I imagine it's almost worse being arrested after-hours, the waiting dragging you through the night like roadkill.

The Department won't know what hit them on this particular morning. The guards will show up, assault rifles in hand. They will file the first Shadester onto the stage. They will watch the Shadester look down and read our message. The Shadester may even smile to themself. They may look the guard in the eye then turn their attention to the crowd, seeing them but not really seeing them at all. They may become a blurry face in someone's photograph, a blurry face someone thinks about for a long time after. The guards will then see the graffiti, they will shut down the stage for the day while they try to figure out how to clean it. For one day, we will have won.

"Ready?" I whisper.

"Ready," she says.

We approach the stage casually, holding hands as we walk, Bear skipping like a much younger child. We are both wearing backpacks. Once we get to the stage, we pull out our spray paint, shake it, and get to work on the floor of the stage, directly in front of the X where each Shadester must stand. We move quickly, our heads on a swivel the whole time. We figure we have just a few minutes before an agent shows up.

Once we are done, we take a step back and examine our work, pride swelling in my chest. We speed-walk to the truck and hop in. Michelle drives away at a socially acceptable speed, and the kid and I hold each other in the back seat.

"We did it, we did it," whispers Bear.

"I wish we could tell Siegfried," I say.

"He knows," says the kid, smiling.

We swing by the park to pick up Julian and Dune and we play musical chairs. I climb into the driver's seat and Michelle moves to the passenger. Julian and Dune get the back with Bear wedged between them. Then we are off.

■

We drive out of the city and merge onto the interstate. I couldn't ask for anything more than this: this in-betweenness, the open-road seduction. My one hand on the wheel and the other on Michelle's leg, Bear on the edge of her seat behind me, arms dangling loosely across my chest, and Dune and Julian arguing about what music to put on first, what constitutes a perfect road trip song—the five of us speeding toward the rest of our lives.

But what about you? Where do you fit in, Beau?

■

FINAL EXAMINATION:

Read each question carefully then choose the corresponding answer. You are permitted to use any and all study materials from the course of your life. You can have as long as you need to complete the exam, but ideally, you ought to finish it before you reach the first rest stop, or else you may miss your exit and run out of gas on the freeway.

True or False (½ point each):
1. Not deciding is deciding, too. _____
2. You can feel the tectonic plates of your world shifting beneath you. _____
3. Love is not a finite thing. _____
4. Your story was never just your story. _____
5. Pleasure can exist on its own, without the intrusion of shame. _____
6. You were right: remembering is a courageous act. _____
7. It's time to tip the scales. _____
8. It is possible for an answer to be both true and false at once. _____

Fill in the Blanks (2 points each):
1. The last stage of grief is _____.
2. Key in _____, key in _____.
3. Love is waking up and _____ someone every day.

Essay Section (10 points each):
1. What's one thing you understand that you didn't before?
2. Where in your body do you store your regrets? How will you release them?

3. Who are you when no one is looking, not even your shadows?
4. What would you say if you learned that Beau has let go? How would you repay her?

Bonus Question (5 points):
Describe the atmosphere of your arrival, the closing of one distance and expanding of another.

■

We drive and drive through the night, the mountains a set of small knuckles before us. Windows down, the cool air laps our faces, and the smell of sea salt slowly drifts away. Cacti. Windmills. Sky, so much sky. Shadows of little creatures dart across the road. Headlights glisten like diamonds. White arrows direct us. East, west. Merge.

There is a reason devotion sounds like motion. I belong to you, kid. You, Bear.

Acknowledgments

Endless thanks to the brilliant people at Catapult, including my all-star editor, Alicia Kroell, whose vision and insight are unparalleled, Wah-Ming Chang, Alisha Gorder, Megan Fishmann, and Rachel Fershleiser—I am so grateful to you all. Thank you to Dani Li and creative director Nicole Caputo, for designing the dreamiest cover—it is everything I imagined and more.

Thank you to my agent, Maggie Cooper. There is not enough space here to express my gratitude for your generosity, wisdom, and care, and for believing wholeheartedly in this book. You always know what's best.

Thank you to the editors who published my previous work, especially Aaron Burch, Aram Mrjoian, Jake Wolff, Steffan Triplett, Katelyn Keating, Jacqueline Doyle, Alyse Burnside, Matt Ortile, Mia Herman, Dani Hedlund, and Stefanie Molina. I will forever be grateful for the support.

Thank you to everyone at the Tin House Winter and Summer Workshops, Bread Loaf Writers' Conference, and Lighthouse Advanced Writing Workshop. I am a better reader, writer, and person for having met you all. And thank you to Bryan Washington, Laura van den Berg, and

Melissa Febos, for being such lovely teachers and workshop facilitators.

Thank you to T Kira Madden, for your curiosity, tenderness, and generosity, and for teaching me to write into the problem, into my obsessions. Oh, and for loving *Titanic* as much as I do. You are a gift.

Thank you to Elizabeth Crane, for encouraging me to make the work I'm excited to make.

To my brilliant writer friends, Ariél Martinez, Marissa Higgins, Kate Sullivan, and Frances Dinger, for keeping me grounded and laughing, even on the hardest of days. You all inspire me.

To my sister, for showing me what it means to lead a life full of wonder and creativity. To my mom, for taking me to the library every week growing up, for showing me the power of words. To my brother and my dad, for instilling a tireless determination in me—writing is just like basketball: equal parts beautiful and frustrating.

Finally, to Ash, my joy, my reason, my let's-not-go-slow love. ITPB. And Wilder, my little light, my love on the move, I can't believe I am lucky enough to be your parent.

© Jerrelle Wilson

MARISA CRANE is a writer, basketball player, and sweatpants enthusiast. Their work has appeared or is forthcoming in *Joyland, No Tokens, TriQuarterly, Passages North, The Florida Review, Catapult, Literary Hub, The Rumpus,* and elsewhere. An attendee of the Tin House Workshop and Bread Loaf Writers' Conference, they currently live in San Diego with their wife and child. *I Keep My Exoskeletons to Myself* is their first novel.